DEADLY THREAT

Cash Gore's voice was touched by hatred. "You were a fool to ride out here, Benbow."

Jim Benbow said quietly, "I came to tell you that I heard this outfit is crooked. But I'm going to wait for proof."

"You can go on waiting," Gore sneered.

"I can wait," Benbow said coldly. "And when the time comes I'll be back. And I'll wipe you off the map, Cash."

"Sounds tough," droned Gore.

"It'll be tough alright," murmured Benbow as he pulled his horse away from the porch. He drifted around the corner of the house holding the shapes of Gore's crew with his scrupulous attention. When he got by the corrals he threw the pony into a gallop and raced up the canyon.

ERNEST HAYCOX

DEEP WEST

PINNACLE BOOKS
WINDSOR PUBLISHING CORP.

PINNACLE BOOKS

are published by

Windsor Publishing Corp.
475 Park Avenue South
New York, NY 10016

First Pinnacle Books printing: October, 1989

Printed in the United States of America

Contents

1. In Two Dance

Jim Benbow dropped off the train at Two Dance and stood on the platform a little while, watching the red and green coach lamps of the westbound slide away and vanish at last in the layered darkness lying over the vast dry sweep of this land.

A telegraph key clattered inside the station. The smell of coal smoke and steam lingered behind. Arapahoe Street ran gently upward between Two Dance's frame buildings, crossbarred with shop lights shining across the loose dust. Horses stood three-footed in front of Faro Charley's and farther along, by the gallery of the Cattle King Hotel, the highwheeled stage was making up for its night's run southward to the reservation. Beyond town the low outline of Two Dance Range made a ragged silhouette. A freight engine's bell began to ring down the siding and Izee Custer strolled out from the thick shadows of the station house.

The two of them swung together and walked by silent agreement toward Faro Charley's, the matter-of-fact Izee Custer stretching out his legs a little to match Jim Benbow's broad stride. There was a six-inch difference of length between these two. "Get your chore done?" asked Izee Custer.

"Yes."

"Pete Cruze," murmured Izee, "is eatin' supper up at

7

the hotel."

"Drop him word to stay there until I give the signal. I want this thing staged right."

Riders were wheeling out of the prairie darkness into Two Dance, swinging at the hitch racks, and lights flashed more brightly from all those buildings as the town woke to its evening's liveliness. Ed Swain came from the hotel, made one long jump to the stage's seat and sent his four horses away from Two Dance at a fast trot. Benbow and Izee Custer were at the open doorway of Faro Charley's, and here Benbow came to a sudden halt, his flat and high shape swinging in the saloon's full glow. Izee Custer laid his hand against Benbow to prevent collision. He lifted a round and stolid face and said: "Huh?" Afterwards he turned to see what drew Benbow's attention. There was a big clay-colored horse standing by the Cattle King porch.

"Yeah," murmured Izee. "Cash Gore came in about an hour ago."

Change stirred Benbow's long lips, a faint impatience cracked the habitual serenity he imposed upon his cheeks. His jaws definitely established the long borders of a big-featured face, shelving squarely at the chin. His eyes were a sharp gray with a light in them that could turn, as now, restless and exacting. Like a hidden heat unwittingly exposed. He had high cheekbones, minute weather lines slanting out toward them from his eye corners across a smooth and bronze-turned skin. When he let the pressure go from his lips they grew fuller.

"Connie's around somewhere, too," said Izee. "Came in this afternoon with Clay Rand. Clay's been at the poker table with Faro Charley ever since."

Jim Benbow stepped into the smoky warmth of Faro Charley's and stopped with a characteristic roll of his shoulders, catching the identity of the crowd at one quick survey. Mirrors flashed up a sulky brilliance in here and Price Peters pivoted from the bar and grinned at him. A few punchers from the Mauvaise Valley—a clannish

8

district—made their own group at one end of this bar; and a man in a loud yellow shirt, looking like a rider on the loose, stood at the other end and whirled a glass between his fingers in a solemn isolation. Shad Povy, roustabout in Menefee's stable, lay full length at the foot of a wall, drowned in whisky.

There was a game going on at a corner table, with Faro Charley dealing and Clay Rand and two other men sitting in. Jim Benbow went over there to lay his hand quietly on Rand's shoulders. Rand looked up, a flushed and irritated expression all across his half-handsome face. When he saw Benbow a swift smile took the irritation away. He said: "How was Cheyenne, kid?"

Faro Charley called: "Open?" It was a thoroughly colorless voice. He let his glance lift to Benbow for a moment and then nodded, his stiff shoulders remotely stirring.

Benbow went back to join Izee and Price Peters; they lined up at the bar and in silence took their whisky. Price Peters had a horse ranch over on the edge of the badlands. Around thirty-five and a graduate of Princeton, '72, he already was beginning to turn gray. There was a kind of ironic reserve about him that repelled most people in the Two Dance country, a let-me-alone manner hard to penetrate. Only Jim Benbow had ever got behind that reserve to really know the man. They made a strange and steadfast group, those four—Benbow and Price Peters and the silently solid Izee Custer, and Clay Rand whose voice suddenly cut through the soft-drawled confusion of men's talk. "Throw this damned deck away, Charley."

The three partners at the bar looked quietly and comprehendingly at that scene. Clay Rand's cheeks, always highly colored, were florid with drink and the sting of bad luck. He tossed his hand to the floor. Faro Charley murmured, "Tough, Clay," and broke open another deck.

Price Peters said softly: "He's been droppin' his

money there since two o'clock. Connie came in with him. Somebody ought to tell him she's probably ready to go home."

Jim Benbow pushed back the brim of his hat in a restless motion, these other two men closely watching him for some break in that tough and smooth and reserved expression. "It's his fun," he suggested, and then looked indifferently at the yellow-shirted stranger standing by the end of the counter. The man's eyes lifted to him for one brief moment, and slid away. Afterwards Benbow's turning glance reached the dead-drunk Povy on the floor. Presently he was smiling in a soft way, in a way that altogether changed him. Both his partners turned to see what had caused that; and by common impulse they walked over to the corner, standing above Povy and commonly speculating on the man.

Benbow said: "Povy, wake up."

"He'll be like that till tomorrow morning," said Custer. "Takes him all night to sleep off his jags."

"You sure?" drawled Benbow.

Izee Custer's eyelids slowly came together and a bright light began to glitter. They stood there, silently considering. Chips made a brittle clack in the room and one of the Mauvaise Valley punchers laughed and struck the flat of his palm against the bar. The steady blang-blang of a freight engine's bell rang over the town's housetops and afterwards they were all thinking of the same idea and considering its possibilities. Benbow waggled his head to Izee who instantly reached down to catch Povy by his armpits and drag him into the saloon's back room, Benbow and Price Peters following. Benbow closed the door.

"The train?" said Price Peters.

"Sure."

"Now wait," Izee broke in. "A little blood—"

Benbow murmured: "Suppose he's got a gun anywhere?"

"An idea," said Price Peters, and made for the back

10

door. Izee Custer called, "Wait for me, Price," and trailed him into Two Dance's rear alley.

Benbow stood there with a little smile breaking its way across his long lips. The ragged light of this back room slanted across his cheeks, turning them irregular and remotely hard. Out front, Clay Rand was swearing again, whereupon Benbow's smile quit showing. He straightened and a dark unruliness had its way with his eyes while he stood there alone, vanishing as soon as Izee and Price Peters came back. Izee had a tin cup in his hand; Price had found a rusty .32. "It was under his bunk in the stable," said Price. "It's loaded."

Izee said: "Ben Drury's wife will sure kill me when she finds out I slaughtered one of her hens." Leaning down he sloshed the contents of the tin cup deliberately across Shad Povy's shirt, that chicken's blood making a wide, irregular stain.

The three of them stood back to observe the effect. "Better hustle," said Price Peters. "The freight's due to pull out."

Izee and Benbow seized the completely indifferent Povy by head and heels and walked out the back way, Price Peters following. Half down the back alley, Benbow thought of something else. "Should have a couple empty shells in that gun."

Price fired the gun twice at the sky. The freight engine was hooting for the switch and the long string of cars jerked into life. The three partners made the moving caboose on the run, lugging Povy inside. A brakeman reared up from his bunk, took one startled look and broke into bitter protest.

"Listen, you fellows. No dead men in here!"

"You'll be stopping at the Mauvaise loading pens," said Benbow. "Joe Russell will be there. You tell Joe that Jim Benbow said to pass Povy along."

"What?"

"He'll know."

The three partners dropped off the caboose as it rolled

11

by the station house. They stood there a moment, and then turned back up Arapahoe Street. "You sure Povy won't wake up till morning?" asked Benbow.

"Never does," said Izee.

"He'll be up in the Yellow Hills by then."

They were in front of Faro Charley's, and Price Peters had begun to laugh immoderately. Benbow said, "I'll be back," and went on toward the Cattle King alone. Constance Dale came slowly down the galleried porch to meet him. She had been standing there; she had been waiting there for Clay Rand.

Benbow pulled off his hat, speaking evenly. "If you're ready to go home, Connie—"

"Where's Clay?"

"I'll get him."

She reached out and touched him with her hand, rooting him to the spot. "Let him play poker." Against the thick shadows of the porch her supple form stirred and made its pattern of grace for Jim Benbow; a stray sliver of light from the hotel window came out to touch her face and though her eyes were hidden from him at the moment he could tell by the lift of her chin and the slow, cool way she spoke that she had been waiting long for Clay, and was hurt by the wait. He knew her better than she knew herself—this child of old Jack Dale. Hat's owner. She could ride the hell out of him, Benbow thought, when her anger was up. And she could go still and distant and try to hold her feelings away from him. One thing or the other—it was that way with them most of the time. But she couldn't hide much from him. She stood soldier-straight, still touching his arm, and her lips made a faint and sweet line in smiling. A strong-tempered and dark-headed girl who could have her way with him any day, and knew it.

"I'll go home with you," she said. "When you're ready."

He said: "You had better break Clay of that habit before you marry him."

"I don't break my men, Jim."

Pete Cruze appeared in the Cattle King's doorway, thinly silhouetted against the light shining through from the hotel lobby. He said: "When you want—"

Benbow's voice sang its soft and thin and wicked tune at Pete Cruze. "Get out of sight." Pete Cruze faded and Constance Dale's head lifted another inch and her eyes were suddenly in the light, round and puzzled and cool. But she didn't ask any questions, knowing Jim Benbow too well. Benbow's fingers were rolling out a cigarette; she could see his narrowing lids deliberately shut away his thoughts. There was a man pacing down the walk slowly, coming beside the gallery of the Cattle King. In another moment she turned to find Cash Gore paused there. Gore said: "Evenin'."

"Good evening, Cash."

Benbow pulled his attention from the cigarette, placing it on Cash Gore with a deliberateness, and there was then in this cool, windless night the faint intimation of some dry and deadly thing creeping up. Gore was a high and narrow shape on the walk. He had paused and removed his hat out of courtesy, his rusty red hair vaguely gleaming under the hotel lights. There wasn't any way of telling what his interest was, for his eyes were too closely guarded to be read and a mustache dropped its straggling ends across his mouth to hide whatever expression might have been there.

"Cheyenne still alive?" he said.

"Yes," said Benbow.

Cash Gore nodded with a kind of saturnine indifference and went on. Benbow dropped his attention back to the cigarette, yet Constance knew he was carefully listening to Cash Gore's footsteps tread toward Faro Charley's saloon. Benbow had mannerisms even in his silence; he had little expressions that betrayed his mind to her always observant eyes. It was something she could not help, this deep interest in what he thought and what he felt. She had known him for years, sometimes hating him and sometimes almost loving him, and never able to release herself from the turbulent pull of his personality.

He bent toward her. "Tell that fool Cruze," he said in a soft-running murmur, "to stay out of sight until he gets his orders," and wheeled away from the porch.

Six horses stood in a row before Dunmire's stable and men crouched at the base of the stable's wall, their cigarette points glittering through the dark. Cash's men. When he came into Faro Charley's again he observed Cash Gore standing alone at the bar, the shackle-jointed frame eased against it and the drawn and quick-tempered face bowed over a glass of whisky. These things Benbow saw in one rapid survey—the stranger with the yellow shirt still immersed in his own isolation, Izee and Price Peters grouped about the poker table, Clay Rand grown more flushed and more irritable from his run of luck. Benbow put his arms on Clay Rand's chair, but his glance went over to touch Izee Custer and tell Custer something; and then dropped back to Clay.

Custer said, to nobody in particular: "Hell, I've had enough of this place," and left the saloon.

Benbow bent over to speak quietly to Clay Rand. "Connie's ready to go home."

"Sure," said Clay Rand, and looked at his cards. There was a bet made. Rand called it and lost. He put both his palms on the table, staring at Faro Charley. His eyes were a deep blue, and unstable with sultry anger. All this blondheaded man's features were full and bold. Benbow said: "Come on, Clay. We're all ready to ride."

Clay jerked his head around. "Good God, Jim—let a man alone!"

Benbow said, "All right, kid," and wheeled away from the table, showing no expression. But Price Peters, still at the bar, sent a rapid glance from Benbow to Clay Rand and gently shook his head. Cash Gore swung to look at this scene with a slicing, taciturn interest.

At that moment Pete Cruze walked into the saloon, a young and grinning boy with an oversized Adam's apple.

He saw Jim Benbow and stopped, and an expression of uneasiness came to his face. He said uncertainly: "Hello, Jim."

Benbow stared at Cruze. "What you doing here, Pete?"

"Just rode in for some tobacco."

"Who's taking your place at the line cabin?"

Peter Cruze dropped his eyes. "Well," he said, "nobody. I didn't figure to be gone long."

Benbow said: "Damn a man I can't trust. You had orders to stay there. What have I got to do—give you a nurse and a guardian?"

"Jim," said young Pete Cruze, all at once losing his uneasiness, "don't talk to a man that way."

The room turned still and the poker game stopped. Clay Rand lifted his head, at once alert and puzzled. Nobody said anything for a moment. Cash Gore swung his lank shape completely around to see what all this was. Benbow spoke with an irony that hurt: "How do you want to be talked to, Mr. Cruze?"

"Well," said Pete Cruze stubbornly, "not like that."

Benbow said: "My apologies for showing a lack of respect for your feelings. Of course, Mr. Cruze, no gentleman wants to be tied down to one spot when he's out of tobacco. I'll just relieve you of the trouble."

"Listen—"

"You've got your walking papers from Hat," stated Benbow bluntly. "Right now."

Pete Cruze put his hands into his pockets and pulled them out. He got redder and redder and his Adam's apple slid up and down. He murmured, "Well, shucks," and then simply bawled at Benbow, "to hell with your damned job! I quit before you fired me!" And having said that, he stamped from the saloon the picture of mortal affront.

Clay Rand said: "Kind of a tough guy tonight, Jim. Who stepped on your foot?"

Benbow had an answer for Clay, a wickedly even

15

answer: "This place seems to be full of gentlemen of leisure. Don't let me trouble your game, Clay."

Clay Rand's ruddy cheeks took on an instant set. He laid down his cards. "You're a little too high, Jim. I don't work for Hat, and my time's my own."

"I'll remember that," said Benbow and turned to Price Peters. "Riding my way?"

The stranger in the yellow shirt moved out from the end of the bar. "If you're in the market for a rider—"

Benbow had started for the door. He wheeled and looked down on this lesser-built man whose face was flat and unsentimental and indifferent. He had a crooked nose scratched whitely by a scar, and a pair of eyes incredibly watchful.

"Where you from?" said Benbow.

"Arizona," put in the stranger.

Benbow said briefly: "It's tougher up here, Arizona."

"Do I look easy?" asked the stranger with a faint insolence.

Benbow stared at the man; and presently grinned in a thin, appreciative way. "If you find the Hat outfit tomorrow, I can use you. Coming, Price?"

Price strolled over, going out of the saloon with Benbow. The man so suddenly named Arizona went back to his corner and wigwagged silently for another drink, Cash Gore's glance following him with a bitter-bright attention. Clay Rand started to lift his cards again. He looked at them, and dropped them abruptly and got up from his chair. "See you next week," he told Faro Charley, and started for the door.

But just before he swung away his glance lifted carelessly and touched Cash Gore across the room. Cash Gore met that inspection evenly and then swung his narrow shoulders back to the bar. He put both elbows on it and his head rolled forward and thus he stood, still and taciturn and engaged in his own secret thoughts. Once his lips moved and he slid a covert look at Arizona, as though some sudden and powerful idea had stirred him;

and dropped his head again.

Clay Rand left the saloon, catching up with Benbow and Price Peters. The three of them walked on in thorough silence for a short distance. Afterwards Rand laughed and put his arm on Benbow's shoulder. "Forget it, kid. I lost a hell of a lot of money tonight and maybe I spoke too fast."

"Sure," drawled Benbow. "Sure," and all at once the feeling between these three men changed and the strain went away. Price Peters spoke with an open relief. "That's better. I don't like to hear you boys wrangle."

Clay Rand observed: "Never saw you work on a man like you did Pete Cruze."

Benbow said: "He was supposed to stay where I put him."

They came to their horses in front of the Cattle King. Izee Custer stood there, talking with Constance Dale; and Jim Benbow saw how Connie's face came around and showed its faint anger when Clay Rand went forward to her. He didn't, Benbow observed, apologize to Connie for his delay. It wasn't in the big, blond man to make amends that way. He had another way, which was to smile at the girl and let the careless, teasing melody of his voice have its effect. "I tried to win enough off Faro Charley to build you a mansion in the Yellow Hills, Connie."

"And didn't?" said the girl.

"I guess Faro Charley will be buildin' the mansion," explained Clay Rand wryly. "Well, another day, another kind of luck."

"I suppose," said Connie in a small voice.

They went out to the horses and swung up. Paused a moment, Jim Benbow looked back toward Dunmire's stable to observe again the shadowy shapes of Gore's men. They had been there all this while, motionless and speechless, and waiting for Gore. Clay Rand was laughing with a deep and reckless amusement at something Connie had said or done; and now Connie turned her horse and fell abreast Benbow. There was a little interplay of feeling

17

here Benbow had missed, for he saw the sudden and desperate set of her face. Somehow Clay had hurt her again. She said, to Benbow, the very coolness of her tone telling him of her stifled pride: "Ready to go, Jim?"

Square Madge Reynolds crossed from Donlake's store to the Cattle King. Near Benbow she lifted her head—this big and buxom and still attractive woman—and smiled at him and spoke with a quick favor: "Hello, Jim."

Benbow lifted his hat, and then she had gone into the Cattle King and Benbow put his horse to a trot, leaving Two Dance behind. Ahead of them lay the formless shape of Two Dance Range. There was a faint and wild-scented wind crossing this night and in the bitter-black depths of the sky all the stars were glittering.

"You have friends in strange places, Jim."

He said, "I take 'em where I find them," and let it go like that. She was thinking of Square Madge, and she would remember that against him. Or maybe it would be in his favor. He never knew about Constance Dale. She had a way of judging his life and sometimes of analyzing it for him with a frankness that was startling, as though her interest in it was too deep to be ignored. As though she had a share in his life. Well, he had been Hat's foreman five years and there was little reserve between them.

Clay Rand was chuckling out his pleasure at something Price Peters had said. Things, Benbow thought, ran this fast for Clay. He could curse at his luck over the poker table; and forget it soon, and find things in the night to set off his gay humor. Always this man lived by extremes, and had his way of making people love him.

Rand said: "What took you to Cheyenne, Jim?"

"Stockmen's convention."

"That all?" questioned Rand idly.

"Yes."

"You can be a close-mouthed sucker," jeered Rand.

Izee Custer's voice came from the rear. "A good habit for these times."

"So," said Rand, a soft curiosity in his talk, "there was

18

something else."

"No," said Benbow. It was the way he said it. Talk stopped there and they ran up the Two Dance grade in silence and alternately walked and cantered along the pine-guarded alley that was the summit pass. Deep in the timber they saw the brief flash of Summit Ranch and afterwards, falling down the slope into the black sweep of Two Dance Valley, the faint and far-spaced glint of isolated outfits began to break that deep plain's mystery. They passed Gay's store and presently reached the valley floor. By tacit agreement Benbow and Peters and Izee Custer drew ahead and halted, leaving Constance Dale behind with Clay Rand. Benbow rolled himself a cigarette, hearing Clay Rand's talk rise and fall in a kind of amused and melodic bantering; and hearing Connie's quiet answer. She would be forgiving him for his sins, as she always did, as all people forgave Clay Rand. There was silence then, back there. After a while Connie said: "Clay!" and Benbow scraped a match across his leg to ignite the cigarette. The planes of his face, against this sudden yellow light, were flat and hard. The light went out as Connie came up alone. Clay Rand was racing off to the southeast, taking the short cut across the valley to where his own small outfit, Short Arrow, lay at the base of the Yellows. They went on, hearing his voice calling cheerfully back: "So long!"

A mile farther ahead Price Peters turned with a brief "good night," and struck for his own place down toward the badlands, westward. Benbow and Connie pressed forward, while Izee Custer dropped discreetly back; and after another forty minutes of steady riding along the flat width of the valley they raised the Hat's lights and passed into its yard.

2. Charity for a Man

Big Jack Dale's voice emerged from the solemn depths of the porch. "That you, Jim?"

Connie said, openly amused: "Is it your foreman or your daughter that interests you the most?"

"My foreman," drawled Big Jack Dale, "is a necessity."

Connie slid from her horse and went into the house, dropping her father a kiss on the way. It was as though she made a reluctant concession to Big Jack; and as though he accepted it reluctantly. There was, Benbow thought, always that unsentimental manner masking the real affection between those two. Izee Custer took the horses away and Benbow stood on the porch steps, idly smoking out his cigarette. Big Jack Dale shifted in his chair and sighed, and said:

"Get your business done?"

"All the cattlemen are cryin' about the rustlers this year," said Benbow. "It's the same story, from Jackson's Hole to Julesburg. We're bein' hurt. So's everybody else. Seems like there's a reason."

"A reason won't help spoiled beef," growled Big Jack Dale. "But what is it?"

"The little boys are growing into big boys. The big idea hit 'em all at once, which is that it's easier to gang up and make a real business of rustlin' than to play a lone hand. There's gangs all over the state. They got a system. A man planted in the outfits to hear things. A bunch to run the stuff. A bunch to hold it somewhere, a long ways off. Another bunch to peddle it. It's what all the stock-men in Cheyenne say."

"You think it's that way here?"

Jim Benbow dropped his cigarette, grinding it beneath a boot heel. He sat down, stretching his long frame forward, pulling his big hands together. Hunkered over that way he listened to the shallow river cluck and ripple its way through the willows near the porch. "I mean to find out," he said.

"How?"

"I fired Peter Cruze in Two Dance tonight. And hired another man."

"What other man?" said Dale.

"Another man."

Big Jack Dale's amusement came along the dark with a husky sibilance. "All right, Jim. All right." He got up then and stamped his walking stick three times on the porch flooring; and went inside the house.

Benbow rubbed his hard palms together, and held them still and stared at a point of light pulsing far across Two Dance Valley, which was Rho Beam's chuck wagon making camp near the base of the Yellow Hills. But he wasn't thinking of Rho Beam or the chuck wagon. It was the softness of Constance Dale's voice when she spoke to Clay Rand that kept ringing like the gentle echoes of a bell in his head.

She came out of the house quickly, passing him and turning to face him at the foot of the porch. He saw the oval of her face shining through the shadows, with that streak of darkness lying like a velvet strip across her eyes. A straight-bodied girl, full of fire, full of hidden wealth. Something struck him and left its fresh shock. He kept remembering her as a leggy kid, built like a boy, without hips and without bosom; but he was seeing something he hadn't seen before. She was a mature woman now, more reticent than she had been; modeled in the way a woman should be.

"Jim," she said, "you're a glum man."

21

"As usual."

She murmured, "As usual," and sank beside him. Suddenly she had tipped against his shoulder, without sound. It startled him. She was too proud to cry, but he could feel her body trembling; she reached out to catch his hand and to grip it in the way of a girl somehow frightened.

He said, as stolid as he could manage: "Buck fever?"

"I'm supposed to be happy."

"Hits some people in strange ways."

She stood abruptly up, and spoke with a swift outrage. "Damn you, Jim Benbow! Don't be so brutal."

He didn't answer that for a moment. He sat there, hands idle and his head inclined toward the ground. After a while he said: "Let a man alone, Connie. I can't help you. I can't even help myself."

He heard her swift, sharp sigh. She murmured: "I'm sorry, Jim. So sorry."

After she had gone into the house he got up and circled the yard, keening this night for what it held. The day's heat was out of the earth and autumn's chill flowed along the valley. Turning back to the bunkhouse, he heard the fast drumming of horses come up the Two Dance road; and in a little while made out a string of riders running by, bound for the Yellow Hills. He could not see them, but he knew who they were. This was the way the men of Running M—Cash Gore's men—used in homeward travel.

Around eight o'clock that evening the train crew laid the loose form of Shad Povy before Bill Russell at Mauvaise station. Part of Russell's crew happened to be there and these men took up Povy and carried him to the near-by ranch house. An hour later, when the Rocky Springs stage came by, they put Povy aboard. At midnight, following his instructions, the driver stopped on the long grade leading up Yellow Hills and lugged Povy to a comfortable spot in the pine timber and left him there. Thus, having come sixty miles from Two Dance in a dead stupor, cheerfully and even enthusiastically cared for along the way, Shad Povy at last rested on the upper edge of Two Dance Valley, stained by blood and with two bullets fired from his gun.

Benbow was at the corrals with Custer and three other Hat men when Arizona rode up, shortly before sunrise the next morning. Arizona eased himself in the saddle and for a moment let his glance have its sharp way with the men scattered about the place. Physically he was not a match for any of the Hat crew, and yet there was something about him that made these other men take their careful look. A steely calm covering the hint of a wildness fitfully asleep. A way of absorbing the world with his eyes.

He said, to Benbow: "You still want a hand?"

Benbow kept his attention on Arizona, as though his thoughts were not fully satisfied. But he spoke to Izee. "Take him over to the line cabin Pete Cruze had."

Custer went off to saddle his horse. Arizona let his legs hang full length, free of the stirrups; and rolled himself a smoke. None of the other men broke the silence and presently Arizona said: "Anything about this line cabin I ought to know?"

Benbow said: "You look like you could take care of yourself."

"My habit," said Arizona briefly.

"Stick to the habit," answered Benbow. "It's all I've got to tell you."

"That kind of a job," observed Arizona, the lids of his eyes drawing together.

Izee Custer trotted up. Arizona joined him and without further parley these two rode over the ranch bridge and fell into a steady canter southward across the flats of the Two Dance. Presently they were a pair of diminishing shapes under a sudden burst of sunlight, the color of Arizona's yellow shirt dying out. Gippy Collins, who was only a kid, spoke up.

"Well, where's Pete Cruze then?"

"Fired," said Benbow, and turned to his own horse. In

a little while he was riding northward through the swell of a fine, brisk morning with a flawless sky above him.

Two Dance Valley ran this way twenty miles with scarcely an undulation, with only the willows of the river breaking the flow of the flat earth. On the north lay the low Two Dance Range in a kind of continuous wall; to the south the ramparts of the Yellow Hills shouldered abruptly up from the valley floor, dark-streaked by pine timber. In the foreground little spirals of dust were rising from wagons hauling hay out of the river meadows. This was the heart of the valley, these miles of Hat lying between the hills and rolling east to Mauvaise siding fifty miles removed. He could not see the quarters of the neighboring outfits, but he had them all in his mind clearly. Rand's Short Arrow tucked in a crease of the Yellows, twelve miles off, Running M two miles west of Clay, its houses backed against the mouth of Granite Canyon, Diamond-and-a-Half more remotely placed in the Yellows. Behind him, in the west, Block T and The Crescent and Price Peters' horse ranch verging off into the chalky color-streaked gulches of the badlands. With a few nesters here and there.

This was the Valley. The year was 1884 and Benbow, cruising on through the strong light of the day, had only to close his sharp eyes to recall in his mind every trail and spring and boundary mark within an area eighty miles square. This summer was his fifth season as Hat's foreman. And his tenth since, as a wild and footloose kid, he had come up the trail from Texas. It hadn't been so long ago that Indians made their lodges along this river; and he could remember seeing Sam Yancey's body lying up by the breaks, naked and without scalp.

Riding this way, studying the ground and horizon always for news, a man often pondered strange things and reached strange answers. Only, sometimes there were no answers. That was what he thought this morning. A man fooled himself into believing he could drift with the seasons, the seasons not changing and himself not changing. It was hard to realize he wasn't a footloose kid any more and it was hard to think that Connie Dale, within the reach of his voice for so long, would presently marry Clay Rand. That would be the break—the end of something. It was hard to figure beyond that break. Was that what Big Jack Dale, hunkered down in his porch chair, was thinking too?

This while, his eyes were running the deep reaches of the valley. He had seen Arizona and Izee Custer vanish at the base of the Yellows and later that morning he watched Izee travel back, shooting up dust spirals as he rode. It was beyond two o'clock when Benbow reached Hat again to find Izee crouched on his heels in the shade of the corral, taking ease. Izee opened his eyes, said briefly, "He'll do," and closed them again.

Benbow ate a solitary dinner and went to the office adjoining Hat's big living-room. Jack Dale sat on his customary wide leather chair, his feet hoisted to the sill of an open window, his attention strayed somewhere beyond the thickening whorls of fall haze lying across the Two Dance. Benbow sat up to the desk and opened the work book. He wrote in it, "Arizona, hired," and added the date—and put after the name a faint cross. The cross represented something in his mind, something he couldn't write in the book.

He set the book aside, and remained there before the desk, his solid fingers idle; and his mind narrowing down to Hat's business. All the life of the ranch, its people, its livestock and water rights, its bank account and its bills on Omaha were there before him, set down by his own hand. He knew more about Hat than old Jack. He represented it, he operated it, he made most of its decisions. Considering the desk, more and more involved in his thoughts, Benbow could hark back and realize how deliberately Jack Dale had thrown this on his shoulders until now the old man was like a silent partner. It was Jack Dale's life—this big and sprawling outfit which lay chunked out between the twenty-mile sweep of the Two Dance and Yellow ranges. But it had come to be his, Benbow's, life too. Until nothing else mattered much. He

25

was, he thought, a fixture, a part of the place.

Yet there was that shadow of change over him, unsettling him. When Clay married Connie, it would properly be Clay who sat at this desk. There wasn't room for two riding bosses on Hat.

Jack Dale said: "Where's Rho Beam?"

"In the Yellows, with the chuck wagon."

"Beef should be heavy this year."

"We'll be shipping out of Mauvaise all the way till early winter. The market is good."

By and by Jack Dale turned his head toward Benbow to catch a careful look. It wasn't like this big, bronzed puncher to be dallying before a desk late of a fall afternoon. Benbow was a restless one, a driver, a fighter. But he sat there, with the steam out of him; with his tough cheeks drawn into tight lines.

Jack Dale said, indolently: "When I was young I had a fever to travel. So I rode till I was gant. Like a longhorn starved for salt and lookin' for it." He let that lie in the still air. And then he said: "You're twenty-five, Jim. Don't your feet fiddle?"

"I got that knocked out of me early, Jack. When I was fourteen, coming up the trail from Texas."

"Man's got to be a little wild when he's young," murmured Dale. "And let the wildness spill. Or he goes sour, like a bad horse. Or flat, like a hand-fed deer." He cleared his throat. "I observe there's some hell in you. It's why I sent you to Cheyenne—to get drunk and wind up in the cooler. You didn't do it."

"Think that would help, Jack?"

Dale's glance sharpened on Benbow. Afterwards he shook his head. "No, I guess that ain't it." But there was something in him that stirred his habitual silence powerfully and had to come out. In a little while he spoke again. "A few women need gentle handling. But it's my observation the rest of 'em like a man better if he makes them cry now and then. Seems to me women have a habit of just admirin' men that treat them softly and with understanding—and fall in love with the kind that give

26

em storm and trouble. They like the rough way better han the smooth."

A rider galloped impetuously into the yard and stopped nd a woman's voice—Eileen Gray's quick, expressive voice—sailed through the house. "Connie." Presently both women were on the porch, talking. Benbow got out of his chair. He stood in the middle of the office, his rough and flat shape making a high presence there. He looked down upon Old Jack Dale's grayly passive face with a full understanding of what the Hat owner was trying to tell him. He shook his head. "It will have to be the way it is, Jack," he said quietly, and strolled out to the porch.

Jack Dale settled more deeply in his chair. Indian summer's haze stirred like fire-smoke all across the Two Dance. Beyond, the ramparts of the Yellow Range were dim and strange—just as they had been fifteen years before when his wagons had ventured to this choice and dangerous ground of the Sioux. Isolated images rose before him and passed on—of men he had known so well, of things he had done in his heartier years. But his thoughts, irritably insistent, returned to this Jim Benbow who was so much like a son—and in whom he had so deliberately entrusted the management of the ranch. Now after five years he saw that hope die; and like an inveterate poker player silently discarding a poor hand, he threw his particular ambition away. And sat wholly still in the chair, watching the day turn on.

Benbow stood against a porch post watching the two girls. Eileen Gray's glance came to him immediately and took a personal notice. She said in a teasing voice: "Don't be so serious, Jim. I'm worth a smile, am I not?"

It drew the smile out of him and then Eileen, satisfied with her accomplishment, turned toward Connie and the two fell to talking about the wedding of the following week. Eileen was marrying Joe Gannon who ran a one-man spread over against the Ramparts.

There was a contrast here Jim Benbow noticed clearly. Eileen Gray was like a flash of restless color, slim and

27

laughter-loving, and with graphic features that kept registering all the sudden changes of her temper. A pretty kid. One that wanted men to like her and was hurt by any man's indifference. Connie sat quietly by, a taller girl and outwardly a calmer one—hearing all that Eileen said and meanwhile listening beyond the words for things left unsaid. Once her eyes lifted to Jim Benbow, as though wanting to know what he thought.

There was a rider coming across the flat on a steady lope, which would be Clay Rand riding in to see Connie. Benbow built himself another smoke, the secret knowledge in his head making this picture very sharp to him. Connie's glance rose to that approaching figure and all the gravity of her face softened, changing the expression of her eyes and mouth—even though she was trying to hide that change. When the hoofs of the horse struck the hard earth in the yard Eileen Gray swung around and then the laughter went immediately out of her, replaced by a dark and half-haunted look. Benbow saw how completely she threw her heart at Rand; and then he pulled his eyes from the girl, silently enraged.

Rand slid from his saddle and came on forward, a high and gallant shape against the sun; he removed his hat and his smile was as it always was on that flushed and handsome face—softening all resentment. He said, "A picture of beauty for a fact," and then his chuckle ran the dry air. "Marred only by the face that's shocked a thousand men. Meaning Hat's hard-boiled foreman."

"Maybe I'm in the way," drawled Benbow.

"Just came over to protect my interests," grinned Clay Rand. "You're runnin' me a tough race."

Benbow said: "Me? I was disqualified at the post, Clay. I grew up with Connie and she knows me too well."

Clay drawled: "Never let a woman know you too well, kid. They like a little mystery."

Connie said smoothly: "If it's mystery you want, Clay, you'd better cover your tracks a little better."

Clay Rand's ruddy cheeks showed a deeper flush. It was a thing that stabbed into his pride; he showed that.

28

Then Eileen Gray stirred to attract his attention and spoke in a begging way. "You coming to my wedding, Clay?"

"I never miss weddings, Eileen."

They made a three-cornered group on the porch, with Jim Benbow in the background, out of the scene. There was something here that excluded him definitely, and he dropped his cigarette on the porch, ground it beneath his foot and returned to the office to find Jack Dale asleep on the corner couch, his face covered by a newspaper. Benbow drew out his hay and stock record and began to work at it. On the forks of the Two Dance five hundred tons. At the willow meadow thirty tons. The Indians on the reservation were saying it would be another tough winter—a starving winter. Sometimes they were right and sometimes they were wrong, but in the cattle business a man had to be smart. Smart with beef and ignorant in the ways of a woman. It seemed to be his story.

He worked on with his mind thus split. Hay and beef and Clay Rand and Arizona and himself and Connie Dale—and the far darkness of Hat's future. Another six hundred tons along the upper corner of the river. His big fingers moved with a steady regularity, pressing the pen point into bold strokes. The voice of Clay and the girls rose and fell along the porch. The day droned on and the hay hands were riding into the yard with the late long-flung shadows. Somewhere Izee said in a quick voice: "Jim—come out here." It was five-thirty then.

When he got to the porch Izee simply pointed toward the farther sheds of Hat, around which came a rider at a jiggling trot. He rode a scrubby horse barebacked, with a piece of rope twisted Indian fashion for a hackamore; a little man all bent over and having a hard time of it.

"Povy," murmured Izee, in his blandest manner. Hat's men were moving forward to see what this was. Clay Rand said: "What is it?"

Shad Povy brought his sweat-caked horse to a stand at the porch. Dry blood stretched all across his shirt and he

29

had the expression of a fugitive on his peaked face. He tried to ease himself and almost fell off. He looked at the encircling hay hands and back to Benbow. A hoarse croak came out of him.

"Jim, before God, I dunno how it happened! I'm a condemned man! Last night I killed a fella! Gimme a fresh horse. I got to leave the country."

There was a shocked silence on the porch. Izee put his hand across his face slowly and looked at Benbow. And then Benbow sat down suddenly on the porch steps and laid his broad palms on his knees for support and let go with a deep, uncontrolled shout of laughter.

Povy said: "What the hell, here? I—"

His lips were moving, but nobody heard what he said. The whole yard full of men were at once whooping, as though they had gone crazy. Izee's grin got broader and broader; and Benbow seemed to be crying, to be praying. It went on like that for a full minute, with Shad Povy staring about him, his expression beginning to break. He said, "Aw," and his jaws dropped. All at once he jerked up the hackamore rope and yelled out: "Damn you, Jim! One of these days you'll go too fur!" And afterwards he galloped out of the Hat yard, his skinny frame bouncing a foot at each forward surge the beast made, the wild howling of the collected Hat crowd following him mercilessly.

Connie said: "You ought to be spanked, Jim Benbow."

Clay Rand stared at Benbow. He hadn't laughed much at the joke. He spoke now with a faint malice, a thin note of envy. "Why didn't you let me in on this last night?"

Benbow got to his feet. He had to wipe the tears out of his eyes. He only lifted his hand at Rand and then went down the yard with Izee Custer, both of them howling.

The supper triangle began to bang behind the house and the crowd broke for the low, long ell running back from the main quarters. The sun dropped over the western badlands in one fast flashing sheet of flame; and violet began to flow immediately across the valley. Eileen said: "I've got to hurry," and went out to her horse. In the saddle, she looked down at Clay Rand in a way that was quiet and rigidly unhappy. "I hope you'll like this wedding, Clay," she said, and then raced out of the yard.

Connie Dale rose from her chair. "Staying for supper?"

Clay Rand shook his head. "No. What did she mean, Connie?"

Connie looked at him. She had a way of going quietly angry that always turned her face slim and pointed and proud. "Clay, I'm not as much of a fool as you might think. Your affairs aren't very mysterious."

He came up the steps to her immediately, not smiling any more. He said: "Connie, can't you be charitable to a man?" She started to speak, but he bent his blond head down and kissed her. They were like this for a moment— long enough for Benbow to see them when he came back from the bunkhouses. Clay stepped back, serious and strained and having a rough time with his feelings.

"I think I'd always forgive you," murmured Connie Dale. "It's something I can't help."

Benbow swung wide of the porch, going deliberately away from it. Clay Rand clapped on his hat. He stood a moment before the girl who was so stirred, who so deeply showed the way of her heart. "Hope for a sinner," he said gently. "Never change toward me, Connie. Never mind what happens—never change."

"Stay for supper."

"No," he said, "not now," and went to his horse and rode away. Connie watched him swing out across the valley toward his ranch far over at the foot of the Ramparts. Dusk whirled along the flats in wide blue streamers.

3. The Grisly Message

It was dusk and then it was dark, with Old Jack and Connie and Benbow on the porch. The hay haulers and the few home ranch riders were grouped down the yard by the bunkhouse and somebody had brought out a guitar, playing "Buffalo Gals." A breeze ruffled up the dying earth-heat and dust and hay smell was very strong. Far over in the Two Dance footslopes the lights of Gay's store were winking and vanishing and winking again. The sound of riders made a trembling echo off in the stillness—riders coming on fast.

Old Jack Dale said: "Takes me back. We used to sit here and listen to horses comin' hell bent like that and wonder if it was the Indians. Trouble out of the Yellows. The Two Dance hills never meant any grief. Riders from that way meant good news. But it was always trouble when they came from the Yellows. Time goes too fast. Cheats a man. Promises him a lot of things when he's young. All of a sudden he's old and it's time to go."

"Dad," murmured Connie Dale.

"Not complaining," said Old Jack Dale. "I've had my fun."

Off yonder the rhythm of the riders was abruptly broken; and afterwards one single horse rushed along the road past Hat, and disappeared. Benbow had been leaning against the steps; he sat up at once, listening into this

32

night. Jack Dale's chair creaked and the old man said: "Which is odd."

Izee Custer's short and rolling shape appeared in the yard. He came on to the foot of the porch, not saying anything, the point of his cigarette making a red hole through the shadows. The lone rider's horse sent back its diminishing echoes and then they ceased entirely. But there was something on the edge of Hat Yard, something that stirred and stopped. Benbow rose. He said, "Put out your cigarette, Izee," and watched that glowing point drop to the earth.

There was a horse drifting in, the shape of it breaking vaguely through this darkness; riderless yet with some low shadow across the saddle. Benbow stared at that a long moment and then murmured, "Bring a light, Izee," and walked out from the house.

The horse stopped and threw up its head, expelling a draughty breath. Benbow said, "Easy, easy," and took his time. But when he caught the dragging reins he stood fast, at once identifying that burden lashed across the saddle. A man there. His voice ripped the shadows. "Hurry with that lantern."

Men ran on from the bunkhouse. Old Jack Dale challenged him from the porch. "What do you see?" Izee trotted forward with a lantern. He came around Benbow and held the light full against that pony's burden. They saw it at once.

This was Arizona, thrown across the saddle and tied there like a sack of meal. His head hung down and his arms hung down and his face was turned to chalk; and he was dead.

Izee said in a singsong voice, "Wait," and reached out to a bit of paper fluttering on a thong attached to Arizona's neck. He passed it over to Benbow, who smoothed it against his knee and held it before Izee's lantern. It said:

Here's your range detective from Cheyenne, Benbow.

33

You didn't fool anybody.

All Hat's crew stood around the horse in a still, shocked circle. Jack Dale came up to have his quick look and Connie walked forward and put her hand on Benbow's shoulder, the sound of her breathing irregular and very small. Izee Custer saw the girl's white face staring at the pony's burden and instantly swung around, putting his body between it and the light. There was a feeling here that dragged its spiderlike tentacles across all of them, screwing up their nerves. Izee Custer's dark eyes lifted to Benbow to reveal a brighter and brighter glitter.

Benbow moved suddenly through the circle, leading the horse down the yard. Izee handed his lantern to somebody else; in front of the crew's quarters he helped Benbow unfasten the dead Arizona and lift him inside to one of the bunks. The light traveled forward from hand to hand, shining down on the man again and showing the blue, pencil-pointed hole centered in his forehead.

"Rifle bullet," said Izee, voice plunking that long stillness like a rock dropped into a well.

Gippy Collins, Hat's youngest rider, said: "Well, who was this fellow? What'd he take Pete Cruze's place for?"

Izee grunted, "Shut up, Gippy," and followed Benbow out of the bunkhouse. Benbow called, "Gippy, come here," and waited until the kid's stringy shape appeared uneasily before him. "Ride into Two Dance, Gippy. You'll find Pete Cruze there. Tell him to come back."

"Whud he do?"

Izee repeated gently: "Shut up, Gippy."

Benbow went down the yard with Izee as far as the porch. Jack Dale sat in his chair, making no motion. Connie stood with her shoulders touching a post, her face showing vaguely to Benbow. Jack Dale's voice ran the silence with an iron distinctness.

"You framed something, but it leaked out. Is that it?"

"I arranged this with Arizona at Cheyenne four days ago. His real name was Jory and he was a detective for the

34

Cattlemen's Association. Cruze knew his part, and played it well when I fired him. But there was a leak." He spoke in a dying, softening voice. Connie turned nearer him when she heard that tone, knowing the fury held beneath it. Gippy Collins pounded out of the yard toward Two Dance town; the shallow river sent its clucking echoes into this deep stillness. Benbow stirred his tall figure. He spoke again. "We're going to have some trouble, Jack."

"You can have it," said Old Jack Dale, "or you can avoid it."

"Trouble will hurt Hat."

"It's your choice, Jim. You're runnin' this ranch. It's your say."

"Hat," said Benbow, "comes first. It always has."

"I built Hat out of trouble," Dale said. "But you can duck this trouble if that's your desire. I make no recommend."

"No," said Benbow. "I'm out to break, or be busted. But I can leave Hat clear of it."

"How?"

Benbow looked up at the girl. "When you marry Clay, Connie, he'll be the foreman here. I'm not desirous of turnin' a wrecked ranch over to him. When you marrying him?"

She said: "Why, Jim?"

And Jack Dale growled: "What's that got to do with it?"

"I can wait my time until he comes. I can hold off on this fight—if it ain't too long. But if it's to be a delayed affair then I'll have to quit and go after these fellows on my own hook."

"Quit?" said Dale in a resounding tone. "Who the hell is pickin' foremen for this ranch, you or me? You'll stay."

But Benbow's answer was softly stubborn. "Clay's my best friend, but there ain't room for two foremen here."

"Who said there'd be two foremen? He'll be Connie's husband, but you'll run Hat."

35

"Connie," said Benbow, "your dad ought to be a smarter man than that. Tell him what he doesn't see."

The silence ran on, Connie Dale not speaking. Izee turned away because he knew he had no place here. Jack Dale pushed himself out of the rocker, his heavy body a painful burden to his joints. "I guess I see," he said.

Connie Dale descended the steps until her eyes were level with Jim Benbow's face. She touched his arm and her voice was softer with him than it had ever been. "I don't know when I'll be married, Jim. But you'll have to stay until then."

"Why?" asked Benbow. "Why?"

Jack Dale went to the house doorway, and paused there. He said: "When I ran Hat I never stepped around a fight. I'd like to see one more scrap before I die." Having said it, he went inside.

Connie said: "What are you afraid of, Jim?"

He swung away from her deliberately. But she was a strong presence at his side, like fragrance riding the night air, like melody coming over a great distance. Well, it was worse than that. Here stood Connie Dale to shake him badly with the hint of a womanliness so fresh and turbulent and strong. All across the flats the full shadows of night pulsed; the faint lights of Gay's store were winking out from the foothills and the near earth had a gray, lucent shine to it. He remembered the way Arizona's body hung over the saddle.

He said irritably: "What do you want to delay the marriage for?"

"I don't know, Jim," she told him, humbly. "I don't know."

"Nobody," he grunted, "seems to know anything."

She repeated: "What are you afraid of?"

He wheeled and reached for her, pulling her down the steps altogether until she fell against him. He had a tight grip on her arms and could feel the sudden tremor running through her body, through all its soft resilience. There was a little moment of passiveness; and then she was pushing against him. He let her go.

She said: "Is that what you're afraid of?"

He couldn't find the right answer. Wildness drifted with the night and the feel of it was queer to him, like the weightless, breathless air preceding the break of bad weather. Only it was worse than that. His thoughts couldn't reach ahead, but off there somewhere—in the farther space and in the future time—lay something that turned him spooky, sending through him a cold thread of actual fear.

He took her hand, holding it without pressure in his own big palm. "It's the end of good times, Connie. For all of us, I'd guess."

4. Women Have a Way

George Gray was marrying off his only daughter and only child, and since he was a large-handed man in a neighborly land, all of Two Dance Valley collected at Block T this crisp morning to help him celebrate.

Standing beside the keg of whisky set up on a platform, George Gray considered the valley men around him with a rather harassed glance. He couldn't, he told them frankly, consider himself in his right mind. Preparing for the ceremony had been just one damned thing after the other, and if he'd known it was to be like this, with the womenfolk crying all over the place and the house decorated up like Fourth of July and the work on the ranch gone plumb to the devil while his riders wore themselves gant running to town for things forgot at the last minute, he'd of put Eileen and Joe Gannon into a buggy and made a shotgun wedding of it long before now. Having said it, he tapped the keg for another drink and took it quick and straight. And said, dismally, "Your health, Joe."

They were all here, Jim Benbow, Izee, Clay Rand and Price Peters, Gray's own Block T crew, Gordon Howland who ran Crescent over on the edge of the badlands, Jubal Frick of Running M and Cash Gore, his foreman, the folks from Summit Ranch and from Gay's store, and Nelson McGinnis of the remote Diamond-and-a-Half up in the Yellow Hills. And the bridegroom, Joe Gannon, who stood uncomfortably and unsmilingly with the group. And a young kid who had ridden into the yard and made himself at home, though nobody knew him. The bishop, who had come from Cheyenne to perform the ceremony, was in the house, rehearsing with the women.

Everybody filled up at the whisky barrel to acknowledge George Gray's toast. Everybody but Joe Gannon. Gannon said, "Thanks, George," and looked around him with an air that wasn't quite easy. He was ten years older than Eileen, a rather somber man who ran his own spread over in the Yellows and had a reputation for a short temper.

Gordon Howland, George Gray's nearest neighbor for fifteen years, spoke up cheerfully. "You can sleep late tomorrow and rest your mind."

They all grinned at that, knowing how much worry Gray's half-wild daughter had caused him along the years. Clay Rand turned to wink at Benbow; and then Benbow saw Joe Gannon stare at Rand with a swift flash of anger. The crowd broke up, loitering around the tables spread in the yard for the wedding breakfast. The youthful stranger stood with the Block T crew, his gawky and immature face turning about in curiosity. Rand and Price Peters and Izee had come up to Benbow, to form the inevitable partnership. Benbow heard the kid speak in an insolent tone.

"I got to get a new horse. A posse ran hell out of me, clean across Utah."

Most of the men in the yard caught that and turned to look. Benbow observed the way the kid reacted to this interest, lifting his shoulders and slyly smiling.

Price Peters looked at Benbow. "Tough. He admits it."

"Fresh from mama," said Benbow. "Just tryin' to cut a figure."

"Bad place to announce his sins," murmured Price.

Mrs. Gray came out of the house and called, "George," and Gray walked away from the party. Clay Rand drove both hands into his pockets, restlessly clattering some silver change. "A wedding's a long time to wait for breakfast." Sudden Ben Drury, sheriff of the county, came curving into the yard, a little man and a close-mouthed man with a clever manner. There was a group half-circled around one of the tables and going over that way, Benbow found a man from Gay's store seated opposite husky Ben Phillippse of the Block T outfit. They were trying out their strength, palms locked, elbows on the table. Ben Phillippse grinned and drove the other one's arm sidewise down to the table, and let it go. He said, "Well, anybody else?"

"Sure," called Izee, "I got a man for you. Sit down there, Jim."

"I'll have some," agreed Benbow and took his place opposite Ben Phillippse, locking his big hand into Ben's. "Say when."

"When," said Phillippse and threw power into his arm hugely. It lifted Benbow an inch up from the bench, but he kept his arms straight. Phillippse quit grinning at once and threw his right shoulder forward to get a better leverage. His lips stretched out from the effort and he began to throw a heavy breathing through his wide nostrils. Benbow said, "It ain't enough son," and forced Phillippse' hand to the board.

Phillippse said in astonishment: "I never knowed you could do that, Jim," and promptly got up from the table.

Jack Dale spoke from the circle. "Hat feeds its men well. Fifty dollars to the fellow that can lick Jim."

"A go," said Clay Rand and sat down in Phillippse' place, matching his palm to Benbow's. Benbow said seriously, "I'd rather not, Clay," but Clay Rand shook his head and said, "Go," and threw his strength into that arm. A moment later he was standing half upright, his knuckles pinned to the table top by Benbow's sudden burst of strength, a swift, rash anger boiling into his bright blue eyes. Benbow let go and sat still and cool. Rand turned his hand around, staring at the fresh bruise across the knuckles; his cheeks were red as fire and all the humor was out of him.

"Kid," he said unevenly, "I hate to get licked."

"A sucker's remark," called Price Peters at once.

Rand wheeled away, not saying anything more. Benbow lifted his attention quietly to the rawboned shape of Cash Gore standing by. Gore's eyes were half closed in the manner of a man deeply considering a fresh, strange thought. He met Benbow's glance carefully and without a change of expression; yet behind that attitude of indifference Benbow saw a white flame burning its wicked light. Benbow said: "Interested, Cash?"

Gore lifted a hand, pressing it carefully across his mustache. He murmured in a dry tone, "I never do fool things, Benbow."

All at once the silence of the circle turned thick and a feeling of strain crept along it. Benbow got up from the table, hearing George Gray's voice summon them all to the house. Nobody else moved for a moment and Benbow, letting his eyes stray to either side, saw the cramped interest of all those faces, the thoughtful attention. They were like men waiting for something they had long expected to hear.

"I always said you were a clever man, Cash," agreed Benbow. Then his added phrase fell with an idleness that was more effective than a rifle shot. "And a careful one, too."

Gore's answer held that same dry rustle. "That's right."

Jubal Frick came through the circle to touch Gore on the arm. "That's all, Cash."

Gore swung on the Running M owner, shaking the man's arm away and speaking to him sharply. "I'll make up my own mind, Jubal."

Jubal Frick spoke with a touch of apology. "I know, Cash, but—"

"Mind your business," said Cash Gore.

He was shaming the Running M owner before this crowd. Jack Dale stood up to his full height, outraged yet silent. Nelson McGinnis of Diamond-and-a-Half stared with an angry wonder. They were all waiting for Jubal to give this overweening foreman his just answer, and shock was a plain thing in the crowd when Jubal, without

41

meeting any man's eyes, turned quietly away.

"A good way," drawled Benbow, "as long as it works." He left it like that and swung toward the house. The valley men broke out of the semicircle as though released from frozen attitudes.

Price Peters walked in audible astonishment beside him. "You see that?" he grunted. "You see that?" But there was nothing more said, for they were all crowding into Block T's front room where Eileen and Joe Gannon were side by side before the bishop. Karen Sanderson, a big and blonde German girl, was playing the old-fashioned organ and some of the women had already begun to weep quietly, instantly reducing every man to a wilted silence. When the music stopped Eileen and Joe knelt before the bishop who began to recite the wedding ceremony.

Clay Rand leaned near Benbow, ironically whispering. "Why do they cry—for happiness or for knowing what marriage is like?" But Benbow was indifferent to that talk, for he saw Connie standing tall and pale and near to being beautiful in the bridesmaid's place; and he saw her eyes turn and find Clay Rand and send something across the room that was sad and strange and lovely—and meant for Clay alone. Benbow dropped his head, listening to the last words of the bishop.

The organ started up again and at once everybody was talking. Price and Izee and Clay were bending their heads together. Price said: "Joe's a jealous son-of-a-gun," and winked. And at once the four of them walked toward Eileen in single file, Price leading.

Price said: "All brides get kissed," and took Eileen into his arms. Gannon stood darkly by, stabbing Price with his eyes; and afterwards Clay came up and caught Eileen. Everybody in the room had been laughing at this, but the laughter died out, for Eileen stared at Clay, suddenly white as paper. Her arms resisted him a little before he kissed her. He had quit smiling and Joe Gannon seized him and whirled him around, ablaze with that quick rage always so near his heart. Gannon said: "You've had your

42

time at that, Rand. The time's gone by."

Clay grinned insolently at Gannon. "When I go to weddings, Joe, I always kiss the brides."

Izee and Benbow took their turns and went on. A plump redheaded, little girl at the doorway said to Izee, scornfully, "I thought you were a bashful man," and went out with him. Benbow suddenly found Connie Dale walking without comment beside him, across the yard to the tables. He turned away, but her hand was in his arm, stopping him, and when he looked at her he saw a hurt pride showing out and a clear call for his help. They sat down together at one of the tables. Eileen came out with Joe Gannon and the bishop and the Grays. They started for this table, and then Joe Gannon wheeled and went rapidly around Block T's low horse barn.

Connie said: "What is he doing?"

Joe Gannon came back, driving a buggy across the yard. He stopped and jumped out and held his arm for Eileen to rise by; and stepped up to the seat again. He wasn't smiling and he wasn't pleased. There had been talk going on and now it ceased and into this quiet he placed his talk with a grudging effort.

"I thank you and my wife thanks you. We'll be at the ranch for any of our friends. But if anybody comes up there to start this fool shivaree business they'll run into buckshot." Afterwards he turned the buggy about the yard and lashed the team into a trot that carried them, unbreakfasted, eastward along the valley.

"Why did she marry him?" breathed Connie.

George Gray pounded a knife into his plate to get the crowd's attention. "What we're here for is to eat breakfast. Hop to it." He sat down and let his body go idle, staring at the table in a strange, troubled way.

The plump redhead came up, holding Izee firmly by the arm. "Connie, did you see Izee kiss the bride? Wasn't it romantic?" Her round cheeks were pink and she was smiling at Izee, though the smile had an edge to it and her voice was remotely exasperated.

Izee said uncomfortably: "Well, it's a custom, ain't it?"

43

"If there's nobody else you want to kiss," said Mary Boring with a restrained wickedness, "sit down and I'll bring your breakfast."

Izee sat down, muttering. The crowd was at the table, with a good deal of talk running around. Clay Rand came up to stand a moment by Connie, his high-colored features ironically amused at all he saw. He said: "When we're married, honey, I'll let you eat before I haul you away in the buggy."

Connie said, "Thank you, Clay," and didn't look up. Benbow had finished. He rose and left them there, going on toward his horse. Price Peters and a few of the younger men made a circle around Karen Sanderson who stood tall and serene and striking among them. Benbow removed his hat and said, "How are you, Karen?"

She gave him her hand and across the enigmatic composure of her features a glow of pleasure appeared. Her voice was even and touched by faint huskiness; she spoke carefully, the inflections of English being still difficult to her. "I'm glad to see you, Jim."

"Women," complained Price Peters, "are always glad to see him. He seems high on the eligible list. Why is that, Karen?"

Karen Sanderson showed Price a slanting, veiled glance. "I have heard you speak German."

"Yes," said Price. "Long ago when I was a gentleman and a scholar."

Karen Sanderson spoke a few quick words in her own tongue.

"I think," said Price, gently, "you're right."

"I hope so," put in Benbow.

Color ran quickly across the girl' cheeks. "You understand?"

"No. But whatever it is, I hope so," said Benbow, and moved away.

Karen Sanderson's azure-blue glance followed him half across the yard and then came back to Price, without expression.

Clay Rand walked up. He said, "Hello, Karen," and

44

Price Peters' sharp senses felt coolness come between those two people plainly. It was that much of a change, Karen Sanderson looking at Rand with a distant pride, with a reserve and a faint shadow of contempt. She didn't speak. Rand let a brief laugh fall and swung away.

"And he is not," she murmured to Price.

Walking toward his horse, Benbow came by a knot of Block T hands in time to hear the strange kid speak up in a bragging voice: "I'm called the Travelin' Kid. Once down in Arizona I led a sheriff three hundred miles—"

Benbow stopped and caught this scene at a glance. The Block T men listened gravely, knowing a liar when they heard one. But Cash Gore kept himself a little aside from this group and observed the kid in a manner that was as sharp as the edge of a knife, as sharp and as predatory. He caught Benbow watching him and made a brief circle on his heels and walked away. Benbow went on to his pony, climbed up and trotted across the yard. He lifted his hat to Mrs. Gray, and said, "See you next week, George," and left Block T behind him.

Price Peters meanwhile had drifted back toward the whisky keg. He stood there idly, displeased with his thoughts as was his habit; and then raised his glance from the ground to follow Clay Rand's retreat toward the horses standing threefooted by the Block T corral. Cash Gore was already over there, fiddling with a stirrup. For a moment Gore and Rand were side by side. Peters' mouth made a downpointed semicircle and his eyes narrowed on that scene. Neither man seemed aware of the other, yet Price thought he saw Gore's lips move just before Rand swung up to his saddle, adjusted his reins and rode after Benbow.

Price was so engrossed in his thoughts that the touch of another man's arm beside him jerked him straight. Looking around he found Izee; and for a moment they swapped glances. Izee cleared his throat, started to speak and changed his mind.

Price said: "Yeah."

5. A Little Shooting

Benbow returned to the ranch from Block T and immediately afterwards struck across Two Dance Valley. At noon he had reached the ramparts of the Yellows and thereafter climbed that stiff edge of the hills and made his way through one and another of the corridors of a thick pine forest where silence lay like deep pools of water. At two o'clock he reached Rho Beam's chuck wagon and stopped for a cup of coffee with Old Veersdorp, the cook. Rho and the four Hat men who made up this outfit were somewhere back in the timber hazing up mavericks. Keeping Hat stock branded and located was a year-round proposition and this chuck wagon seldom got back to the home quarters.

"Tell Rho," said Benbow, "to kill a two-year-old and send a quarter to Frank Isabel. I'll be back here late tonight to get the other."

"Goin' tords Granite Canyon?"

"Maybe."

Old Veersdorp let his eyelids droop. "Rho went over that way last week and had a shot took at him."

Benbow went on at a leisured gait. Later reaching a naked dome on the edge of the Ramparts he climbed it afoot to have his look at the valley below, all aswirl with the powder-blue haze of Indian summer. Far across the land's yellow and chrome surfaces Hat's buildings lay as a faint blur. Dust rose from the hay wagons on up the river, and dust made its ribbonlike shape along the Two Dance-Running M road. Those two horsemen creating that bannered signal would be Cash Gore and Jubal Frick returning to their ranch. And across the valley another rider, seeming motionless because of the distance, ripped up his smoky trail. From this vantage point he could see the wide gap in the northeast where the valley ran between the prows of the Two Dance and the Yellow ranges toward the railroad of Mauvaise station.

He traveled on without hurry. Crispness lay under these trees, foretelling winter. Somewhere a shout sounded and ran on in a thinning echo. He passed a bunch of Hat stock in a little meadow. The trail, never very even, began to rise and dip to the more abrupt contours of this tangled land; and at five or thereabouts he reached the edge of Granite Canyon.

At the bottom of the canyon a small creek, laced whitely by the foam of its fast travel, dropped toward Running M out on the edge of the bench. In the other direction the high rock walls made a sweeping turn, carrying this natural highway deeply on into the heart of the rugged Yellows. A wagon trail marched crookedly beside the creek.

He put his horse back into the trees, himself taking position at the edge of the canyon. He had brought along his field glasses and from time to time he focused them on the outline of Running M's quarters just visible at the canyon's mouth, half a mile away. Men were moving around the yard, and around six o'clock a rider came into the canyon at a rapid gait. Lying flat on his belly, Benbow watched the man come forward and pass directly beneath. At this distance he had no trouble recognizing the husky, tublike shape of Indian Riley swaying with a characteristic looseness in the saddle. Once Riley's very dark and very round eyes lifted, his eyes sweeping the rim of the canyon; afterwards he rounded the upper bend and was out of sight.

47

Benbow went back to his horse and rode into the trees, taking a faint trail that paralleled the rim of the canyon. Going upward at a casual trot, he finally bent away from the canyon and came at last to a little meadow occupied by a gray log hut. It was sunset time, with long and hard flashes of light streaming above the timber and shadows banking themselves palely against the pine trunks. Stopped at the margin of the meadow Benbow called across it:

"Pete."

Pete Cruze was somewhere along the far edge of this meadow; his voice came back. "That you, Jim?" and afterwards he walked forward into the open patch and met the advancing Benbow.

Benbow said: "You campin' over there?"

"I like it better than in the cabin," Cruze said dryly.

"Trouble?"

"Shot at this mornin'. Before daylight—through the window."

Benbow nodded. "I thought it might come that way. Take up your belongings, kid, and join Rho Beam's chuck wagon."

"I can stick it out here," said Pete Cruze stubbornly. "To hell with Indian Riley's crowd."

"You'll join Rho's outfit," repeated Benbow, and then remained silent a little while, his long jaw crawling forward and settling his lips into a broad, thin crease.

He said softly, "You come with me, Pete," and waited while Pete Cruze went back into the timber for his horse. The two of them turned on up the trail.

The sky light faded and shadows were running thicker all through these pines, with a little wind springing up. The trail here struck straight into heavier timber, climbing steadily, and at the end of a half hour shot off to the left and led them to the canyon's rim again, dropping into it by sudden switchback turns. Below them directly, at a point where the canyon widened into the falling slopes of the Yellows, three gray houses sat elbow to

48

elbow beside the creek.

Lamplight glimmered through the windows and men moved along the yard; and behind the houses somebody stood in a corral roping out horses. There was this much visibility left in the fading day. Benbow got down from his horse and drew his rifle from its boot. Seeing that, Pete Cruze followed suit. Both of them dropped flat at the rim's edge.

"It's always polite to return a callin' card," said Benbow. "We'll concentrate on the windows. Indian Riley might be pleased with the compliment." He let go then with his shot, the dreaming stillness of the hills burst apart by the long and sharp clap of that explosion. One huge shout raced above the shot echo and all those men below turned to weaving shapes, racing to the rear of the houses. Pete Cruze had opened up, pleased with himself as he fired. Lights went out down there, one by one leaving the settlement presently in its half-darkness. Indian Riley's outfit, crouched out of sight, set up an answering fire. A bullet went whining past Benbow, high over his head. Benbow rolled on his side to refill the gun; raked the settlement with another calculated burst of firing; and stopped then.

"That's enough, Pete."

They crawled back from the rim and got into their saddles, diving back down the trail. At the cabin he said, "Get your stuff and join Rho," and went on alone. When he reached the main trail he dropped immediately into the canyon's bottom and followed it toward the open plain, with darkness falling fully across the world. Running M's light winked in his face and Running M's dogs, hearing his approach, began to sound. He curled past Jubal Frick's corrals into the front yard and dismounted there. Somebody's high shape retreated around the far corner of the house; and two men rose almost in unison from Running M's porch chairs. Jubal Frick was there, but it was Cash Gore's voice that laid a toneless challenge on Benbow.

49

"Who's that?"

The front door stood wide, with lamps throwing a fresh, butter-yellow beam through it. When he stepped onto the porch he had to cross that light; and Cash Gore's voice came again, flatter than it had been before.

"You're draggin' your picket, Benbow."

Night's wind roved the yard, bringing up the scent of dust and drying grasses; bringing up too the scent of trouble. One man had retreated around the corner of the house, but a dark knot of Running M hands emerged from the shadows and stood at the porch's end—waiting. Jubal Frick's breathing came sighing out of him and Cash Gore was a thin, still shape. Benbow caught it all—all that it was and all that it meant; and stepped through the doorway. "Jubal," he said, "come in here."

Jubal Frick followed him and then Cash Gore walked in and closed the door and rested his thin shape against it. His eyelids squeezed down into angular frames, half hiding his taciturn attention. His lips were hidden behind the rusty-red mustache. A stiff and uncompromising man; and a crooked man.

"Jubal," said Benbow, "your foreman's a scoundrel. You know it?"

He looked at Cash Gore when he said it and saw the light of Gore's eyes change, throwing out a gleam that was ironic, that was somberly amused. Jubal Frick brought up both his hands and rubbed them down his gray cheeks. He had been a proud, peppery man once, as Benbow recalled; but the look on his features was deadened and furtive. Without looking at either Gore or Benbow, Frick muttered, "Go out a minute, Cash, I'll talk to Jim."

Gore said: "You can talk. I'll listen."

"Cash," Frick groaned, impotently angered, "why don't you get out?"

"Jubal," said Benbow, "is this your ranch, or ain't it?"

"I'll answer that," broke in Gore indifferently. "He owns it. I run it." He showed Frick a dry grin. "I'm a good

50

foreman, ain't I, Jubal?"

Frick jerked up his head and meet Benbow's glance with a dull resignation. "I guess," he said slowly, "you can see how it is for yourself."

"Sure he can see," put in Cash Gore. "But what do you see, Benbow?"

Another rider came out of the canyon, his pony's fast-striking feet telegraphing along the hard earth. One of Running M's crew ran along the porch and the dogs streamed around the house in full voice. The rider trotted to the porch, his voice sounding clearly through the wall. "Cash here?"

Another man spoke softly. Cash Gore's eyes widened a little, cold and wicked in the way they watched Benbow's face. The arriving traveler was being warned, but Benbow lifted his voice so that it would carry through the house wall. "Come on in, Riley."

"Smart," gritted Cash Gore. "Was that what you wanted to know?"

Indian Riley opened the door, pushing Gore aside; and came into the room and shut the door. He stood beside Gore, a short and round-bodied man with huge shoulders and a copper skin, against which the color of his eyes established a brash light. He said quickly: "What's this, Cash?"

Benbow spoke up. "I thought you'd come here, Riley, but I wasn't sure of the tie-up between you two. So I thought I'd find out. You liked the shootin'?"

Riley's dark, moon-shaped face went blank; only his eyes showed what he felt, suddenly rolling out a faint wildness. He didn't say anything.

Gore said: "So now what you got?"

"I never condemn a man till I see him stealing. That time will come too, Cash."

"Men that know too much don't live."

"Maybe so," gravely assented Benbow.

There was a thought here that loosened Cash Gore's lips and fashioned them into a semicircular half-grin.

51

Indian Riley stirred away from Gore, prompted by an unspoken impulse. Jubal Frick backed across the room, out of range. The edge of that fast-traveling thought had struck him, too. These other three men made a triangle there, with Benbow watching what went on. He had his hat tipped back and his palms rested on his hips; and his long jaw lay in its silent, stubborn line.

He said, "Move out to the porch. I've found out what I wanted to know."

Indian Riley cast a swift side glance at Gore. Rash instinct stirred his flat lips. Gore remained wholly still, weighing all this in his secretive way. Benbow's talk crept into the stillness in a sleepy, suddenly tuneless manner.

"All right, Cash. I'm willing."

Gore jerked his head faintly higher. "Wait," he said. "Open the door, Riley."

Indian Riley obeyed, standing in the aperture, slowly adjusting his thoughts to the change that had flashed over the room. He said to Gore: "Well?"

"Go on."

Benbow moved for the door. Riley gave way and then Cash Gore stepped cautiously backward to the porch. Out there, Benbow saw the shadows of other Running M men ranged across the darkness. They had all come forward. They were waiting and listening—Cash Gore's crew. He slid over to his horse and stepped up to his saddle. Nobody stirred, but trouble whirled around the yard in mute violence and Benbow felt all those eyes targeting him in this darkness. He sat there alert and not sure, one arm idle at his side, his big shape stiffened against the break that might come.

Cash Gore's voice was as dry as dust; it was thin and remote—and touched by hatred. "I never underestimate a man, Benbow. But you were a fool to ride here."

"No," said Benbow quietly. "I came to tell you something."

"Tell it," droned Cash Gore.

"This outfit is crooked, which I know without proof.

But I'll wait for proof."

"You can go on waitin'," said Gore wickedly.

"I can wait. But when the day comes that I trace a Hat cow to this outfit," said Benbow, "I'll be back here." He let that fall, seeing all those Running M shapes shift and turn on the edge of the yard. Then he added coolly, "And I'll wipe you off the map, Cash."

"Sounds tough," droned Gore.

"It'll be tough," murmured Benbow.

Cash Gore intoned: "Better get off the place."

Benbow said nothing more. Pulling his horse gently away from the porch he swung a little, holding the shapes of the Running M crew with his scrupulous attention, and thus drifted around the corner of the house. When he got by the corrals he threw the pony into a gallop and raced up the canyon.

Indian Riley said: "You had him, Cash. Why'd you let him go?"

Gore said noncommittally: "There's other places and other times. What you want here?"

"They poured lead into my houses."

Gore said: "We'll pour it back. Ride along."

He waited until Riley galloped away. And went into the house then. Jubal Frick sat in a chair, his fat arms limp across his spread knees. Frick stared up at Gore, uncertainly, with a dumb anxiety in his eyes. "Cash," he murmured, "you're too brash in front of company. I—"

"Be quiet, Jubal," interrupted Gore. "And next time we have company you keep your damned mouth shut." He stood there momentarily, letting the strict and altogether arbitrary weight of his mind play against Jubal Frick; and then he lifted his watch from a vest pocket, saw the time, and left the room.

He stepped into his saddle and said to the crew loitering about the porch, "Stick here," and rode out from the ranch. A few hundred yards away, at a point where the timber ran fully down the Ramparts to the edge of the valley, he turned into the pines and stopped. A man

53

rose up from the scattered rocks there. He said: "I've been waiting here for a hell of a long time."

"Your friend was here, Clay."

Rand said instantly: "What'd he want?"

"Just a visit."

Rand said, after a thoughtful pause: "Some day, Cash, you'll die. I know Jim Benbow when he gets his back up. I know what he can do."

"So," murmured Gore. "And what's your ticket, Clay?"

"Me?" said Rand. His voice sank to a lower note, to a saddened and frustrated tone. "I think I died when I took up this game."

"For a corpse you make a good livin'," suggested Gore dryly. "Anyhow, I got a job for you. Ride up through Hat's timber and see where they got the stock held. It's time for a little business."

6. Trouble in Cherokee

Benbow rode directly from Running M to Rho Beam's traveling outfit in the Yellows. Rho and Pete Cruze and the other Hat men attached to the wagon were hunkered around the fire. And one other man—the Traveling Kid who had done his boasting in the Block T yard—was also there. He had been talking, for Benbow could see the noncommittal expression on the faces of the Hat riders. They had the kid's number already.

Veersdorp got up to rustle a supper for Benbow. The kid stared closely at Benbow and said then, in his half-insolent way: "Guess I saw you this mornin' at the weddin'."

"That's right," agreed Benbow. Veersdorp came back with a bait of short ribs and potatoes on a tin plate, and a cup of coffee. Benbow fell to eating and for a little while let the conversation slide around him. The kid said:

"I never forget a face. When a man's on the run he's got to be careful that way."

"Sure," agreed Rho Beam. "You can't be too careful." The smooth way he said it lifted Benbow's glance. Rho's left eyelid fluttered faintly at Benbow, but nothing stirred the grave expression of this bully-chested, black-haired *segundo* of Hat.

"Yeah," growled the kid. "I been in some tight spots."

"Guess you've had to kill your men from time to

time," suggested Rho Beam gravely. The kid flashed him a half-distrusting look. "Well, I've had my troubles. But I'm still alive."

"Tells the story complete," said Rho Beam, permitting admiration to shade his talk. "I slaughtered that two-year-old, Jim."

"How's the stock running?"

"Pretty high up in the timber. Fat this year, too."

"We're shipping again this week, or next. Cut out five or six carloads and hold them here. I want big mossy horns. Then I want you to start drifting everything else down from the high timber. I'm counting on a heavy winter and it won't do to have the beef caught up there in the deep drifts."

He had finished his meal. Rising, he inclined his chin at Rho and presently the two of them were beyond the fire, beyond the kid's big ears.

"He ain't dry yet," opined Rho. "But he'll stub his toe, the way he talks. You want Pete Cruze to stay with me? Who's going to keep an eye on the canyon?"

"Never mind the canyon."

"Changed your mind?"

"I've found out what I wanted to know. And I don't want anybody shot."

Rho Beam said, "All right," in a way that wasn't quite satisfied. "But we're bein' rustled plenty." He walked back to the fire. Benbow turned to the cook wagon and got a fresh quarter of beef that Veersdorp had wrapped in a gunny sack. He stepped into the saddle, holding the meat across his thighs. "Kid," he called, "come here a minute."

The kid rose unwillingly and took his time in walking over. His thin, immature face tipped toward Benbow, half sullen and half uncertain.

"Listen," Benbow told him gently. "You're welcome to ride any part of Hat country. But just as from one man to another, don't talk so much. There's some people around here that might cause you trouble."

56

The kid grumbled, "I can take care of myself," and went back to the fire.

Benbow watched him a moment, irritated and yet troubled. The kid was greener than grass, just a boy impatient to be a full man; and he rode now in a country that had no mercy on innocence. He thought about this and dismissed it from his mind and went away from the camp, going along the edge of the Yellow ramparts.

This was the main-traveled trail, from which other trails switched off, either to the higher hills or to the plain below. From its occasional vista points he made out the faraway glint of Hat's lights and the remote blink of other ranches nestled along the edge of Two Dance Range entirely across the prairie. Wind brushed down-slope, ruffling the trees, and suddenly it was crisp and cold, carrying on the hint of winter. He was thinking of Cash Gore at that moment and of Indian Riley; thinking of them in relation to Hat.

It was his way, to balance all things against the ranch. He could not escape that loyalty. It was a condition of his being, a singularity of reasoning that made all things good if they were good for Hat; and all things bad if they were bad for Hat. There was this simplicity about Jim Benbow, with always a slowness in coming to judgment, and always a hard adherence to those judgments when he had made them.

But while he bored into the problem of Running M, he was also conscious of the night world around him, keening the wind, catching the quality of the surrounding shadows. And so he saw the shape of horse and rider in the trail when still fifty yards away. He let his pony trot on, meanwhile straightening his shoulders, letting his right arm swing closer to the gun in its holster.

The man's voice reached toward him, flat and unfriendly. "Who's that?"

He recognized Joe Gannon's voice and drifted on until he was a yard from the man. Downgrade, not more than a mile, Gannon's ranch lay at the edge of the prairie, its house lights shining.

He said: "What's up, Joe?"

"Benbow? That's all right. Thought it was somebody else." Gannon's voice eased away from its high-keyed tone. The man's sigh cut the night air. He moved himself nervously around the saddle.

"Trouble?" suggested Benbow.

"You seen Clay Rand?"

"No."

"He was driftin' around here before dark."

"Going home, I suppose."

"Home?" growled Gannon. "Home, hell! Listen, Jim. You tell him something for me. Tell him to stay away from my place or I'll kill him on sight!" Then he let a swift grunt of wrath fall out of him and whirled his pony around. He said, "I know what he's done," and raced headlong down the hill toward his ranch.

Benbow went on along the main trail a half mile and curved into another one which led him upward through the full blackness of the pines. He thought to himself, "Clay's a fool," with a deep bitterness. This full-blooded friend, this smiling and handsome man was, in many ways, as unstable as sand. It made Benbow think of Connie Dale again—and then morosely close his mind. There was no hope to be had there.

Three miles back in the Yellows the trail slid down into a twenty-acre meadow set like a shallow bowl into the forest. A creek flowed windingly across the clearing, and by the creek a small house sent out its glow. A dog barked furiously when Benbow forded the water; and then a woman came to the door and stood in tall and shapely silhouette against the light.

Benbow said: "We killed a beef today, Karen. I brought you a quarter."

Karen Sanderson's slow voice lifted to a musical and pleased tone. "Come in, Jim."

* * *

Passing by the Gannon ranch at dusk, Clay had seen Eileen standing in the yard. There was no particular thought in his head concerning her then; only a knowledge that he might have married her had he wished. But after meeting Cash Gore he came back along the main trail, dropped quietly down the Ramparts and halted in the trees near the place. Thus he saw Gannon leave the house and ride up the Ramparts. A little afterwards Eileen came to the porch and stood with her back to one of its posts, looking out across the valley in Hat's direction. There was nobody else here. Gannon's handyman, he knew, had gone to Two Dance. Leaving his horse, he went on across the yard. She heard his footsteps and turned; he was at the base of the porch before she recognized him.

A quick, gusty breath fell out of her. "Clay!" And then she was in front of him and he could see the dark and desperate look on her face. He laughed a little, reaching out for her, and having his way with her.

"Kid," he said, "why'd you marry that fellow?"

"Don't, Clay. He's a good man."

"Sure," said Rand, smiling as he said it. "But you don't love him."

She said: "How do you know?"

"Eileen, honey. You don't. Or else you've been lying to me a long while."

"No," she told him, dully. "No, I never lied to you. Maybe to a lot of other people, but never to you."

"Then, why?"

She said: "I'm twenty-five, Clay. Almost an old maid. That's why."

"With all the valley men to pick from—"

She said, "Clay," in a breaking tone. It stopped him instantly. It erased his smile. He stood there, hearing bitterness come out of this girl. "All the valley men! No, Clay. The valley men remembered I had been going with you. Joe's the only one who didn't mind that."

He said, "I'm sorry, Eileen."

59

"Then why are you here? Joe's good enough to forget I was your girl. But he won't stand you around. Go on away. We're through, Clay."

He said in that easy, teasing way: "Eileen—you sure about that?"

She put her hands behind her and stared at him. "Now I know something about you. You don't care much for things you can have. It's the things you can't have that you always try to get."

He took her by the shoulders and kissed her again. She did not resist him. She didn't draw away. It was Clay who, hearing the swift slash of a rider racing down the Ramparts, stepped back. He said: "I'll be here again, Eileen."

She said, half in despair and half in contempt: "What for? To sneak around at night? You fool, I loved you—and you knew it. Don't come back—don't ever come back!"

"I'll come again."

He was out of sight and she was crying. Joe Gannon's horse rattled along the rock of the lower half of the trail. Eileen turned swiftly into the house and went to the mirror tacked to the living-room wall. She pressed away the tears with her fingers and stared at herself with a strange, dead feeling in her heart. There wasn't any mercy in her eyes for the woman she saw, only a belief that that woman was old and hopeless and lost. Gannon, coming rapidly into the room, saw her standing there.

"What's the matter?"

She didn't turn. "Nothing, Joe. I just don't like to be left all alone."

He came over, not touching her. He said, humbly, "I didn't mean to. It was just a chore. Listen, I'll do whatever a man can to make you pleased."

She whirled about at once and looked up at this tall, homely man whose face was beginning to show the hallows of a hard-worked life. Her tears were fresh again. "You're a dam' kind man, Joe. I'll do my best by you. You won't ever have reason to complain."

"I've got no complaint, Eileen."

She went across the room and into the bedroom, closing the door. Gannon dropped his glance to the floor. He pulled out his pipe and packed it and stood there, sucking stolidly at the smoke, his shoulders rounded. She was unhappy and he knew it; and knew why. There wasn't any power in him to handle that unhappiness and nothing he could say to her that would help. Being a man who had seen time change and erase many things, he had hoped she would some day forget Clay Rand. It was his only hope, and one to which he doggedly clung. Presently he went to the door, calling quietly:

"Where do you want me to sleep?"

Jim Benbow carried the quarter of beef into the kitchen and went back to the log house's only other room. Karen Sanderson stood against a wall, not saying anything for the moment. She was a big, hazel-eyed girl with tawny blond hair massed above a wide forehead, above a gravely serene face that had its own kind of beauty; a sturdy woman who had done a man's work in these hills and still kept her cheeks smooth and her hands white and slender. She didn't talk much, but when she did there was always in her slow words the inflection of something strong and richly emotional hidden far down. She had a way of looking directly at a man, quietly and without shyness; as though to appraise him and store that appraisal away in her head.

She said, "Sit down, Jim," and went into the kitchen to pull the coffeepot over to the stove's hot lid. She was, Jim thought, thoroughly German in the way she kept the coffeepot ready for whoever might drop in. Building himself a cigarette, he looked around at the perfect order of the living-room. She had come to this country as a stranger, two years before, and still was a stranger in many respects. Big Jack Dale had helped her locate this homestead and the Hat men had put up the log cabin. All the rest of it she had done alone, chinking in the

61

crevices with her own hands, wielding the saw and hammer like a man. She owned a milk cow, some beef stock, a few chickens, and a garden that she had plowed and planted and tended. In almost every way she was self-sufficient, asking no favors she couldn't repay; friendly with the valley folks, yet saying nothing of her own history.

She came in and handed him a cup of coffee, and stood back against the wall again, her eyes quietly on him. She said: "You're riding late."

"Going up to Cherokee."

"It is not a friendly town, for you."

He said: "You've learned a lot about this country."

"I listen."

He had finished. He carried the empty cup into the kitchen and returned; and stood there, a big and solemn man whose features were touched by the hint of unruliness hardcurbed. "Ever get lonesome up here, Karen?"

She said, "Yes," quietly. Her lips were long and pleasant in the way a woman's lips should be. There was a generosity about her, and a courage. Her eyes were proud, with something in them that seemed to carry the image of Benbow backward into deep and distant places. Color tinted her cheeks more deeply as that silence ran on.

He said: "Then what?"

Her shoulders shrugged that away. "Loneliness is something we must all stand."

"I know."

A ripple of pleasure broke the even, dreaming gravity on her face. "I thought you would understand that."

"Why?"

The melody of her voice was slower, it was softer. "We are a little bit alike."

Her personality stirred him in strange ways. He couldn't help saying what he did, bluntly and without trying to temper his meaning. "You ought to have a man,

62

Karen. You're missing too much."

She smiled at him, her hazel eyes glowing. "Perhaps," she murmured. "Perhaps." And when he turned out to his horse and got into the saddle he saw her posed against the light again, tall and strong and still. She said in a demure voice: "I'm grateful for the beef. Will you come again?"

He said, "Yes," striking at once up the meadow trail and passing into the solid blackness of the timber.

The trail swung eastward in steady ascent, threading its way toward the broken backbone of the Yellows. Five miles from Karen Sanderson's meadow Benbow reached the lip of one of the many low passes which broke through the irregular spine of this rugged range and came into Cherokee.

Cherokee was a hotel, a saloon, a stable, a store and three other frame houses seated in the pine forest. It sat on the edge of the reservation, by daylight doing its lawful trade with the Indians, by night selling its liquor illicitly to the reservation and sheltering all those fugitive men riding the hills for their own secret purposes. A dozen Indians crouched stolidly along the hotel wall, half a dozen squaws sat in the ramshackle buggies, stolidly waiting. A few white men stood at the hotel door, and at the stable's arch. Benbow saw all this in one quick, thorough glance and went on to leave his horse in the stable, out of sight. He said to Ambrose McRae, the owner of the stable, "I'll be back," and headed for the saloon.

It was a touchy little town, its nerves keyed to catch the sound of any arriving rider. Benbow realized this the moment he stepped inside the saloon. A man was at that moment sliding quietly out the back way. Two others had withdrawn to the far end of the bar, and stood there now studying him with an aroused, friendless intensity. Donner, the proprietor, came forward and said, "How, Jim," in a cool way. His saloon was dangerous ground, a spot frequented by the fiddle-footed ones, and a poor

63

place for any Two Dance rancherman to be; and Donner, carrying water on both shoulders, had long ago learned to ask no questions and to answer none. He reached to the back bar and produced a bottle and glass, watching while Benbow took his drink.

Benbow said: "What's the weather going to be?"

"Indians say a hard winter." Donner quit talking, his head bowed thoughtfully over. Those two men at the bar's end were altogether still, their silence an attentive and listening silence. "Nights are gettin' cold already up here."

Benbow laid his two-bit piece on the bar. Donner shoved it back with a soft, fleshy hand. "On me, of co'se. Glad to have you pay the visit."

The two men came behind Benbow on the way out. One of them said, "Donner." Donner's glance lifted and then Benbow felt a signal being made behind him, for Donner's sake. Afterwards they left the place. Benbow stared at the saloonkeeper and saw the man's expression definitely freeze up. Whatever the information passed, it sank instantly behind the surface of Donner's eyes.

There was at once the sound of wagons rattling down Cherokee's street. Turning to the saloon's doorway, Benbow saw all the Indians rising from the walk to their wagons and putting this town behind them. It was a thing too definite to be accidental; it was like the answer to a warning softly spread along the street. Benbow crossed the dust casually and stepped onto the hotel's porch and took a seat there, his back to the hotel wall. From this position he saw a man stop at the stable's black archway and take root there. Up at the head of the street a cigarette sent its telltale glint from this night's deep shadows. And suddenly life seemed to drain out of Cherokee.

Benbow tilted his chair back against the wall, the knuckles of his down-hanging arms faintly tapping the wall. All the sins of men, all their violences lay along the surfaces of this town, ground into its very boards; and

64

out of those boards now was the faint emanation of that wickedness, clearly registering. Cherokee had no marshal and no law. High up in the pines, it served as a refuge for those whose hatred for law was wild and everlasting. His own presence here seemed to set up an actual disturbance.

A man came out of the hotel—little Sawmill Baker who owned it. Sawmill strolled to the edge of the porch and stood there, lighting a match to his half-chewed cigar. He bent over, throwing the match into the dust, and his voice ran its faint tone as far as Benbow and no farther. "They been workin' the north pass trails recently. You better get out of here." He turned indolently and went back into the hotel.

Up from Granite Canyon way came the strike of ponies' hoofs in swift tempo, that rumor bringing the man at the head of the street out of the deepest shadows into the middle dust. He was there like that when the shapes of half a dozen riders scudded forward from the timber into Cherokee. He was there, raising his hands and saying something that the run of the horses drowned out; and then he stepped aside and this outfit rounded up at the saloon. Indian Riley dropped his tublike body to the ground and made a complete circle to have his look at Cherokee's street. Afterwards he passed into the saloon, the other men following.

The fellow self-posted at the stable came immediately toward the saloon and waited for the one who had been at the street's head; they followed Indian Riley's crowd into the saloon. Dust, ripped up by the horses, drifted with the slow, sharp wind. The sound of voices over there lifted strongly and then fell away. One man was speaking; the others were listening.

Benbow stirred in the chair and laid his two hands idly together. At the head of the street something vaguely appeared and quickly disappeared. The voice in the saloon quit on a rising note and boots afterwards dragged along the boards. Indian Riley came out, swinging his shoulders from side to side as he crossed the walk and stepped into the dust. He stopped there, his torso jerked into a set position; light from the hotel slanted across his moon-round face. He called, "Benbow," and stared into the darkness of the porch.

Benbow hauled himself slowly from the chair and came down the porch steps until he saw Indian Riley's murky eyes begin to squeeze out warning. He stopped then. Riley's men were slowly spreading, up and down the street; restlessly spreading, lightly sliding their feet along the dust. He was a target for all those narrowing glances, and the evil of this town was an actual smell in his nostrils.

Indian Riley's lips stretched flat against his teeth. "Benbow," he said, the hard temper of this man coming out in each gusty word. "You made a mistake shootin' out the windows of my place."

"The habit," stated Benbow, "is getting to be common in the Yellows."

Riley's men kept sliding their boots through the dust. They made a semicircle now, covering him on either side. Indian Riley's cunning eyes slipped a glance in either direction. He jerked up his head. "You want trouble?"

Benbow struck into this man's half-breed pride deliberately. "How many men you need for protection?"

Riley yelled, "I'd like to send you to hell a-kickin'!"

"Proud talk."

The smell of evil grew stronger. The outflung light of the hotel touched Riley and Riley's men, showing the dull set of their features, showing the way savagery pinched and thinned those features and engraved its mark there. They were all a single step from the killing moment. He knew that, and could not help it and would not help it. He had passed by his own mark of safety, and stood before them now coldly agreeable to it. Keyed like this, surrounded like this, the thought of mercy and of safety went out of him, and left him as cruel as they were.

7. Deep Trails

He droned: "Send your men down the street and we'll have to try."

"Why?" grunted Indian Riley.

Benbow threw his wicked stare at Riley like a bullet. His voice lifted to a higher pitch, metallic and calculated. "You're a bastard-born mongrel with your tail draggin', Riley."

A call drove forward from the darkness. "Hold that," and Riley threw his head around, clapping one hand against his hanging gun. Rider and horse drifted into the street from the town's high edge, into this gray-yellow light. Clay Rand's tall shape weaved as he dropped from the saddle and he paused with his horse as a barricade between himself and Riley's men.

"Riley," he called, "get out of here."

"There's no fight in him," said Benbow.

Rand answered that swiftly. "Be quiet, Jim. Go on, Riley. Go on."

Riley had been facing Rand; he let himself turn back to Benbow with a straining care, the palms of both hands clamped at his hips. Sweat greased his cheeks and the hotel light established their oily shining. The silence ran on in this singing way until he broke from his long rigidness, stepping backward to his horse. He was in his saddle and his men were in the saddle before he spoke again. "Benbow," he said, calmer than he had any right to be, "I'll find you soon." And then the group went storming out of Cherokee.

Benbow wheeled on Rand, his talk very sharp. "What are you doing up here?"

"You ought to be glad of it," retorted Rand. He left his horse and went on until he could see the stiffness of Benbow's face, the accented boniness of that face. The gray in Benbow's eyes shuttered out a pale glow, the headlong temper still having its wintry way with him. Clay Rand saw that and shook his head, marveling.

"Never saw you go so far. You dam' fool!"

Benbow repeated his question. "What you doin' up here?"

"Traveling," said Rand irritably.

Benbow's answer was dry as dust. "You got here in a hurry from where you were last."

Rand said in a dying, guarded tone: "Where was that?"

"Listen, Clay. Keep your hands off married women."

"When I want advice I'll ask for it, Benbow."

They were riding their nerves, with a smoky anger whirling around them. Rand's temper was always a quick thing, and Benbow still was swayed by the headlong rage. So they stood, tall and unyielding before each other— friends on the dangerous edge of quarreling.

Benbow spoke his mind at once. "I'd go a long way for you, kid. But Connie's in this and I won't stand back watchin' you make a fool of her. Remember that well. I won't say it again."

He swung down the street. Rand said, "Hold on, Jim," but Benbow's high legs carried him directly into the stable, to his horse. One of the men he had earlier noticed in the saloon stood vaguely against a stall post, saying nothing. Benbow stepped up to the saddle and then was motionless a moment. "You got anything to say?"

"No," grumbled the man.

"Then get out into the street where I can keep my eyes

on you."

The man wheeled through the archway, walking on to the hotel porch and halting there. Rand had mounted. He drifted forward. "Kid," he said, "why do we always get in a wrangle? You can have my shirt any time you want. Where you going?"

Benbow's horse paced down the street, with Rand instantly following. They were beyond Cherokee and Cherokee's inquisitive ears. "Up to the north pass," said Benbow.

"That's no place for you to be at night alone," said Rand instantly. "Let's go home."

"So long."

"Wait a minute," argued Rand. He drew a long breath and Benbow, considering him with a hardening and dismal curiosity, saw the lines of his partner's face go thin and deep. All the laughter was out of Rand, and he was speaking quickly. "Well, I'll trail along."

"No."

"What's the matter with you?" snapped Rand.

"Nothing. So long."

"You can be tough with a man, Jim."

Benbow shook his high shoulders together and said in a gentler manner: "This is my business, kid. I'll have to do it my way."

"All right." But Rand kept his station, the surface of his cheeks becoming gray and odd. His tone fell and its wistfulness was very definite to Benbow. "Jim," he said, "we've had a lot of fun together. I hope the day never comes when that's finished. There ain't a hell of a lot of mercy in you sometimes. I'd hate to buck up against you. I hope it never comes to that."

"Better get out of these hills yourself," was Benbow's laconic suggestion; and he waited there in the chilly blackness until he saw Rand's retreating pony pass through Cherokee's street and drop out of sight beyond. Then he traveled on down the reservation road a mile or so and stopped again, listening into the pure silence of

69

the night. Satisfied, he left the road, diving directly into the timber. Pressing northward and upward, it was his intention to go as far as the high pass trail of the yellows. Indian Riley, so Sawmill Baker had whispered, was working along that country. And he could trust Sawmill who, though nobody else knew it, was his friend.

He was calmer now, the deep beat of his temper dying out and leaving him with a gray aftersight of what might have been. Once before in his life, when only a kid, coming up the Chisholm Trail, he had been forced into a situation such as this. Hemmed in and without the possibility of escape, the same freezing rage had closed down on his mind, turning him into another man. That time he had fought his way clear. This time Clay Rand had broken up the coming gunplay. But there would be other situations like that soon enough in the Yellows. He saw them advance out of the dark and he saw himself stiffened up again by that wildness over which he had no control; and he saw darkly across that interval, the inevitable ending. He could not avoid being what he was and he could not soften the ending. This night he had in effect declared open war on Cash Gore and Indian Riley and they would not spare him, since they knew at last that he understood their partnership.

Traveling forward, with the fall of his pony's hoofs muted by the soft-carpeted trail, his mind caught fugitively at the edge of things he deeply felt and could not explain. Like Clay Rand's gift for seizing the good moments of life and finding laughter in them. Like the sweetness of Connie Dale and the softness of her lips and the loveliness shining through her eyes. For some men there was an ease and a comfort in the world; for some there were rewards. He didn't belong to that class, and never could. Except in the matter of honesty he was another Cash Gore with the same wildness deep in him, with the same ability to kill. It was a way of thinking and of feeling—grained into him in his earlier years when nothing mattered as much as the simple ability to stay alive. His boyhood days had ended early and life along the trail had been rough.

These were his riding thoughts and they carried him on up the pitches of the Yellow Range until he reached a broader trail cutting directly north and south. This was the main way through the pass, with a message in it for him. The quick, cold breeze ran this narrow slash between the trees; and in the breeze lay the keen smell of recently risen dust. Indian Riley had traveled by only a short while before. He turned with the trail, his senses whetted against the black. After a short interval the trail tipped over the Yellow's summit and fell in quick pitches into a tangle of gulch and ridge and timber and swift creeks boiling across bedrock four hundred feet below. A quickening breeze ruffled sound out of the pine tops. The darkness was like a bottomless hole. Dust still registered in his nostrils, but he swerved away from the trail and quartered back along the edge of this high ridge. Nothing tangible warned him yet he felt the strong instinct to turn aside and he obeyed it now as he always obeyed that obscure impulse.

Thus cruising, with the canyon sheering through the Yellows on his right hand, he saw presently the glow of a light appear and disappear away below.

He turned immediately and rode out to the canyon's edge. Down there a campfire made its round, tawny shape against the gravel of a creek. One man moved into the range of light, bent over, and moved back from it into the farther darkness.

And at that moment a gun began to lay flat, spanging sheets of sound through the rustling night, the marksman evidently not more than a hundred yards from where he stood. Stiffened to the saddle, he heard that echo and the subsequent ones roll out through the hills, rebounding from point to point and at last sink. He counted six of them, hearing no bullet wake near him; and as he counted he saw somebody below run to the campfire, kick its burning wood into the adjacent creek

71

and step aside. The last rumor fainted far along the hills and the marksman's horse was rushing away through the trees furiously, and the little glow in the canyon faded completely. A man in the canyon launched a long, deep yell.

When Clay Rand left Benbow he rode straight through Cherokee's street and far enough beyond it to escape Benbow's following glance. At that point Rand turned northward, found a trail, and pursued it at full gallop. Benbow, he knew, would never let a fight die. Slow-moving and slow-thinking, this big man had an intensity in his actions more pronounced than that of any man Clay Rand ever had known; a single-mindedness that carried him terribly on. Benbow would be riding up to the north pass trail. That way also was Indian Riley bound, in obedience to Cash Gore's instructions. If Benbow collided with Riley's party it would be the end of Benbow.

This was the conviction that drove Clay Rand along and later turned him into the main pass trail. The dust of Riley's passage was fresh and thick in the wind when he reached the edge of the canyon; and here he stopped, drawing back into the timber. Far down he saw the first small spirals of Riley's fire burst into full glow. And listening painfully to the little echoes washing along the night, he made out, a quarter hour later, the shuffle of another horse on the trail. Brush rattled over there, and ceased to rattle; and then, knowing that Benbow had spotted Indian Riley's fire, Clay Rand lifted his revolver, fired six times into the night, and raced back toward Running M.

He had played it as impartially as he could, warning Riley and thereby keeping Benbow out of a fight. It was the most he could do, and the least he could do. This one time it lay in his power to break up that collision. Probably he would never have that chance again; the game had become too bitter.

Racing down the slope, Clay Rand saw himself with the sunless clarity of one condemned. It was the turning points of his life that clung so unmercifully to his memory. At each turning point he had stopped to listen to a faint voice speaking, and then had ridden down the left fork, unmindful of that voice. From the very beginning it had been this way, himself believing there was a time when he could turn back, cover his tracks, and take the honest road. This, he realized, was his last chance. He turned back now, or else he was forever lost.

In that frame of mind he threaded Granite Canyon, came about the Running M and stood off in the shadows to send his whistle toward the house. He waited like that, on guard against any of Cash's men riding out to spot him; and finally seeing Cash's flat and angular shape march from the house and come on.

Gore stopped twenty yards away, suspicious as always. "All right," murmured Rand. "All right, Cash." Gore advanced then, his boots striking the loose rubble fallen down from the Ramparts near by. There was a black area behind them where the last row of pines made a stand against the prairie; out of that prairie the yellowed grasses sent a dim shining. Running M's dogs were running the night, heavily howling.

"I met Benbow up at Cherokee," said Rand. "Indian Riley had him cornered."

"So," said Gore.

"No," answered Rand. "It didn't happen, Cash."

"Why?"

"I stopped it. I bluffed Riley out."

Gore's thin jaws ground gently on a cud of tobacco. Some husky sound crept up his throat. He shifted his weight, staring at Rand. "Where's your bread buttered, Clay? Don't you know yet?"

"Never mind. Nothing happens to Benbow while I'm around."

"You're smart, Clay. Smart enough to know how far this goes. You been foolin' yourself. You're no use to me

73

if you string with Benbow."

"It's time for me to quit."

"I guess it is."

"All right."

"No," said Gore in his expressionless way. "The time for you to quit was a long while back."

"You're stopping me?" asked Rand, his voice becoming reedy.

Gore lifted one hand slowly, rubbing it across his mustache. "Me? No, Clay, I never hold a man that's restless to go. You stopped yourself when you started workin' on Old Jack Dale's beef."

"I'll do my own judgin'."

"Sure. And you'll be a hard judge, kid, with what's on your mind. There's different kinds of crooks. Honest ones and crooked ones. Man has to stay by some sort of rule. I've stayed by mine and I can sleep well. It's a thing you can't say." He permitted himself one quick expression of real contempt. "You been a fool from the beginnin'. What in hell did you want to go stealin' for in the first place?"

"Never mind," snarled Rand. "I'm telling you to count me out."

He backed to his horse, never letting his glance drop from that thin shape before him. And swung into the saddle and cut a wide circle away from Cash Gore. He was fifty feet away when he heard Gore speak in an ironic and amused tone. "Maybe."

Rand called back. "What are you afraid of?"

"Me? Not a thing. You're the boy that's got something to be afraid of." And then Rand, running northward toward his own ranch two miles ahead, heard Cash Gore's laughter suddenly rip the darkness like metal fragments flung out, and as suddenly die.

Rand was gone and Gore had returned to the house when a thin little shape reared up from the near-by pile of

74

rocks and stood half bent and very still. Running M's house door slammed shut. The little figure wavered gently in this darkness, breathing quick and soft; and then trotted past the rocks and up the rampart slopes to where his horse stood. He said, "I got to get out of here," but when he pulled himself to the saddle he rested there.

Five minutes later, having made a roundabout circle to kill time, he came into Running M's yard and was stopped by a man's sudden challenge. "Who's that?"

"I want to see the boss," said the Traveling Kid.

"Gwan, get out," said the man.

"I want to see the boss," insisted the Kid.

Running M's door opened, letting Cash Gore through. Gore said: "Who's that, Ben?"

"You got a job?" called the Traveling Kid, and rode directly to the porch steps. Gore saw him and recognized him then; and let his narrowing glance have its long effect. "Where'd you come from?"

"Through the hills. Et with an outfit up on top."

"What outfit?"

"Said they was Hat men."

The fellow in the yard stepped rapidly forward, but Gore said evenly: "That's all right, Ben. Why pick on this outfit, Kid?"

The Traveling Kid said in a husky voice: "Maybe I can do the sort of work you like to have done."

Gore said: "Put him up, Ben."

"I work here?" asked the Kid.

"You work here," answered Gore, and went back into the house. Halfway across the room he stopped, his head dropped down. He brushed the back of a hand across his roan mustache, staring narrow-lidded at the floor. There wasn't any change on Cash Gore's taciturn cheeks.

8. A Light Goes Out

Returning to Hat around one o'clock of the morning, Benbow found Izee restlessly tramping the yard while the rest of the ranch slept. Izee said, with a gruff relief: "When you go on the scout, Benbow, I wish you'd let a man know. Where you been?"

"Cherokee."

"A dumb thing to do. What'd you find?"

"Nothing." But afterwards Benbow asked: "You know the country beyond the high pass pretty well?"

"Some of it. Spots I never got into—it bein' mighty rough."

"We'll have a look at those spots one day."

"Indian Riley knows every foot of that country."

"I know. Which is why we'll have a look." Benbow turned out his horse and pegged his gear and came back across the yard again. Izee still stood there, a short and stolid shape in the dark, ridden by a fretful gloom.

"Jim," he blurted out. "What you think of marriage?"

"Depends on who's getting married."

"That's the trouble. It might be me."

"Mary Boring's a fine girl."

"Yeah," said Izee dispiritedly. "Yeah, sure. I ought to know. We been goin' together four years." He scuffed his heels into the packed earth, staring down. "I get to thinkin' it would be swell. She can talk to a man and make him feel like he's seven feet tall and fit to lick lions. Ain't no woman in the valley that can cook any better and she'd save a man's money better'n a bank. I get kind of lonesome when I see all the boys pickin' their girls and settlin' down."

"What's holdin' you back then?"

"Well," said Izee in a foreboding manner. "I been my own boss a long time and it goes hard to give that up. I see these married fellows that used to ride anything that had four feet and which used to drink the night plumb through down at Faro Charley's. Then they got married and the ginger went out of them. I ask 'em how they like it and they say fine. But they don't look me in the eye when they say it. Mary now, she's got a determined character. What'd you do in a case like that?"

"Have a try, Izee."

"Aw, hell," sighed Izee and paced back to the bunkhouse.

Benbow stood momentarily still, the outline of Hat's buildings lying blackly against the night. There was a little wind running its cold breath over the valley and the nearby river clucked in the marginal willows. Other than that there was no sound and no motion. He went on to the big house and let himself into the office. Lighting up a lamp he sat down before the desk, feeling no need for sleep.

The night had solved some things and some things it had left tangled. He had always known—in common with the valley—that Indian Riley was an ordinary thief who escaped being hung only because he covered his tracks too well. He had also always known that Cash Gore was a crooked man. Suspecting a connection between Riley and Gore, he had at last satisfied himself of that fact by putting a few bullets through Riley's settlement windows. Riley had run back to Cash Gore with the news. The evidence there was complete.

Jubal Frick's buckling under to Cash Gore was something he had not understood before. Jubal lived there in obvious fear of his life and Gore operated Running M as he pleased. What he also knew beyond doubt was that Gore was the power behind all the country's rustling. Under shelter of Running M he had picked a crew to his liking; and it was his word that put Indian Riley to work up along the Yellows.

This much he had established; this much he had proved. He could erase from his mind whatever doubts and whatever compunctions he might have entertained. There remained now the job of discovering by what route these men slipped valley beef through the Yellows and to what destination they were sent. Until he knew that, and until he actually saw stolen beef being herded out of the country by this outfit, he could not act.

There was this quality of exact justice in Benbow that he himself failed to recognize. He was certain of Gore's guilt but he had not seen any Gore man rustle beef. He had to see that. Slowly considering the chain of evidence, he sat solemnly before the table, his big fighter's body relaxed in the chair. There was a battle coming that would spread its bloody, brutal tracks all over the hills. He knew Gore's kind too well to expect surrender; he knew himself too well and the valley cattlemen too well to expect mercy. It was why he wanted to be sure.

It was winter now, and Gore's men would be rustling out matured stuff, chasing it on down into the adjoining state somewhere, doctoring the brands and shipping to market through some rancher in on the deal. This was one way. Men clever with the running iron could change Hat so that only a careful examination of the skin side of the hide, after slaughter, could tell the tampering. And the Cattle Associations didn't yet have that careful an inspection system at the big slaughterhouses. Leaning forward, he reached for a pencil and began to blow out a few variations of the Hat ⬜ brand. Some of them were pretty obvious, like Box Arrow ⟼, H on a Rail ⊢⊣, Tent △, Broad Arrow ▽, WA on a Rail ⩗. With a little more doctoring it wasn't hard to produce The Hub ⟨brand⟩, Chain ⟨brand⟩, Dugout ⟨brand⟩, Broken Heart ⟨brand⟩ or Split 88 ⟨brand⟩. The variations, to a clever brand changer, were infinite. He had seen plenty of it done.

There was another way. When the calves were dropped in early spring, Gore's men would take them before branding, run them into the hills, slap on a brand and parcel them out amongst feeder cows. And many a Hat cow bereft of her calf up in the Yellows would be bawling miserably with a bag full of milk.

Yet in the end he knew he'd see what he wanted to see—a Gore man behind a Hat cow. When that time came, the valley would hold its bitter man roundup and the crop from that roundup would hang down in a stiff row from suspended ropes, turning slowly to the wind. He dreaded its coming—and knew it would come.

All this went through his head in its dark, slow fashion, and he sat in the night-still house with a sense of loneliness that grew and could not be shaken off. Hat was the valley's great ranch, and he ran Hat, and it would be to him that the rest of the valley turned when killing time came. It would be his responsibility; and it would be his word that hung or saved a man. His conscience had to hold all this.

His thoughts had a way of sliding off to other people, to Connie Dale, to Joe Gannon who was a better man than the valley believed him to be—who had married Eileen Gannon knowing her heart was on another man. To Clay Rand. His thinking halted there and he reviewed the scene in Cherokee with a puzzled, alert consideration. Earlier in the evening Clay had been near the Gannon place; then he had appeared in Cherokee. What for? The man was notoriously a restless rider—always on the move; and of late more secretive and less gay. His gambling debts, Benbow guessed, were bothering him. He couldn't keep his hands off a pack of cards. There was that streak in Clay always disposed to take chances, to make a long bet, to choose a short cut.

It grew colder in the room and darkness pressed against the windows. Connie said: "Of what are you thinking, Jim?"

He turned to find her standing at the office doorway, her arms holding a faded woolly robe closely about the shapely slimness of her body. Sleep had softened her cheeks, it had stained them a rose color, it had loosened the arrangement of her hair. Framed against the yellow light, she made a picture that hurt Benbow to see.

"Better go back to bed, Connie."

She came over and sat down in Jack Dale's favorite leather chair, studying him. Her eyes were wide with what she felt, with what she wanted to know. It was the way she always looked at Benbow, personal and intuitive, and terribly frank. She could not ever escape that odd, half-wifely instinct of possessing him—of sometimes wanting to hurt him and yet always standing instantly by him when she felt that others were hurting him. This little flash of loyalty came to her now that she saw how hard his thinking had been. When he was tired his long face had a way of settling and losing light. When trouble came to him he showed it, by the unruly expression of his eyes.

"I can make you some coffee, Jim."

"Never mind."

"Where were you tonight?"

"Up in the Yellows."

She had her father's way of listening to an answer and catching what lay behind the words. She had her father's way of cutting through the things that didn't matter. Laconic. "Find anything?"

"Yes," he said.

She let her shoulders rest in the chair and turned one leg idly across the opposite knee, swinging it up and down. It was an old habit, a gesture of boyishness still remaining; he had his look at its smooth, white lines and

80

lifted his glance away, and something of what he felt then went across to her. She straightened in the chair, her color more distinct than it had been. But she wanted to know exactly what he was thinking, as she always did. "Jim—what?"

"You're not a kid any more."

"You've seen my legs a good many years," she told him tartly.

"I know."

She dropped her eyes and her hand folded the edge of the robe in more secure arrangement around her knees. She said, gently: "We've had a lot of fun together, Jim. Will it all stop when Clay and I are married?"

"You'd better ask Clay," he said dryly.

"I'm asking you," she told him.

"I won't be here, Connie."

She spoke with a quick lift to her voice. "Don't say that." She rose from the chair and stirred uncertainly around the room. Afterwards she came to stand behind him. Her fingers touched his hair, smoothing it down, and then she let her hands fall to his shoulders. Her talk ran its soft way through the chilly stillness of the room.

"You're kind of tough, Jim. Sometimes I watch you in a crowd of men and I see how all of them swing around you. You can make people mind. You can always make them do what you want done. I don't know why—it's a trick you have. I've watched men drift your way, wherever you happened to be standing. It's made me feel funny. Proud. You never lift a hand, or raise your voice. But they come."

"Go back to bed."

She said: "I have tried to imagine this ranch without you on it. I can't do it. It wouldn't be Hat any more. I'd keep remembering back to the time when you were here. You see? Whether I like it or not, I'm the same as all the others. I look for you."

He pulled himself from the chair and turned. Her eyes were slow in lifting; but when they rose they were altogether candid—holding the strange and terrible honesty there for him. She was trying to tell him something she couldn't say aloud; and she was reading him anxiously for an answer. "If you went away," she said, faintly above a whisper, "could you forget me?"

"Connie," he said, "it's Clay you're marrying."

She dropped her glance. "Yes," she murmured. "Yes." He heard the strange, falling cadence of that answer. The top of her dark head was ashine under the lamplight, a fragrance rose sweetly from her. He put his big arms behind him, hands locked together. When she looked at him again a self-imposed reserve seemed to cover her feelings. Her lips were gently curved. "It's strange, isn't it, Jim? How can I tell you what I feel? I don't know—I don't know."

He drew a long, long breath. Fire flashed its way through him, freshly and hungrily burning. Restraint cramped down on his big muscles and left them with an actual ache. "Connie," he said, "it's Clay you're marrying. I've been a kind of fixture around here. Something maybe you'll miss for awhile when it's gone— and then forget. If it does you any good, kid, I'll tell you—"

He stopped on that, afterwards adding: "Let it ride like it is. Sure we've had fun. I can remember that, too. But you've grown up and you can't hang onto memories. Every now and then I've had to say good-bye to a part of my life that was all finished. I've had to make the break. You'll have to make that break, too, like every living soul. Don't look behind you, kid. That's the one thing I've learned. Yesterday will always make you cry. I know. It's tomorrow you've got to look for."

She said, near tears. "When you go—I'll lose so much!" And for a moment they stood like that, something whirling rashly between and swaying both of them in its violent compulsions. He broke it brusquely. "Other things come first. I'm taking Hat into a war, Connie. It may come this winter or it may be in the spring. God only knows the answer to it. The valley we had our fun in is all gone."

82

She whispered: "That bad?"

"Somebody," he told her gently, "has to be killed."

She turned back to the doorway and wheeled there a moment, a supple-shaped girl turned mysteriously into the fullness of a woman, with a sudden grace and a sudden richness putting her beyond his reach. All her face was in the lamplight; yet shadow made its deep pools in her eyes. This way she momentarily stood, studying him with an odd intensity; and then went back up the stairs.

He was at once bone-tired, isolated in a dead-black world. Turning out the lamp he went to his own room. Usually a sound sleeper, he lay long awake listening to the quick wind whisper at the edges of the house. Winter was on its way.

Cash Gore crossed the Running M yard, roped out and saddled his pony and stepped into the leather. The Traveling Kid stood near by, watching Gore with his bright, adolescent eyes; the ranch crew came up slowly from the corrals and stopped in the background. It was the way Gore sat in his saddle that told them of trouble. He loosened his rope and shook it out and whirled a tentative loop and let it fall. Yet the crew saw his hand hold that loop in its half-built position. Morning's fresh sunlight burst along the valley and a cool breeze played out of Granite Canyon's mouth. There was a nip in this air. Gore let his taciturn stare fall on the kid.

"Know anybody at that weddin' the other day, Kid?"

The Traveling Kid said: "I don't know anybody."

"How was it you stopped to eat with the Hat chuck wagon last night?"

"Gettin' dark and I was hungry."

"If it was dark what kept you from sleepin' there?"

"Me? Say, I don't stay long no place. A fellow on the dodge learns that."

"Then why'd you come here?"

"Maybe," said the Kid mysteriously, "I figured this

83

kind of a place was a good place for a fellow like me."

"What kind of a place?" pressed Gore.

"I got ears," said the Kid. "I hear things."

Cash Gore swung his loop idly, his stony eyes watching the loop widen and fall. "Where you from?"

"New Mexico."

"Know Jim Benbow?"

"Seen him. Don't know him." The Kid shifted his boots around the dust, and looked behind him to the row of men ranked so still-shaped there. At once he jerked his head back to meet the full slantwise glitter of Cash Gore's glance. The Kid's big Adam's apple slid up and down and his callow cheeks whitened. He said, nervously: "Well, what—"

Gore said, with a softer and softer voice: "You come straight down from the Hat chuck wagon last night?"

"That's right."

"Straight down—no dallyin' around?" urged Gore.

The Kid's pallor was distinct. It accepted the angularity of his cheeks, the thickness of his lips. He moved his feet again and said in a cracked, dry voice: "Yeah."

Silence dropped like a vast tent over the whole yard. Gore's eyes were narrowing out a raw light and his lips showed a vague change beneath the rust-colored screen of his mustache. His hand turned the loop of the rope idly beside the horse; he looked down at it, swung it up over his head in one sudden throw. The Kid saw that loop snake forward and lifted his arm, yelling:

"I never—"

The rope bit instantly around his waist, pinning one arm. He fought the rope with his other arm and then Gore's horse, training to hold anything that fought, backed away step by step, holding the tension while the Kid scuffed up the dust with his boots.

Gore said: "You been lyin', Kid. Your boot marks show where you squatted in the rocks out there last night. Benbow put you up to this!"

"By God," cried the Kid, "I got nothin' to do with

84

Benbow!" He flung one wild look back to the Running M hands who made no motion and no sound. "You goin' to see him do this!"

Gore wheeled the horse and dug in his spurs. The rope snapped the Traveling Kid's thin back and turned him completely through the air. He was still fighting when he fell, fighting and rolling and screaming as Gore's horse plunged into a dead run across the valley. Dust rose around the Kid and one arm lifted and made a faint signal for mercy; after that his head struck a rock and his feet wheeled through the air. He was through fighting then. Gore dragged him a few yards farther and stopped. He got down, walking back to the Kid, slipping off the rope.

The Kid was dead, with blood creeping out of his nose and a look of terror not yet dissolved from his battered, immature features. Gore stared down at him, showing no expression. Then he rolled up his rope, climbed back into the saddle and returned to the yard. None of the crew spoke.

"Hat," said Gore, "is havin' hard luck with its spies. Dump this kid in Jack Dale's yard tonight, Ben."

Ben Kell muttered: "All right."

"When I don't trust a man," said Gore evenly, "that's his end. I trust you boys. Think it over."

All along the Two Dance and Yellow ranges roundup fires burned their holes into the black and chilling nights; and by day the long files of cattle ruffled the valley dust in steady line as they moved on toward the railroad at Mauvaise siding. Big mossy-horned steers tossing their horns rampant, wild with the long isolation in the hills and with an unmixed Texan blood; and blockier, gentler steers bred to the new Hereford strain. Looking at this improved stuff as it surged up the chute at Mauvaise into the cattle cars, Nelson McGinnis of Diamond-and-a-Half parted his whiskers to drink his coffee out of a tin cup and opined that the cattle business was growing up. He could remember the time in the

Southwest when beef was simply beef. "A steer wasn't much tamer or slower than an antelope. Mean to meet and worth next to nothing. It's growed up to a business and I can't say I like the change." He recalled the past regretfully and then snatched the flaming hot cup from his lips with the enraged bellow of a bull. Out in the darkness riders of all the different outfits circled the herds' edges and grumbled their soothing songs, waiting turn at the loading chute. The glare of the freight engine's headlights shot far down the track and the smell of cattle reeked in the night and tallymen were yelling and the engine bell rang and brakemen's lanterns wove white circles on top of the cattle cars. Thus loaded in sweat and haste, another train moved off for Omaha and another string of empties slid along the chute.

Somebody yelled: "Crescent—git your beef up here!" And Gordon Howland's shout sailed forward and Crescent steers surged restlessly forward from the dark.

It went like that throughout the fall, the columns of beef debouching from the timbered uplands and marching on across the valley. Diamond-and-a-Half, Block T, Crescent, Hat and Clay Rand's little jag of Anvil stuff. With the ranchers beyond the Yellows making their long drives from the south; and with the Mauvaise Valley people coming down from the north. Converged at this lone siding in the middle of the flat lands, week after week, the punchers of the various outfits worked and slept and swapped and quarreled and visited and went on their respective ways. Chuckwagon fires bloomed awhile and died; and outfits moved in and out and friends met and bad blood boiled, and then chuck wagons and outfits rode back across the plain and at last Mauvaise siding was still again, with the packed ground bearing the scars of the fury that had been, the blackened fire circles, the tin cans and broken bits of men's living.

It was October and then it was November, with a premature white dusted along the heights of the Yellows. In sixty days of riding, Benbow had touched the home ranch but three times. With the shipping done, there was still the job of drifting all the rest of the Hat stuff down from timber to the flats. Purposely, he left a small scatter of beef along the edge of Granite Canyon; and in three weeks of solid, bitter rain he wound up the season.

In December it was done. Winter was on them, winter and the dreary business of riding line. He established his men in the cabins along the Ramparts, freighted their winter's grub out to them, turned the extra horses loose and came riding back to Hat fifteen pounds lighter than he had been.

Sitting in the office with Jack Dale—the old man didn't move much from his favorite chair these days—he made his report.

"I left some beef up at the edge of the canyon. Bait for rats. Pete Cruze will do the watching."

Old Jack shook his head and spoke with a weary remnant of anger. "That Travelin' Kid—they handled him pretty brutal. I keep rememberin' the young lad's face. Just wanted to be tough, like any boy. And got killed for it. They figured him one of your men—like that Arizona." Dale swung to have his direct look at Benbow. "I never was quite sure if you had the kid hired to do this."

"I didn't know him at all. He just fell into the situation at the wrong time. Same man killed him as killed Arizona."

"Know the man?"

"Yes."

Jack Dale reared up growling. "Why in God's name you hanging back then? You got the whole valley to choose your help from."

Benbow slouched forward, resting his arms across his knees, rubbing his tough palms together. He let the silence run on, having a hard time finding the proper words to express what lay so blackly inside. "There's a chore here that will stick in my mind the rest of my life. I can stand that, if there ain't any doubt afterwards. So I've got to prove what I know, before I start."

Jack Dale lighted a cigar, looking through its smoke and through the window to the long sweep of the yonder valley. He said irrelevantly: "A pretty land. I've had my luck here and my fun. When you think the showdown will come?"

"By spring. Or, if a break comes, sooner."

Jack Dale slowly shook his head. "I wish," he murmured regretfully, "I could be here to see it."

Benbow lifted his eyes immediately. The window light made Jack Dale's face quite gray. The steam was gone from this hearty old man and the flesh along his jaws was loose and wrinkled. "You seen a doctor?" asked Benbow.

"I've lived long enough with animals to be like one. A hound knows when it's dyin'. I know—just like that hound." He added instantly: "Don't say anything to Connie."

"No," murmured Benbow, and stared down at his big hands. He cleared his throat, slowly locking his hands together. The light of the room dimmed for him. Old Jack's voice was remoter than it had been—a voice that had been so strong and alive and now was slipping away into a far land.

"I'd like to last long enough to see the end of the fight," repeated Jack Dale wistfully. "I ain't afraid to go. It's the uncertainty as to how you come through it I hate to feel. You been my son, Jim. I couldn't of had one of my own I'd of liked or trusted better."

"It'll come out all right," Benbow told him gently.

"I don't know. I feel trouble. I feel a lot of trouble up ahead. An Indian is sly, but a white man turned crooked is worse. Well, it's that I don't like. And Connie marryin' Rand. I'd meant this to be your ranch, son. Now you're pullin' away. Nothin' solid in the world any more."

"I won't be goin' till the trouble's settled. And Rand will make her a fine man. They don't come any better, Jack!"

Jack Dale made no answer. His eyelids narrowed down as he watched the land outside. It was a way he had, of closing his mouth definitely, of withdrawing from people when he had contrary thoughts. Benbow could feel the old man's opposing judgment ride this room, and it puzzled him. But he held his tongue and long afterwards Dale said enigmatically: "You've got more to contend with than you now see. Remember I told you that. I dislike to know what you'll have to face. It'll be a hard day for you when it comes."

Benbow got up. He stood high and husky over Jack Dale, unable to speak his feelings. He said briefly, "I keep rememberin' the day I rode up to Hat, a raw kid, and you took me in," and swung out of the room at a fast step. On the porch he stopped to build himself a cigarette, scowling at his finger tips. Early afternoon's sun lay somewhere above a winter's milky storm haze, spraying a strange mist-light across the range. The rising wind bit its cold way through his clothes. Clay Rand trotted into the yard and rounded up at the porch. A moment later Connie came out.

"Come in for coffee, Clay."

Rand stepped to the ground and stamped his stiff legs. Wind had ruddied up his cheeks and his grin was as white and fine as anything in the world. He looked at Benbow cheerfully. "You been workin', kid. Thin."

Benbow drawled: "I'm no wanderin' minstrel."

Clay Rand's laughter was a huge shout, echoing still as he tramped into Hat's house. Connie waited at the door. "Coffee for you, too, Jim?"

"I'm going to town early. I'll see you there tonight."

She said: "Promise you'll come to the dance hall?"

"Yes," he said and went across the yard. She remained in the doorway until he came riding back with the Hat crew behind him. And watched him swing down the road.

9. Betrayer

Nelson McGinnis came over Two Dance's crowded street and touched Benbow's arm. "Back room of the Cattle King in ten minutes," he said, and walked away. Frank Isabel tramped down the walk, a dark-stained and barren-faced man. Jim said, "Howdy, Frank," and watched Isabel's squaw tramp behind him, carrying their five-year-old. Price Peters idled up, time heavy on his hands. He stood there, his restless and sharp eyes seeing things in this town other men never saw. "A drink?" he suggested.

"Try a dance first."

"And then a drink," murmured Price, "to drown the memory of that impertinence."

"Don't follow you, Price."

Price's grin was a rare thing—lighting up the settled and disbelieving shadows of his face. "Never mind. I read Omar once, and never forgot him. My education has been comprehensive. Like the education of other fools. So we dance."

They strolled toward the Masonic Hall, countering the steady traffic of valley riders drifting down toward Faro Charley's. Diamond-and-a-Half was in, Crescent and Hat were in; and at this moment Block T's crowd came riding out of the windy blackness with a long, wailing halloo. Three Running M hands stood in studied indifference by the Cattle King porch. One of them said, "Hello, Hat," in a way that was narrow and touched by plain insolence. Benbow stopped and made his slow, deliberate wheel. He said, "Hello, Ben," and watched Ben Kell's muscles go straight and flat. There was something here, like the smell of smoke from a fire he could not see; as definite as that. The other two Running M riders showed the obscure and shineless surfaces of their eyes to him, neither moving nor speaking. But the smell remained here.

He said in a summer-soft voice: "That all, Ben?" And waited until he knew there would be no answer. He turned deliberately and went on, Price Peters' boots striking more exactly beside him. Price murmured: "I don't know those other two fellows."

"Cash hires his men from the other side of the Yellows."

Price's shoulders moved impatiently. He wasn't satisfied. It was the way of his mind, to keep digging deeper into the motives of men, the dark areas of their minds. He said: "What'd he speak for?" in a discontented way, and then looked along the street, his interest honed by Ben Kell's talk, to a razor's hungry edge.

Wind thrust its keen chill down the street and Two Dance began to glow and glitter, like a woman receiving the attentions of men after long loneliness. Price and Benbow edged themselves through the crowd at the Masonic Hall's doorway and were struck at once by an outdraft of warm air and the steady beat of fiddle, guitar and accordion lifting and falling in the rhythm-swing of a schottische. They joined the solid line of men along the wall.

There was always something strange about Price Peters, a compound of bitterest cynicism and of a sadness that would never let him alone. Watching him, Benbow saw how the sight of all those couples wheeling and balancing out on the floor seemed to strike the raw edge of a memory never quite healed. Price's exact face showed it. He wasn't smiling; he had gone a little pale, a little unsteadied. And then Price saw Karen Sanderson turn by on the arms of a Crescent man and stepped to the floor, displacing that man with a remote flourish of an elegance. A gentleman, Benbow thought, remembering manners long unused.

The music stopped just as Connie and Clay Rand came up. They walked over to Benbow, Rand as ruddy and restless as Benbow had ever seen him to be. There was something pulling at this handsome man, at his nerves and at his impulses; plainly he wanted to be somewhere else. Connie wasn't smiling. A fellow yelled, "Pick 'em, boys," and the music sailed into a waltz tune. Benbow took Connie's arms and started for the floor. Rand said, with a hurried relief, "I'll be back in a little bit, Connie," and made an instant bolt for the door.

Benbow saw Connie's glance follow Rand and then they were into the crowd, gliding with it and being turned by it.

Benbow said: "Quarrelin'?"

Ray Dedman, who was Block T's riding boss, caromed against them and pulled his girl away; Ray had shucked his coat, exposing a pair of pink sleeve holders clamped around his arms. He pumped his arm up and down and there was a rapt and desperate expression on his long cheeks, and a beaded sweat.

Connie said in a small wistful voice: "Nothing holds Clay's interest very long, does it?"

He said: "I keep rememberin' a night last year when we danced at Block T. Then Clay came and something happened."

"What happened, Jim?"

"You grew up."

Izee and Mary Boring stalked past, more walking than waltzing. Mary Boring's voice was remotely exasperated. "You could dance better if you'd practice."

Izee said in pure desperation: "Practice with what—heifers?"

92

Connie said to Benbow gently: "No matter how much we fight, I keep coming back to you for support. For help—when things go wrong."

He said: "That's the trouble."

She looked at him directly, throwing back the smooth black surface of her hair. "You've very wise sometimes."

The music quit. They strolled on toward the door. Men advanced to claim Connie, pushing Jim away. Izee and Mary Boring floated on, Izee's face showing signs of doggedness as he listened to her. "I suppose you've got to go and spend your money at Faro Charley's." Izee didn't say anything; he simply plowed through the crowd, outward bound. Ray Dedman claimed her; she made a futile gesture with her arms but Dedman pulled her out upon the floor. There was a crowd around Karen Sanderson and Benbow watched the way she stood before them, graceful and slow-smiling and mysterious to a man's eyes. Her glance lifted past them and caught Benbow's attention; and remained on him, enigmatic and deliberate. Connie, lifting her head, suddenly saw that little scene of two striking and self-contained people exchanging some strong thought across the interval. She looked swiftly at Karen and as swiftly back at Benbow; and at once dropped her glance, a feeling like fear and like jealousy racing through her, to change the whole evening. When the music started, Benbow slipped out of the door.

Price Peters stood at the edge of the walk, raking the street and all the shadows pressing upon the street with a careful and restless attention. He said: "Cash Gore went over and said something to Ben Kell. Then Kell and those three other fellows dropped out of sight."

Benbow said, "Come on," and crossed with Price to the Cattle King. Back beyond its lobby they found the Two Dance valley owners waiting for them. Nelson McGinnis said: "Where the hell you been?" agreeably. Tobacco smoke fumed around the small quarters in solid blue clouds. Gordon Howland was squatted in the middle of the floor drawing a picture, Indian fashion, for George Gray of Block T. Rand had come in and stood by himself, hands plunged into his pockets and staring irritably at the bare wall. Mayne Riley, who ran Hogpen away up north beyond Mauvaise siding, was also here, with Chuck Fentress whose outfit was beyond the badlands.

Price said: "If it's business, let's get started. I still got my drinking to do."

Nelson McGinnis said: "Boys, listen—" and stopped. Jubal Frick came into the room slowly. He lifted his shoulders and looked around the circle with an uncertain air. He said: "A meetin'? Didn't know it till this minute. Why wasn't I told?"

Silence settled at once. Gordon Howland rose from his squatting position and made a deliberate turn, putting his back to Frick. George Gray stared at the floor. It went on like this until Price Peters said: "Well, Nelson."

Nelson McGinnis was older than the others; a blunt and aggressive man never known to hide his feelings. But he was uncomfortable and he seemed saddened when he lifted his voice. "You better go, Jubal."

Jubal Frick stiffened his shoulders and let them fall. Age had broken him down. Age and something else, Benbow thought. Frick said: "That's all right, boys. I understand," and turned out of the room.

McGinnis growled: "I came up the trail with Jubal years ago. He used to be a fine man."

Price Peters was impatient. "I still got that drinking to do."

McGinnis turned to Benbow. He said with a driving briefness: "How much help you want—and when you want it?"

It was like that, the blunt expression of what lay in all their minds, without need of any explanation. Benbow drew out his tobacco and framed himself a cigarette, staring at his finger tips. He said: "Not yet."

Nelson McGinnis shot out his question: "Why?"

Price Peters moved around, impatient with his

94

interrupting talk. "All you boys seem in a hell of a sweat to push Jim into this chore. If you're in such a hurry why not get your own outfits out and do the work?"

"Now look, Price," put in George Gray, "we're all in it and we're all ridin' with Jim. Get off your corn."

"Sure, sure," grunted Price Peters. "You're all ridin'. But you want Jim to pull the trigger."

"Somebody," pointed Nelson McGinnis, "has to give the orders."

"Well," argued Price, strangely stubborn, "why not you? Or Gordon here?"

"Sometimes," stated Nelson McGinnis definitely, "you're a dam' fool, Price. It takes a smarter man and a tougher man than I am or you are to ride the trouble out this country, without gettin' half of his own men killed. It's a delicate business at best. The fellow that takes a committee into this brush has got to know the way. It's worse than you think. I saw a posse slaughtered cold once, down in Texas, bein' led by a foolish man. There's going to be a fight and there's going to be grievin' at the end of it. I'll do anything or go anywhere that Jim tells me, but for no other man. That's the way it is."

"To hell with it," said Price, his dissatisfaction mounting. "You're making a target out of Jim."

Benbow, listening all this while, suddenly said: "That's all right, Price. It's Hat's chore, and I'm working for Hat. But I'm not ready, Nelson."

"Why?" insisted McGinnis. "You know enough to be satisfied in your own mind, don't you?"

"I know—"

Gordon Howland whirled and said in an even, warning voice: "I wouldn't tell what you know, Jim."

Silence flattened through the room again. Nelson McGinnis looked at Gordon Howland and afterwards pulled his thin lips together. George Gray slowly scrubbed a hand across his cheek and tipped his eyes with a certain obscure interest on the ceiling. Benbow, weighing Howland's startling warning and the quality of

95

stillness that followed it, saw Clay Rand's cheeks turn smooth.

McGinnis said: "Who don't you trust now, Gordon?"

Price Peters grated out his own warning: "Let that pass!"

"There is no man in this room," stated Benbow coolly, "I wouldn't trust. If you've got a doubt, Gordon, speak up."

"Let it pass," repeated Price.

"I've said enough," grunted Howland.

"Better that way," decided Nelson McGinnis; and then there was no more talk.

Clay Rand went out of the room first, his boots scraping sound along the floor. Benbow, altogether puzzled, turned to watch Rand go; and so missed the swift negative gesture Price Peters made to the other men in the room. Afterwards the meeting broke up. Out on the Cattle King porch, Benbow stopped to light his neglected cigarette. "What in thunder's eating Gordy Howland?" he grumbled.

Price Peters said carelessly: "I want a drink."

They drifted down the street, into the condensed crowd of Faro Charley's. After the bleak chilliness of the street, the warmth and the smoke of this place enveloped them like a blanket. Talk hummed through the room and all the tables were going; and in the corner a ring of heavy-coated men stood about a table watching Faro Charley and Clay Rand and two others carry on a stud game. Benbow made a path through that ring with his elbows, not gentle in the way he used them, and had his look. Clay Rand sat stiffly at the table, the ruddy mantle deeper and deeper on his cheeks, an expression of strain and irritation flickering out of his eyes. Luck, Benbow understood, was running against his partner again. He pushed his way over to the bar, joining Price and Izee. The three of them stood comfortably there and had a drink. Price studied the saloon with an inscrutable indifference, his feelings seeming to be past rousing. Izee showed Benbow a harassed expression.

"Women," he groused, "never know when to quit."

Price's answer flicked Izee with an irony so light that Izee never caught it. "That's only the first lesson in the book, Izee."

"What book?" demanded Izee.

"Never mind. Better philosophers than you have tried to read it through, without luck. And when you get lost in the dark, remember this: A woman is her own question and her own answer and neither you nor any man can do a thing about it. It will save you a lot of grief if you stick to that."

"Aw, hell," grumbled Izee, "come down to earth."

"Where's earth and what's real?" murmured Price gently, and then let his attention fall on Cash Gore who stood now near the far corner of the bar. The Running M foreman wore a blue army overcoat buttoned up to his neck. Two spots of wind-whipped color made round brands on his sharp cheekbones; and he stood taciturnly against the bar, his morose and gloomy attention lowered to the glass before him. Price Peters' banked interest was at once fresh, at once strong, and that old dissatisfaction began to pinch his features. He moved his shoulders in a restless way and searched the crowd with a keening glance.

Shad Povy came in from the windy night, working his way persistently toward the bar. It brought him before the three partners and he stopped there and said: "Hello, Benbow," guardedly. All at once Benbow and Izee and Price Peters were considering him with a deep and personal and benevolent interest, and Shad Povy, feeling the effect of that thoughtful scrutiny, threw up his hands and backed away. He said: "No, you don't. No, you don't," and disappeared from Faro Charley's. Benbow's grin was a sudden streak across darkness. Suddenly they were all laughing in a soft, soundless way. Clay Rand, coming nervously away from the poker table, found them thus.

"What you fools grinning at?"

"Have a drink," suggested Benbow. "What you so jumpy about?"

"I've lost enough in half an hour to pay for this place," grunted Rand. He wiggled his finger at the barkeep, and got his drink and downed it. Benbow studied him without much expression. "As to poker, God sure made you a sucker."

"Oh, let a man alone!" snarled Rand. But he whirled around after he had said it and laid his arm across Benbow's shoulders. "Never mind, Jim. I'm in a bad frame of mind."

Price Peters lifted his glance to the back bar's mirror and saw things there with a sly absorption. Cash Gore pushed himself away from the counter and turned, and let his attention cross over to Rand. Rand was drinking; yet Price Peters, missing none of this secretive byplay, saw Rand look at Gore and receive something that seemed like a message. Gore left the saloon.

Rand laid down his glass. "Let's get out of here. The place stinks."

"Maybe it needs air," suggested Benbow. It was the softness of that phrase which snapped them around to look at him. He was faintly smiling; and then all of them were alert, and all of them speculatively eyeing him.

They tramped out of the saloon together. Five yards up the street he turned into a side alley, led them back beside Faro Charley's place to the town's cluttered rear lots. Sheds and broken wagons laid their dim shapes against the night black. Beyond stood Hoffmeier's corral.

"Ned Steel's got some beef in there," said Benbow.

They stood still, digesting the information, worrying it around their heads. Izee caught it first and turned like a dog on a scent. "Need a horse," he called, and was gone.

Clay said, "Wait," and walked back toward the back end of Faro Charley's. They saw him vaguely slink through a door. After a while he reappeared. "There's a middle door opening into the barroom. I pushed it a little bit open."

"Need some rope," said Price.

"Wagons," said Benbow and led them toward the corral. The wind lifted its pressure, rattling the loose edges of Two Dance. These three men tracked back and forth through the bitter blackness, hauling and boosting at the discarded wagons and ancient buggies. Returning with his horse, Izee found a runway thus built irregularly between the corral and the back of Faro Charley's. Clay Rand came up, breathing hard. "Hell of a lot of work for a little fun. You fellows all set?"

"Open the door and get ready to jump," called Benbow.

Izee rode to the corral gate. Benbow opened it and let him through, and climbed out of the way. Izee went into the corral and set the cows there into a mill, driving them out through the gate. Price and Benbow, perched up on the wagons, began to yell, and the cattle, lumbering out of the corral and hemmed by the loose line of wagons, bolted straight for Faro Charley's back door. Rand yelled against the wind: "All right!" Then the leading cows hit that frame building with a crash that thundered up into the windy sky. Izee and Price and Benbow were howling at the hind edges of the stock like Indians, keeping up a pressure that shoved the front cows on through the back door, into Faro Charley's.

"That's enough!" yelled Benbow, scrambling out through the wagons. Price and Rand stumbled after him; and Izee scudded instantly out of sight. Benbow came up behind the Cattle King on the dead run, ducked beside it and arrived at the street, breathing hard. The three of them stopped there, Benbow and Price and Clay.

Men were trotting across the street. The sound of splintering furniture and bursting boards came out of Faro Charley's place like the rattle of a snare drum. One lone cow hooked its way through the front swinging door, with a man hanging to its tail; and then the whole jag of Ned Steele's cows simply tore Faro Charley's front door into a wide hole, running out of the place in one frantic stream. Ned Steele came down from the dance hall on the high lope, indescribably cursing. A gun went off in the saloon and men were turning and clawing and trying to get clear of the jam, and the racket in Faro Charley's got wilder and wilder. Cattle drifted aimlessly along the street; and riders scrambled for their horses and began to drive the stock on down toward the depot.

Shad Povy appeared from the cow-stream as though bodily thrown. He hit the sidewalk on his shoulders, jumped to his feet and broke into a fast trot. When he got as far as the Cattle King he stopped dead. The tail of his coat hung in sections and one eye was beginning to turn a delicate blue.

"You fellows!" he panted. "I knowed it!—I just knowed it!"

Izee strolled over from the stable. "Somethin' the matter?"

"I hope you burn in pitch—all of yuh!" shouted Povy and limped away.

"Want to go look?" suggested Izee.

"Gentlemen," said Benbow, "it might be best to withdraw from these shambles," and led the way into the Cattle King lobby.

They stood there, listening to the yonder fury subside. The music in the Masonic Hall began to swing up again. A semblance of order returned to Two Dance, leaving these four partners alone in their bland innocence. Benbow slowly tapered himself a cigarette, the glint of humor slowly fading out as he stood there.

"I can remember a lot of fun like this," murmured Price. "It's about all there is to remember. A few fires burning on the back trail, with the shadows getting deeper. And no light ahead."

Benbow looked up from his fingers. "Beautiful but slightly sad."

"I guess I didn't drink enough."

"You'll get no help from Faro Charley for a while."

Nelson McGinnis put his head through the door and looked at them with a faint grin. "One day," he observed, "you boys are goin' to get shot or hung." And then he went on.

Price said: "A prophecy spoken in jest, but true." He spoke it in so sharp and narrow a way that the other three stared at him. Izee presently lowered his head, drawing a pattern on the floor with his toe. Clay Rand made a high and gallant shape in the room, but the sparkle of pleasantry was out of him and he met Price Peters' eyes with an expression drawn thin and shadow-haunted. It was like this. The ease and the thorough understanding and the voiceless thing that held them together seemed to die; and left them as strangers.

Clay murmured: "You give a man the creeping willies, Price," and went abruptly from the place. Izee said something about Mary Boring, also leaving. Price spoke very quietly.

"Always an end to fun. I was born to expect too much of it—and I got too little. I wish I had your nerve, Jim. Come rack and ruin, you'll never budge. The thunder rolls out and the heavens fall in and men betray you and you'll reach the bitterest situation that can ever come to a man. But you'll still be the same. The most solid thing on this crazy earth."

"Time to dance," observed Benbow.

"I'm still thirsty," said Price and left Benbow there. Later, following as far as the porch, Benbow watched Price cross the street and go into the dance hall, which struck him as being odd. Clay and Izee had vanished, and his questing glance found neither Gore nor any Running M man in sight. The ruckus down by Faro Charley's had died away, with all the cattle herded from the street.

Winter whirled down from the Two Dance heights, slicing through the crevices of this town and ripping up the street's dust. All the ponies along the walk racks had swung around, their rumps into the wind. The sky's blackness was pure and deep, the stars sparkling like frost particles. He stood there thoughtfully, a premonition having its way with his deeper mind; feeling it as clearly as if it were a tangible bit of evidence, yet not knowing from what quarter it came. Nursing the last smoke out of his cigarette, he kept thinking about his cattle placed at the edge of Granite Canyon, of Cherokee and the trails running through the Yellows. Of Indian Riley. And, finally, of Cash Gore.

A man came from the alley between Dunmire's stable and Withrow's store, crossed the street's dust and paused at the porch. He looked around him cautiously and spoke then. "Square Madge says to tell you she's got something you'd better come and hear."

Benbow didn't know the man, but he said, "All right," and then watched this messenger stroll down toward Faro Charley's. Benbow ground out his cigarette, had another look at the street and crossed it, entering the alley.

Price Peters left the Cattle King closely on the heels of Clay Rand. He saw Rand go up the street and turn out of it near the Masonic Hall. Waiting a moment, Peters strode diagonally as far as the Masonic Hall, entered its front door and slipped out of it by a side exit. He stood here in the favoring darkness, the wind nailing him to the building wall, with his instincts aroused but not clearly shaped. And then, on the point of circling behind the hall, he saw Cash Gore leave the street and come across the vacant lot adjoining the hall and vanish at the hall's back side.

Price followed immediately as far as the rear corner. There was no light here and no way of seeing what stood ahead of him. But, paused this way, feeling the savage force of his suspicions, he heard Gore's voice coolly lift from that black area. "Clay."

Price's eyes were focussing. He saw a figure slide slowly forward; and then those two shapes seemed to blend into one vague blot of darkness. Clay Rand's tone

102

was too plain not to be identified. "All right, Cash," he said.

Gore said: "Listen to this . . ." and his voice became a thread of sound stretched meaningless by the rising wind. It was only for a moment. Placing himself flat against the wall, Price watched one of that pair come back into the vacant lot and reach the street and the street's light. It was Rand. Gore had retreated farther behind the town.

Price Peters slid along the building wall as far as the side door. He started to open it when he saw a figure hoist itself from the vacant lot and travel toward the street. It was, he saw a moment later, Izee, and the moment he recognized him he ran out from the building, calling Izee's name. Izee whipped around, his right arm drooping toward the skirt of his coat. There was a look in his eyes unfriendly even to Price.

"Where you been?" challenged Price.

"None of your damned business," rapped out Izee.

But he stared at Price and saw what was on Price's face. He came nearer, seizing Price by the arm, his fingers biting into Price's skin. "Listen, kid. Say nothing to Jim. He's been Clay's friend since the beginnin'. You know how Jim would feel about that? You keep your mouth shut. We got to figure another way."

"I know the other way," was Price Peters' even answer. "I—"

A shot burst over the Masonic Hall and bucked the rush of wind; and then a general firing lifted across the town.

103

10. The Fight

Benbow walked into the alley between Withrow's store and Dunmire's stable, an utterly black little lane no wider than the spread of his two arms. The sound of music ran with the wind and voices sent their little echoes in dim pattern through the board walls of the store. Fifteen yards from the street the alley opened upon a compound bordered on three sides by the store wall, the back end of the stable and a long low wagon shed. The fourth side was Cheyenne Street, which ran obscurely away from the main artery of town toward Square Madge's house. He turned diagonally across the compound, bound for that street.

On his left he could see a light seep through the loose cracks of the stable's closed rear door. Above him the stars washed the sky with a frosty and lightless brilliance. The wind left this black area alone, and a kind of uneasy quiet pervaded it and somewhere along this quiet he made out the soft scraping of an object moving in the wagon shed. He was half across the compound, but at once the negligent fires of his attention licked a fresh heat through him and stopped him stone-still in his tracks.

A voice called from the wagon shed: "Benbow."

He didn't recognize it and didn't answer it. Situated thus he could make out nothing—and was instantly and

104

bitterly aroused to his own exposure. That surrounding blackness grew more absolute, and seemed immediately to swirl like smoke. Somebody struck a foot against one of the parked wagons in the shed. His name was called again—not from the shed this time, but from the wall of Withrow's store, directly behind.

"Benbow."

He let his arm fall and lift the gun tucked inside his waistband. There was a moment of delay here while he swung the gun guardedly up. Hardened to the worst of what was to come, he realized he had been sucked into a trap; and was profoundly disgusted with himself. In that faint space of time he had turned stiff and motionless; he had turned nerveless. He failed to identify the voice that ran with an out-breathing care across the compound.

"It's Benbow." Afterwards one shot exploded into this stealthy creeping quiet, its echoes cracking against the walls of the compound and caroming upward into the windy whip of the night. The force of that bullet slapped narrowly by Benbow; he had been turned toward the wagon shed, and so saw the long leap of the gun's muzzle light. On that flash he threw his own answering shot.

They had been waiting for that and it was like the release of thunder—the sudden howl and blast of gunfire opening up all around him. They had him corraled here; they had posted themselves on all four sides. There was a moment in him then, targeted as he was by that bitter hail of lead, when he gave up hope and felt the wild touch of death. He had fired and plunged forward, diving straight at the spot in the shed where he had observed the first gun flash. Its muzzle light bloomed again, round and sultry before his eyes. He fired at it; and heard a man expel a low and whining grunt, as though struck in the belly by a fist. And then that one's shadow capsized from a wagon's seat and hit the ground directly at the feet of the onrushing Benbow.

Dust made its fresh and strong smell in the compound, ripped up by the low-striking crossfire. Flattened against

105

the side of a wagon, with a dying man's hand slapping futilely at his boots, Benbow saw guns all along the far edge of the compound flash and die and flash again. Slugs were searching the wagon shed, crushing through wood snarling against iron parts, spitting and whining at him, searching for him with their little passing fingers of disturbed air. The compound was a-roar and men were yelling and this boiling, down-crashing furor shook the shed on its foundations. The fellow under his feet was dead. In the far part of the shed some other man, trapped by the fire of his own partners, had set up a wild crying:

"Not here—not here!"

Benbow heard the steady fusillade strike nearer his position; and understood they were seeking him with deliberate method. He opened up then, carefully pinning his shots on the flashes across the compound. A man yonder howled with a rising voice, like the howl of a lone wolf dying. And then Benbow's hammer struck a fired shell and he dropped his gun and crouched down and fell across the dead man's body. It was a tell-tale silence, and one that the quick ears of all those other men understood, for their feet were scudding the dust rushing toward him. Hard-breathing and wickedly pushed, Benbow dragged the dead man around and sought and found that one's gun. He had to pry it free from stiff-set fingers. These other fellows were gray shadows dead before him when he turned his borrowed gun on them and fired from his crouched shape. And then those shapes faded and the stable's rear door opened sidewise on its squealing runners and street light faintly pierced the compound and Izee Custer was calling into a sudden full silence.

"Benbow."

Bodies were rushing away to the rear of the wagon shed, their sounds dying behind the deepening howl of the wind. He could see the stable's doorway fill with men piling through from the main street. Price Peters' voice was high and sharp.

"Sing out, Jim!"

"All right."

A lantern flashed through the stable's runway and threw its fractured beams palely across the black. Benbow stepped from the wagon shed. The lantern swayed forward and the crowd came on. Someone said: "Powder still stinks. Who was it?"

"Bring the lantern here," called Benbow. Izee and Price Peters and Clay Rand came forward together, Izee carrying the lantern. Benbow could see the wild flash of all their eyes by this yellow light; he could see the odd whiteness of Clay Rand's cheeks.

"You're all right?" called Izee.

Benbow took the lantern and swung it behind him. The dead man lay face up, his body curved oddly at the base of a wagon wheel. He heard the flat intonation of Rand's voice. "Who's that?"

Price Peters said: "Taggart. A new man who worked for Running M."

"So," said Izee, "Running M."

The compound was filling. Hat riders crowded around. Nelson McGinnis forced his way forward to have his look at the dead Taggart. There wasn't anything said for a minute, but Izee did a strange thing. He lifted the lantern until its shining light struck Clay Rand's face fully and directly. Izee and Price were staring at Rand in a way that was strange, that was wholly dark. Rand put out his arm and shoved the lantern away. He said quietly: "Don't throw that damned thing in my eyes."

Gordon Howland pushed his way through. George Gray was coming up to join them; the surrounding crowd of riders thickened. A gust of wind slammed through the stable alley and raked this compound and turned the lantern light to a thin, flittering wisp. Benbow saw all those faces dully shining in the semidark; he saw the restless turning of their eyes.

Nelson McGinnis said: "Running M, of course. You satisfied now, Jim?"

Howland said at once: "My crew's all here."

Nelson McGinnis caught briskly at the idea. "We'll get everybody together. Jim can—"

Benbow said: "Go ahead and do your riding. I'm out of it."

"What in God's name?" exploded McGinnis.

"When I'm ready I'll tell you," said Benbow. "If you don't want to wait, it's your fight, not mine." He had one more look at the dead Taggart and shook his head a little, and pushed his way across the compound. He went through the stable as far as the street and stopped there, with Izee and Price and Clay closely following. Izee still held the lantern. Clay said irritably, "Put that confounded thing away," and stepped back a pace, until his face was beyond its yellow reach.

Price said, coldly: "What are you afraid of showing, Mr. Rand?"

"Hurts my eyes."

"Maybe," suggested Izee in the softest voice possible to him, "you been usin' your eyes too much."

Rand's tall body swayed. He did not answer either man. He lifted one hand and rubbed it slowly across his face, and jerked his hat brim well down. "Jim," he said, "take Connie home for me, will you? I'm stayin' in town tonight."

He took Benbow's assent for granted, swinging on his heels and going down the street at a fast clip.

Benbow said: "What's prodding you fellows?"

Price turned the subject at once. "I'm cold."

"Time to pull out," Benbow said. But he added, "Kell—I recognized Kell's voice in that racket."

Izee dropped the lantern, going back into the compound. Price said: "See you in a minute," and headed for the Masonic Hall.

Benbow went slack against the stable's wall, building up a cigarette. He had to cup the match in his hands against the wind; and the light of it sparkled brilliantly against the narrowed and thoroughly inexpressive

108

surfaces of his eyes. Afterwards he stood in the howling darkness while men of the various outfits filed past him; hearing their talk but not paying attention to it. The fight had screwed his nerves tight; and now they were loosening up, and weariness fed into his blood. His mind kept feeding him flashes of the fight in grotesque pattern; he could still taste the pungent powder smoke rolling along the wagon shed and he could still hear Taggart's last breath bubble through his throat. It was a forerunner of worse things to come, and as he remained there he viewed that uncertain future with a more and more closed mind. No mercy and no trust for anybody.

He left the stable, going to the Masonic Hall with the full wind shouldering against him, stinging his cheeks with its needling strike. There was a gap at the Cattle King hitch racks, which was where Running M's horses had stood. Only one pony there now, which would be the dead Taggart's. They had ridden out in a hurry.

He stepped into the Masonic Hall and found all the women waiting there. The music had quit and all the gaiety was out of the place. This, he considered, was what gunfire meant in cattle land—a reminder of the old, old hatreds that followed cattle and cattle people wherever they went. Connie came quickly across to him, bundled in her heavy coat, and looked up to him with her eyes very black. A long silence ran between them until she spoke with her father's stark simplicity. "I'm glad you're not hurt, Jim."

He said: "Clay's staying in town, so I'm taking you back." Men were returning to the hall to claim their women; and couples were filing out into the bitter night to make the long trip homeward in the teeth of a half-unexpected blizzard. Izee and Mary Boring walked by, with Mary talking at Izee in a way that was too sharp to sound pleasant. Nelson McGinnis came up with Karen Sanderson. Nelson said: "That's all right, Jim. I'll wait your word." There was this little moment of pause in which the tall, blonde girl's eyes looked straight at

109

Benbow in a way that was unsmiling and without reservation, with a far thought mirrored in those hazel eyes and meant for him alone.

Connie touched his shoulder, drawing his glance down. Her chin had lifted, reminding Benbow of their old days of give-and-take quarreling. Faint color stained her cheeks and she held him with a glance half possessive and half sultry with quick hurt. He took her arm, leading her through the crowd. The Hat outfit was waiting there, with the buggy. He tucked the heavy blankets around Connie, got in and took the reins; and trailed Hat's riders out of Two Dance. Other outfits were coming along behind. No calling and no laughter lifted over the heavy run of wind.

At one o'clock in the morning Hat's cold and weary people reached home. Benbow found Jack Dale and Pete Cruze in the office with a bottle of whisky between them.

Cruze said directly: "I came in from the canyon about three hours ago. The beef up there is gone."

"Drifted with the wind?"

"No," said Cruze. "Gone. Yesterday when I rode a circle, it was there. Late this afternoon I went back. Wasn't there. That's what you want to know, ain't it?"

The big sheet-iron office stove was red hot, and a teakettle, from which Old Jack concocted his toddies, spouted out steam. Benbow pulled off his overcoat and reached for one of the glasses. Connie came in quietly and stood across from Benbow, one hand dropped affectionately on her father's shoulder. Benbow measured a little whisky into the glass, filled it with hot water and passed it to Connie. He took his own drink straight.

"You're sure they didn't drift?" pressed Benbow.

"They didn't drift. The trail leadin' into the canyon above Riley's place was scuffed pretty deep. It's where they were driven down, all in a bunch. You told me not to follow if they was taken, so I didn't. They didn't stray

110

down there without help."

"I wasn't sure Riley would bite," reflected Benbow. "Or that Gore would let him. They're smart enough to see it might be a trap."

"Smart, sure," agreed Jack Dale. "But maybe they ain't afraid of your trap."

"It's what I hoped," murmured Benbow.

"What?" said Jack Dale, and stared.

Benbow ducked his head at Cruze. "Ask Izee to saddle the black mare for me. I want the rifle boot put on, and a blanket roll with two-three days' grub in it."

Cruze left the room. Benbow said, "You always buy good whisky, Jack," and watched Connie's chin rise at him again. The toddy and the room's heat colored her cheeks a little; it softened her lips a little. She had been a leggy, half-wild kid with a terrible frankness and a never-ending curiosity, with a way of badgering him incessantly. She was a woman now, with a woman's mystery covering the frankness, with a woman's softness and fullness shaping her overnight. He had seen all this happen to her in the past year. It struck him now that the change was complete. Here she stood, poised and still, her dark eyes carefully reading him, yet veiled so that he might not read back.

"And," he murmured gently, "your little girl has grown up."

Jack Dale got out of his chair with an infirmness that was painful to Benbow's eyes. Dale said: "There was times after her mama died I felt a little afraid of the job. You went through some godawful stages, Connie, and I couldn't help you none." He was always brusque, because he could be no other way. "But I guess you're a pretty good crop. Hat's best harvest, I think. You goin' on the trail, Jim?"

"In a minute."

"Come back," said Dale briefly and let Connie slip her hand under his arm. He had never done this before; it was a tragic recognition of something that had at last caught

111

up with a man who never had needed or tolerated help. Benbow felt that; and Connie felt it, for her glance came around to Benbow and showed him a silent sadness. Benbow watched them leave the office; and later heard their footsteps tread the stairs very slowly.

Benbow carried his revolver tucked inside his pants as a rule. Now he laid it on the office desk, took down his gun belt from a peg and cinched it on. He thumbed fresh shells in to the piece and dropped it into its holster, fastening the flap; and then lifted a rifle out of a corner case and sought the desk for a box of ammunition, and turned to go out.

Connie was in the doorway. She had been there a little while, watching him.

"How long will you be gone?"

"Depends on the trail."

He picked up the rifle and walked toward the door. But she didn't withdraw to let him by. She stood in her place, bringing him to a stop. She still wore her dancing dress, her white shoulders showing. All the quick curves of this girl's healthy, supple body were plain to him; a faint lift of her head set pearl earrings into faint motion. And something then in the long depths of her eyes was fully shining.

She said, evenly: "You're fond of Karen, aren't you?"

"Yes."

It disturbed her. He saw a faint flash of the old and familiar storminess rise. "Jim—what's there to make you seem so straight and so strange when she looks at you?"

He said: "School's out, Connie."

"No," she said. "I don't want any woman making a fool of you!"

He said irritably: "You've got a man to worry about. Let me alone."

Her tone dropped all the way down from anger to gentleness. "I know you so well. There's too much loneliness in you. Any woman can see it, and play on that. And then you've made a mistake."

112

"What?"

She met his glance coolly. "You know what I mean. You're a homely brute, but you have something in you that attracts women. I've watched them, and I know."

He said: "What of it, Connie?"

She whispered: "I don't want you to make that mistake, Jim. Any other man in the world, but not you."

"The time's past for this sisterly interest, Connie."

A little silence came on. She stood before him with a disturbed and uncertain expression in her black eyes and a pink stain turning her dark features lovely. When she spoke it was as though the words were wrung painfully from her. "It isn't all sisterly, Jim." Looking down at the strange excitement she showed him, he felt the quick violence run between them again, and he did a thing he said he would never do. Reaching out with his one free arm, he brought her small, willowy body forward and kissed her. Ungently. With a tempest howling like the winter wind through him.

He stepped back, thoroughly outraged with himself. "Somebody ought to kick me. And you ought to be slapped until your ears ring."

But she was smiling, her lips half parted and faintly crooked. "I'm not sorry. Listen to me, you big, dumb rider! I'm Clay's girl and I can't help that. But there's one corner of me he never owned and never will. I've got to tell you. That corner belongs to you. It's a silly thing to say, but it's true. Some day you'll get married—and I'll hate the woman as long as I live!"

He said, very softly, "Growing up's a hard job, kid," and went by her, through the dark living-room to the porch. She followed him and her answer followed him, dismally, "I know that better than you do." Then they were out on the porch, the backlash of the wind stinging through their clothes.

Izee stood patiently at the steps with Benbow's big mare. Izee had to lift his voice against the rip and run of the growing storm. "Ain't I going along?"

113

"No."

Connie's hand gripped Benbow's arm with a sudden strength, turning him around. He saw her shivering in this cold, he saw the oval of her face whiten in the dark. She said, "Come back," and was still there on the porch when he settled in the saddle leather and trotted from the yard.

Across the river bridge and away from the lee shelter of Hat's houses, the wind pressed against him like a giant's hand, sweeping all across the valley. He could feel the black mare settle against it, push her muscles against it. There were no lights showing along the land; above him the wash of stars glittered faintly in an overwhelming blackness. Reversing his neckpiece, he lifted it across his nose against the scorch of that frigid blast.

Three hours later, having crossed the Two Dance under the shelter of this wild dark, he circled the faint outline of Gannon's ranch and crawled up the Ramparts. A first bitter streak of light had begun to crack the eastern sky when he passed above Indian Riley's settlement, via the rim of Granite Canyon. It was a sleezy, indistinct dawn when he traveled over the canyon bridge above Riley's and entered the higher timber of the Yellows. Traveling the upper pass trail he at last reached the edge of that ravine from which he had noticed Riley's campfire two nights before; dipping into the ravine, he went a good mile along a distinct road, turned out of it finally and tied his horse in the heavy thicket, himself rolling up in his blankets for a chilly rest.

He had reached rustlers' country without observation, which was as he wanted it to be.

11. Clay Rand

At nine o'clock, the faint strike of hoofs on the hard trail roused him from a sleepless resting; and crouched back in the brush he saw a man travel by him with his head carefully bowed over, intently studying the trail tracks. It was one of Riley's men, bound eastward from Riley's settlement and ranging this stretch of country like a regular patrol. Benbow waited until the sound of the rider had died entirely out before crawling to the edge of the brush. From this covert he had his look at the trail. The marks of cattle were plentiful here, their hoofprints frozen into distinct ripples; his own pony tracks were likewise already frozen, spoiling the freshness of imprint that might otherwise have warned Riley's man. Two hundred yards southward the trail marched up another slope of the Yellows and curved from sight. Benbow drew back, saddled his horse and rode through the covering brush, paralleling the trail.

Going on this way, he reviewed his own solitary thoughts. No man crossed the Two Dance and entered these Yellow Hills without being spotted. It was a fact he had long understood. Cash Gore kept his men moving around to watch for travelers, as had been the case with Arizona. Once Gore had information of somebody riding these hills, that news went out to Riley. And Riley had his own hands scouting, one of whom had just passed.

It made the Yellows a closed country; and in this closed country, with its hundred ravines and its tangled bypaths, Riley ran the stolen Two Dance beef, pretty much insured against pursuit. So far, Benbow knew he hadn't been traced, but it was only a question of time when Gore would find out he had left Hat; and then they would be roving the hills for him.

Of one thing he was certain. The trail he now laboriously paralleled was the main run, the chief highway through the Yellows. The Hat beef had been driven along this route to some destination ahead. The question was one of following these churning tracks as they threaded the hills. So thinking, he pushed his way up to a small knob overgrown with pine, left his horse and walked on until he had sight of the trail below. It made its brown ribbon deviously along the footslopes of all the close-crowded ridges, crossing a creek that sent up a dull flash through the windy winter's day, and vanished again in the continuing green forest ahead. All around him the broken land reared shoulder after shoulder.

Somewhere in this gusty day a gunshot made a thin and wavering echo, whipped soon out by the wind. Standing there in close speculation, Benbow presently saw a rider wheel into sight from the south and gallop full tilt back toward the Two Dance country. Benbow returned to his horse, slid down through the timber and crossed the trail quickly, taking his look at it in passing. The beef had been this way.

Deep in the timber he let his horse have its drink at the creek and pressed on, swinging as the trail swung, cutting across it quickly from time to time to see what was there to be read, and continuing generally southward. At noon he retreated from it a good distance, boiled himself coffee, and fell to riding again. Around three o'clock he had entered a section of the hill strange to him; and shortly thereafter the trail made a quick bend to the west. This way it traveled on a more level course; and now and then Benbow entered and followed it at a fast canter for a quarter mile or more at a time. Once, drawing quickly into the brush, he heard another rider clipping out of the Two Dance country and saw him pass by; some strange hand he didn't know.

Meanwhile the terrain was changing. The trail fell down from the spine of the Yellows to the flatter and less timbered lands bordering the reservation. Now and then he had a view of an Indian shack out on the plain; and when quick dusk began to drive in with the hard wind, he passed a side trail leading in Cherokee's direction and reached the last margin of timber and saw the trail cross this open strip boldly toward the yellow and brown upthrust of the badlands.

There was a shack sitting off from the trail, a quarter mile out on the plain, with a light shining in its window. He had, he guessed, traveled a hard forty miles since daylight, swinging a giant circle around Cherokee far back and high up. This was near to the state line and a part of the range he didn't know; and those yonder badlands were a continuation of the broken country that stretched northward in a straight line to the lower end of the Two Dance valley—and southward to some faraway point.

The beef, he thought, crossed this plain and dropped into the deep breaks of the badlands—and ran southerly on. It was early dark then, with the wind lifting its pitch shrilly in the trees. Leaving the timber he rode for the shack ahead of him, came straightforwardly into the yard and let his horse drink at a well trough beside the house. There was an old, old Ute standing in the doorway to watch him come; he looked carefully at Benbow, having nothing to say, and then withdrew and slammed the door behind him.

Benbow let his horse have a moment's pull at the water and wheeled away on the run. There had been a little light left in the sky. A mile from the Indian house, darkness swept across the world as violently as the wind. Clay dunes struck up from the ground, roughening the earth;

and then the trail dipped downward between walls a-drip with shadow and the wind ceased to press against him and presently he rode fifty feet below the level of the prairie, the trail striking directly into the tangled passage ways of this broken country. The chalky walls shed a faint glow and the sky remained dimly shining above. He pushed on, giving his horse its head.

He had taken one last look behind him before descending into the badlands' deep gullies, and had seen nothing behind. But after he had dropped from sight, a rider came from the trees, pounded across the plain, and slowly followed Benbow down.

When Gore met Rand behind the Masonic Hall the previous night he had said: "Go to Hat in the morning and see if Pete Cruze has come down from the hills. And if Benbow's left the ranch I want to know it."

"I said I was through," answered Rand.

"You do what I tell you," said Gore, his voice giving Rand no consideration at all.

"Listen, Cash," Rand said heavily. "I—"

But Gore swung about on his heels and strode on into the darkness. And a moment later the sound of gunfire raced up from the depths of the Dunmire compound.

After the fight was over and the Two Dance outfits started homeward, Rand strolled down to Faro Charley's. But there was nothing here to hold his interest. The place was wrecked and empty and Rand, who always needed the stir and excitement of a crowd around him to feel happy, bought a bottle of whisky and tramped back to the Cattle King.

He went into the dining-room, got a water glass and returned to pull a table and chair nearer the big center stove. He had the place to himself except for Jack Auslander who ran this hotel; and after a while Auslander said, "If you're stayin' over, take Number Ten," and went off to bed.

Clay filled up the glass, listening to the corners of the hotel cut the driving wind with the sound of a steam saw

118

snarling into wood; he felt the big building shake as that blast piled up broadside against the walls. The big bracket lamp across the room hurt his eyes with its steady shining; he got up and turned the flame down and settled into his chair again, the heat easing him and the whisky loosening his muscles.

There was that power in whisky—to cut him off from the past, to blur those things which, though behind him, still clung to his memory. When he drank, it was for that reason—to bring on that forgetfulness. Yet now when he had emptied the glass there was no peace. He could see himself as he was, cruelly shaped in the strange lucid light of his mind. He could see what he had done, and how little there was left for him to do.

To this point he had always believed he could stop and back up and take the honest road. To this point. Tonight, after meeting Gore, he at last knew that there was no hope of ever retracing his way. In the relentless clarity which illumined his thinking he could see each step of that crooked way which had led him into partnership with Gore. And now Gore—so smileless and obscure and merciless a man—had ordered him to trace Benbow, and there was no way he could avoid hurting the only soul left in the valley who still trusted him.

When he thought of it, the light of this room got dimmer and dimmer. He had known for some months that there was a tide running against him and that somehow the valley had caught on. There were no telltale tracks behind him; yet the valley knew. He could read it in men's attitudes toward him. The warmth had gone out of their talk and a feeling lay reserved in their eyes. Gordon Howland had almost spoken that suspicion and then had stilled his tongue because of Benbow's presence at the cattlemen's meeting. Benbow didn't know; and there was a kind of conspiracy of silence here to keep from breaking the news to that big, solid man whose loyalty was like a hoop of steel.

They weren't protecting him, Rand understood. It was

Benbow they were protecting, remembering how deep and how solid Benbow's affections were.

He filled his glass again, but left it on the table, his hands dropped between his knees and his handsome face reddened and pulled into long, slack lines. He thought of Connie and for a moment one wild thought ripped its way through him, leaving ruin behind; and then he tried to think of what he could do and afterwards his thought whirled out into emptiness and he was once more, as so often, a man adrift on the turbulent surface of his own ungoverned and unstable appetites.

He took his glass of whisky and crossed the lobby and climbed the stairs, with his legs stretched to brace him and went into Number Ten. His exploring hand swept across the darkness, struck the table lamp and sent it crashing to the floor. He downed the whisky and sat on the edge of the bed, loose and lost in a world that had no light; and then, thoroughly drunk, he rolled back on the bed, clawed the blankets awkwardly around him and fell asleep.

Early next morning, he rode through Hat's yard and found Izee coming out of the house.

"Jim here?"

Izee stared at him, obviously in no cheerful frame of mind. He said, after a deliberate and thoughtful pause, "Think he went to see George Gray."

"What's the matter?"

"Nothin'," said Izee promptly. Then he added, "Ole Jack ain't so well," and turned to watch Rand go inside.

Clay found Connie in the office. She was at the window, and had been looking out across the misty wind driven valley. She turned and her glance had its careful look. He hadn't shaved and his eyes were bloodshot and his nerves kept shifting him about, and seeing all that she turned back to the window in a manner that freshened his irritable temper.

"That's a cheerful way to meet a man. What's the matter with me?"

120

"I wish I knew, Clay."

"What?"

"If I did, perhaps I could do something about it."

He was surly with his answer. "If a man wants to go loose once in a while, what's wrong with that?"

It whipped her around. She was angry with him and her pride was stung. All this came rapidly out. "Go loose, then! I didn't ask you any questions and I don't need any answers. But after you go walking through the mud, don't come here and leave it on Hat's carpets."

He said, "Oh, Connie," with so changed a manner that she quit talking and stared at him. He looked beaten, and unsure and half bitter. "Don't rag a man. When are we going to put all this waitin' behind? It's time to be married."

She said: "You've never mentioned it before."

"No, I guess not. I guess I've been waiting to get a little money ahead. Man hates to take a woman off a rich ranch to a poor one. But it's a long drag, and I'm tired of waitin'. And I'm tired of the outfit I'm trying to run. I've got enough money to get married and move on. California's the country. Let's try that, Connie."

She said: "What's better than Hat?"

"Hat's yours, not mine."

"Half of it is mine, some day. The other half is Jim's—though he's never been told."

"Your dad," said Clay in a dry tone, "is generous to his foreman." He was considering it, watching Connie Dale with a close and narrowing glance. "So that would make the three of us living on Hat. You and me and Jim. And I'd be the stranger moving in. Not for me, Connie."

"He's your best friend, Clay."

"Sure. But friend or no friend, that's too damned close. Not for me." He was irritable again. "Anyhow I'm tired of the country. Let's move out. I've had no luck here and never will."

She said: "I was born here, Clay. I'd hate to go."

"I thought," he said sourly, "a woman was supposed

121

to take her husband's side of it, for better or for worse."

She let a small, appealing cry escape her. "Oh, Clay, why make it so hard! If nothing can hold you here, where will you ever find anything anywhere to hold you?"

He shrugged his shoulders. "Let it go. Where's Jim?"

"He went out last night."

"Up in the Yellows?" he asked.

She hesitated a moment, her lips changing; her eyes carefully studying him. A long moment later she said in a half reluctant voice, "Yes."

"What's the matter?" he blurted out, angered again. "Ain't I to be trusted?"

She said nothing. Izee came into the house and crossed to the office. He looked at the two and then put his hands over the stove. "Damned cold."

"Izee," said Rand ironically, "I thought you said Jim was down at Block T."

Izee threw a quick glance at Connie. "Maybe," he said, "I was wrong," and then the room was very still and these three were uncomfortably face to face in it. Abruptly Rand turned out. He was at the front door when Connie caught up with him.

"Clay," she said, "If you must leave the country, of course I'll go along. But not now. Dad's sick."

He swung about and the inconstant temper of the man made him smile and say indifferently: "Sure. There's other lands as green as this one." He went out of the house and was soon gone from the yard.

She stood a little while in the living-room, saddened by what she knew of this man. It was hard to think of leaving Hat; it was like throwing all her past life away. But he had not seen that. There was little understanding in him for the troubles of other people. Things came so easily to Clay; he took so much for granted, and was so swift to resent anything that blocked his desires. She couldn't help remembering Jim Benbow just then; the way he sat so patiently in his chair, tied to Hat and to the valley by a sense of loyalty and obligation Clay could never understand. Tied even to Clay by ropes of affection that Clay indifferently realized.

She went into the office. Izee was at the window watching Rand trot through the down-sweeping mists of the incredibly cold day. He did not look at her, but she knew he had something heavily on his mind.

"You didn't want to tell him Jim was in the Yellows. Why?"

"Guess I just can't break the habit of keepin' my mouth shut," said Izee awkwardly.

"Izee," she said, the tone of her voice bringing him around, "what is it?"

"Nothin'," he said, and she knew by the dogged set of his chin that nothing would ever make him say more. He was disturbed and embarrassed and escaped her quiet appraisal by ducking suddenly out of the room.

She climbed the stairs to her father's room. He sat in his bed, shored up by pillows, and the sight of him thus helpless knifed through her painfully and turned her mind strangely back to her girlhood. He had always been so robust, so hearty and arresting a figure. Through all of those years she could remember him as a solid rock in times of trouble, the boom of his voice always comforting to hear.

He said: "What was it, Connie?"

"Clay."

The same change she had noted in Izee came over her father's graying face—the same shutterlike drop of something inside to cover what he knew and what he felt. It made her say: "What, Dad?"

He shook his head.

"Is it something I ought to know?"

"The only thing worth knowin'," he told her quietly, "is what a man finds out for himself. When you were a kid I put you on a horse. It hurt me like hell to see you take your falls, Connie, but it was the only way to learn. It's got to be the same way now. You got some falls comin'. That's all I can tell you. It's tough to think I can't be around to maybe lend a hand."

"You—" she began, and stopped and looked down at the floor. He didn't want any tears out of her; he had always told her that. So she waited a little before going on. "Don't you worry. Jim will be here."

"I'd like to depend on that."

She put her hand on his arm. "I wish it could have been the way you wanted. Jim's always been your choice. Would it sound funny if I told you that sometimes I wish I hadn't ever known Clay?"

He turned his head and looked at her, shrewd and penetrating with his glance. "No," he said. "You can't do much with your heart. But I started puttin' things into your head long ago, Connie. I'm countin' on that, in the end. I'm countin' on your head, in the long run."

She wanted to ask him what he meant, but she saw weariness pull the blood from his face; and so she rose and fixed his pillows and left the room. In the hall she stopped, silently crying. He had been a great man, always; filling her life with courage and kindness. And now that he was sinking away it left her with an unutterable loneliness, as though all that she could believe in was being withdrawn. Thus empty-hearted she thought of Benbow, with an acute desire to have him near. Going to the end of the hall she looked into the yard and saw Izee still standing against the heavy rush of the wind, staring up the valley in the direction Clay Rand had gone.

Clay trotted northward from Hat until the milky mists of this bitter day closed down and erased the ranch from his back-glancing eyes. At that point, beyond detection, he swung south, crossed the valley and reached the Ramparts at a spot between Gannon's and Running M. He knew that Gore waited for him and would see him make the crossing. Climbing the Ramparts he dismounted in the usual meeting place; and was impatiently

124

smoking out his third cigarette when Gore arrived.

Gore didn't dismount. He swung his horse around—all this Rand observed with a growing alertness—so that his gun side was nearest. And said: "Where's Benbow?"

"Cash," said Rand, "I told you once I was out of this."

"When I want you to do business for me, you'll do it."

"We'll do business," countered Rand. "I've changed my mind again. I need some quick money."

"Damn a man that keeps changin'," observed Gore, no emotion in his talk. "I always did figure you as a switcher, and I don't trust you none at all."

"Fifty-fifty," observed Rand. "You hoe your row and I'll hoe mine."

"One word from me, Clay, and you're ruined in this valley."

"And when you speak that word," retorted Rand, ironically amused, "you're caught in your own trap. Ever think of that?"

"Maybe."

Rand grinned in a hard and confident way. "You figure another way to handle me, when you're through. But listen, I'm not as easy to kill as Arizona was."

"Maybe," breathed Gore, still unstirred. "Where's Benbow?"

"I get my share of this beef?"

"Yes."

"Benbow's up here somewhere."

Cash Gore said: "You took your time tellin' it." And then those two faced each other with a faithless wire-drawn attention, until Rand said: "Scare him out, but if you kill him I'll kill you." Gore pulled his horse back into the brush; and later Rand heard him galloping along the Ramparts' main trail.

Rand stepped to his saddle and turned down to the flats, aiming for his own place. After he had gone—long after he had gone—Eileen Gannon came from the heavy brush near the meeting spot and went to her horse not far away.

125

12. In the Badlands

The trail ran broadly through the badlands, beaten solid by the traffic it had borne. Benbow's horse traced the way at an alternate walk and canter; and now and then he looked above him to see the rim of the gully cut its faint shape against the sky's overwhelming black. Up there the wind rolled wildy, sending its hollow reverberations all along these buried corridors.

For a while the trail was straight, but an hour from the entry point his pony began to swing around a series of chimneys rising up like huge thumbs. Erosion began to tangle the gullies, one feeding into another. He passed beneath a natural bridge, the blackness about him almost tangible. Beyond that it seemed the trail dipped deeper and deeper and there was no true direction at all. Once he stopped and dismounted; on his hands and knees he struck a match—and saw plain prints in the chalky soil. In a manner reassured he went on. Yet he had lost his bearing and felt unsure of his progress. And then, long after, he passed by a solid shadow on his right hand and caught the smell of wood that was burning, or that had been recently burnt.

It stopped him, it pulled him off his horse. Crawling quietly back, his outstretched hands felt a tunnel's mouth open before him, and then rising to his feet he crept slightly inside this aperture and stopped agan. The faint smoke-scent drifted out of it.

Gently stepping, he saw a coal's red eye gleam farther ahead; and immediately dropped to his haunches into a stillness only faintly disturbed by the down-telegraphed wail of the wind. Smoke smell and horse smell. He went forward a yard or so, crawling with the gentleness of a cat, with his nerves as alert and as spooky as a cat's. Halted once more, his hand touched a clod of earth the size of a walnut. The single eye of fire was not more than ten feet ahead of him and nothing was in this cavern that gave him any clue. Lifting the clod he tossed it ahead and heard it fall with an audible "clunk."

One long-drawn minute later he let his breath run freely out and rose and walked on until he stood above the single eye of light. There had been a fire here as late as dusk, for a remote heat rose from that almost extinct bed of ashes. The cavern seemed to run farther back, for he had no feeling of anything immediately in front. To either side its walls were near enough for his stretching arms to span. This much was all he cared to know. He went out to his pony, brought it in and wrapped himself in his blankets.

The restless stamping of the horse brought him out of his stiff half-sleep and at four o'clock he lighted a fire from the fragments of previous fires that had burned in this cavern, boiled up some coffee with water out of his canteen and fried some bacon. Afterwards he rode into the gray and bitter blackness just preceding dawn. The wind still drilled relentlessly overhead, the coldness still held; but there was, he noted carefully, a rawer edge to it—a touch of moisture brought in from a different point of the compass. Blizzard weather.

By degrees, as he rode, light began to seep down and the gaunt outline of chimneys and tangled bluffs appeared before him. By-passes led away from this main trail, into the thousand alleys of a tricky land. He could presently see the print of cow tracks plainly on the trail; and now and then he had a vista of the turreted bluffs heaving away to the deep distance. Drawn into the middle of this broken country he could no longer find the solid

127

edge of the prairie. Shortly beyond full daylight he left the trail to angle from one detour to another; frequently losing himself and frequently back-tracking. Around ten o'clock he sensed an opening not far ahead; at noon, crawling forward on his stomach, he reached a wide bay surrounded on all sides by eighty-foot walls dropping down from the prairie level.

A low log ranch house squatted grayly in this hole, with a barn and corrals behind it; beyond that lay a corral in which he saw cattle moving and men at work. Smoke lifted from a fire over there, and men were rising from it and returning to it while riders milled the held herd. He counted three of them before he drew back to his horse. He was apparently off the main trail and so considered himself safe here; yet he took care to pull the black mare farther into a little blind gulch before returning to his observation spot. A single heavy flake of snow stung him on the cheek, fast-driven by the wind; and then in a quarter hour's time the whole scene ahead of him slowly sank behind a rising, thickening wave of whiteness. They had quit working in the cattle pens. He counted them again as they filed back toward the log house—that same three. Flattened to the earth, so cold that ice seemed to grit its way through his arteries, he watched premature lights spring through the log house's windows. In the middle of the afternoon there was nothing to be seen except that light faintly shining; everything else lay blurred and without substance beneath a wild-whirling snow.

This was south of the border of his own state in a land strange to him. He knew nothing about the ranch, but the trail he had so steadily followed led straight into that deep bowl that seemed to go no farther. And there were cattle held in the corral and men had been working over a branding fire unseasonably. Considering it in his own slow way he knew that he had reached the last link in the long chain and that nothing remained now but to cross to the corral and read the flanks of those cows with his own eyes. He was certain of the answer, yet as certain as he

128

was the knowledge of the brutal chore waiting him back in the Yellows demanded an exactness of proof that would lock his mind beyond any doubt, beyond any least regret.

Numb of leg and arm, he watched grayness drop prematurely from the sky. The storm came out of the blank and hidden plain in a huge, howling furor, with the snow so thick as to create a solid screen his lifting hand could cut by a downward stroke. Even the ranch light had turned vague; and seeing that he rose and shook the snow from his shoulders and returned to the black mare.

He turned out of the gully into the bowl; made a semi-circle of the bowl and drove directly upon the corral from the far side. He was within ten feet of the corral before its posts lifted from the weather's dense drive. He climbed over the corral's top and dropped down inside, directly against a cow, the sudden appearance he made sending the cow away from him wildly. That stampeded the whole bunch. He crouched there, seeing those flanks mill by him, reading the familiar Hat brand upon them; and afterwards, rising to the corral's top as one wild mossy horn charged out of the mist, straight upon him, he saw

another brand freshly scarring that one's hide: ___.

He dropped into his saddle and held the restive mare still a moment, his mind identifying Hat's brand beneath the change. Somewhere in this bowl a voice hallooed and he observed a vague strengthening of the ranch house's light, although he could not define the house itself. Somebody had opened a door over there. He was more than halfway around the corral, with the mouth of the badlands trail off to the left, drowned in the storm. Following the corral rails closely, he came at last to the ranch house side and thought he recognized the blur of a man's shape wallowing forward. It set his spurs promptly into the mare's flanks. She jumped forward into a sudden run, racing back to where the mouth of the trail ought to be.

One moment she was in full gallop, with Benbow

turned sidewise to watch that man's figure swiftly materialize. The man lifted his long call through the weather and the next moment the black mare's front legs were trapped by some unseen obstruction and she went wheeling over in a great circle. Benbow left his saddle as though thrown from a slingshot, turned through the air and landed on the point of his shoulder.

The snow was deep enough to soften the fall. He rolled over and over, badly shaken, and stopped and was on his feet; the black mare struggled up, stood with its head lowered, with one front leg lifted. There was more shouting along the yard and Benbow, rushing back toward the horse, saw two things at once. The stretched rope that had tripped him, and the stout, broad shape of a man whose lifting gun covered him.

"Hold on."

For one moment his jarred senses held him still; and afterwards when the instinct to fight hammered through his long body and wakened it the one instant of chance had passed by. Another man broke the snow screen, rushing on with his body bent over and his hands hanging to this rope which had been stretched between house and corral for guidance when the blizzard closed down.

The man with the gun spoke through a full beard. "Turn around."

Benbow made the turn and felt his gun slide out of its holster. The man said: "Get into this rope and follow it to the house. Watch this fellow, Turk."

Benbow made a careful pivot. The day was darkening on them; he could see neither man's face clearly. He said: "That horse is hurt."

"I'll take care of the hoss. Do like you're told."

He marched beside the rope, both men behind. The house light strengthened and a wall emerged from the weather and he came to the door's square patch and found another man standing there. That one stepped back, permitting Benbow to pass into the sudden and almost painful heat of the room. Stopped in its center, with the rays of the lamp burning his eyes like hot irons, he

130

heard the door slam shut. The bearded one's voice ran the silence very cool and very sure. Blinded as he was, Benbow could see nothing, yet he knew even then that this man was dangerous; it lay in the unhurried way he handled this trouble.

His vision was slow in clearing. Somebody stood in front of him, still-shaped and slim. One man went out of the room—and another came in. His count had been wrong. There were three inside this place—and one outside. He pulled off his gloves and began to rub his ears.

"Frostbit?" asked the deep voice.

"No."

"Should think they was. You been layin' out in the weather long enough."

His enlarging pupils brought the room and its people into exact focus. He stood near the stove, with the slim young man beyond it resting in pure silence against the rough wall. And then he saw that he had made a mistake. This was a girl, dressed in a man's clothes—a dark kid with a half-wildness printed on her quick features. She watched him in a strange way, her eyes wide and alert as though his presence here struck deep into her thoughts and upset them. He let himself turn then, catching sight of the two men standing behind. One was that fellow who had dived forward through the snow at the bearded man's alarm. Benbow remembered his name then—Turk. The bearded man remained near the door, his immense shoulders almost spanning the door's width. His beard ran straight down to the second button of his vest, and had been cut off there, shovel-shaped. He had huge eyebrows bushing out like canopies over sparkling, drill-black eyes. Such skin as was visible above the beard was heavily weathered.

The ——☐☐—— brand had been burned in the wood
         C
above the door; Benbow nodded at it. "Yours?"

A gusty chuckle came up from the tangle of the older man's beard. "The C is for Carter, which is my name."

131

His eyes held the frosty flicker of a well-nourished humor. It was the laughter in this man that made him twice as dangerous.

"A good brand," agreed Benbow, "for your purpose."

"Turk," called Carter, "you know him?"

The high-built one moved a pair of vast hands up and down his coat's front. "Yeah. Saw him once in Two Dance. Hat's foreman. Benbow, ain't it?"

"Heard of you," said Carter. "Expected you some day, but you been a long time comin'. Rody—when's supper? It's dark enough to eat."

The girl came away from the wall, stirring the kettles on the stove. There was a table running across one side of the room, a door leading back to a narrow hall which seemed to feed another room as it passed on to a rear door. A ladder led straight up the wall to a trap in the ceiling above the table. Saddles and blankets and a stand of rifles held the corners of the place; it wasn't a woman's house. Benbow watched the girl's face dip toward the stove and reveal no more expression than the face of a Ute squaw. It licked a little interest through him. White women didn't have that stolidness without some reason. Her glance lifted and crossed the room and caught his eyes, and showed him nothing but a covert brightness.

The rawboned Turk seemed to fire up with a sudden resentment. "Keep your eyes where they belong, Rody."

Carter's deep chuckle rustled like the sweep of a broom. "Always have trouble with your women. She's Turk's woman, Benbow. Don't know where she came from. Where'd you come from, Rody?"

Nothing broke the silence or the reserve that seemed past the point of feelng. Benbow turned to have his look at the men. Carter's eyes were sprung to a triangular shape by the flash of his heartless amusement. Turk's heavy-boned face showed the sultry stain of his anger. He let his stare fall like a weight on Benbow. The back door opened and another fellow came down the hall, and stopped. Just a kid, with a kid's unfilled and bony frame. He looked at Benbow and dropped his eyes. Carter said:

"You put the horse away, Johnny?"

"Yeah," said the kid. Silence ran on. Nothing seemed to hold these people together; they were all strangers moved by their own obscure desires.

The girl walked from stove to table, carrying the kettles; she laid the hot kettles on the table's bare top and stood back against the wall. Turk went down the hallway and the back door slammed and cold air poured in; and the storm shouldered against this low-built house and moved it faintly on its foundations. All the daylight faded from the windows. Turk came back, and everybody sat up to the table. Turk was beside the girl; he bent over and put his heavy hand on the back of her neck, closing his fingers together. She did not move until he had pulled his hand away and then Benbow saw the white print of his squeezing fingers against her skin.

"Turk," said Carter in the same hard amusement, "why don't you hit her and be done with it? Pass the beef. You'll like this meat, Benbow. It's a Hat cow."

Benbow said: "How's the mare?"

"Lame," said Johnny, the kid.

They ate like that and when they were through Benbow remained in his chair while the others got up and moved around the room. The girl came into his vision and went out of it, cleaning away the dishes. She did not look at him again, for Turk was a somber and threatening shape in the corner. Benbow watched her hands rise with the dishes—small and square and hardened by work. Carter's pipe smoke rolled its blue layers across the light.

There was a restlessness here—an uncertainty. Idle in the chair, Benbow narrowly observed these men and caught the silent signals passing between them. Turk and the kid went out together. The girl was near the stove, washing up the dishes. Carter came across the room and sat down opposite Benbow. He put his elbows on the table—and suddenly his eyes were without mercy.

"I never been over in the Two Dance. But I hear you make big tracks when you walk. Ground trembles and the trees shake. It's the story I get. I been sittin' here and waitin'. Knew you'd come sometime, and so finally you stumble over my blizzard rope."

He had been holding the pipe in his hand. He lifted it now and opened his mouth and caught the stem between his teeth and for one moment Benbow saw his lips, small and red, appear behind the covering beard. It was the steely calm of this man that warned Benbow.

Carter said: "I never saw the man a bullet couldn't kill. You been lucky. You ain't lucky now."

"Gore here lately?"

Carter said: "Only when I got money for him."

He was easy about it. He was passing out a secret to a man who would soon be dead. Benbow understood that; and he knew Carter meant for him to understand it. Cold little points of light danced in Carter's eyes. "You did well," Carter admitted, "to get past Riley. He keeps this trail pretty well watched."

"He been here?"

"Brought your cattle in day before yesterday. Kell was here last night. He followed your trail down. You slipped aside from him somewhere in the badlands."

More information carelessly given. This was the way Carter's mind worked. Carter sat back in his chair, one knotty fist closed around the bowl of his pipe. Those bitter-black eyes kept eating away at Benbow, sharp and curious and without human feeling. Benbow had his story of the man completely then. Carter was of that type born nerveless and without the impediment of a conscience. Something had been left out of him, so completely that he never realized the lack of it. He had the equipment of a cougar, with a feral instinct to kill, with a faithless guard risen against every living thing. There was enough of the animal in him to make him restless and spooky—to make him use his eyes and ears with a ceaseless vigilance.

Turk and the kid came in through the front door, their faces raked raw by the storm. Wind and snow rushed across the room and the howl of the wild night was a sudden violence in their ears. Turk braced his broad

134

shoulders against the door before he could shut it; these two came over and sat down at the table and Carter rose and found a deck of cards somewhere and began to deal around, as though this were an old ceremony.

Benbow looked idly at his cards and threw them to the table. He said: "Poker without money is like a pipe without tobacco." Rody filled up the stove, moving softly behind him. He felt her come near his shoulder and stop there, and then Turk jerked up his round sullen eyes and hit her with a hard glance that sent her softly away. In a moment Benbow saw her stretch out on the floor at the base of the wall behind Turk. She propped up her head with one arm and lay loosely and speechlessly there, her eyes on Benbow. The flannel shirt she wore dropped back from her neck to show the white skin beneath.

The game went on, without chips or money, without talk. Strain piled up, riding the kid hard. Benbow noticed his lips turn at the corners, and sag, and turn again. Turk's big shoulders lumped forward and his broad hands handled the cards awkwardly. Carter's glance showed a colder and colder brilliance. Loose in the chair, Benbow shut his eyes in a seeming sleepiness and saw each detail of this room with a hungering attention. The gun he had surrendered lay on a shelf by the door, where Carter had put it; the stand of rifles was in the corner behind Turk. This one lamp on the table supplied the only light. Beyond the fifteen-foot-square room was a hall with one other room leading off. The attic hole yawned above his head.

There was no sound inside this room. The sliding of their hands along the table had quit; the fall of cards had quit. He opened his eyes and saw the three of them settled in their chairs, watching him with the dark stain of their thoughts showing through. The kid was afraid; he was deathly afraid and showed it.

Turk said in a quick way: "What if he wasn't alone?"

Carter turned the quickening flash of his eyes on Turk and Benbow could make out the bearded man's under-lying contempt for Turk's dull mind. "If there's another one what'd he be doing now?"

His head rolled faintly to indicate what lay outside. The wind slid over the roof like the boil of water and the wind struck its hammer strokes against the weather wall. The blackness showing in at the windows was an absolute blackness. Snow sifted through the door's warped edges. Benbow observed Carter's eyes quicken with a thought.

"Want to take a horse and try your luck?"

Benbow said: "Why?"

"You might make it out," drawled Carter, and showed the thin edge of his humor. "You might."

Benbow murmured: "No hurry."

It brought him a fresher attention from all of them. Turk's scowl cut two deep lines across his low forehead. The kid pulled his chair away from the table. Carter removed the pipe from his mouth, his red lips showing and disappearing. Benbow laid his hands on the table and spread and closed his fingers and watched them and saw that the others were watching them, trying to read what he was reading. He made a problem for them and there was an end to that problem they could not quite reach. Not the end, but the way of getting to the end. Tension kept keying up. The room turned warmer and warmer. The windows were icing over and the girl on the floor dragged a leg indolently along the boards. His eyes went down there and her lips formed a word he couldn't read.

Turk blurted out: "You got another man out there?"

"That's your worry."

Carter drawled: "Kell said there was just one."

It brought an easy question from Benbow: "Where's Kell?"

"Went back when he lost your trail."

Turk said, to Carter: "You waitin' for Kell to come?"

"I don't need Kell," said Carter.

"Then what the hell you waitin' for?"

"Like to let a man get the benefit of his supper," said Carter; and his soft amusement sent its broomlike rustle along the room.

Benbow didn't speak again. He pulled his hands from

136

the table and bent back in the chair, and rocked on its two hind legs, showing no feeling to them. Turk's eyes kept watching him from a darker and darker doubt. The man was spooking up. The kid had meanwhile hitched himself to his feet and had taken a place by the wall, completely outside this circle. Turk dropped the flat of his hand across the table, sending up a sharp report. "There's another man around here." And rose, kicking his chair away.

Carter repeated: "If there was another man what'd he be doing out there?" But Turk's doubt was having its way with him, the points of light in his eyes more brightly sparkling against an increased chill.

Turk said: "A man could make out by crowdin' in with the beef. Or he could be in the barn."

"He'd get gored in that bunch of beef," said Carter. "Go have a look at the barn."

"Why don't you go look?" challenged Turk sullenly.

"Go look, Turk," said Carter, never raising his voice.

Turk swung around. The girl lay full length on the floor, her legs and arms flung out loosely, immodestly. Turk stared down and started to lift his feet over her body; and changed his mind and dropped the toe of his boot across her fingers. She jerked her hand away and sat upright against the wall, rocking sidewise and making no sound. She kept her head down but Benbow saw her lips were shaking.

"Get up to bed, Rody," said Turk; and never moved till the girl had risen and climbed the ladder. He put on a buffalo coat hanging on one of the wall pegs, and looked down at a lantern on the floor; the man's thoughts were all slow and cumbersome. It took him a long while to reject the use of the lantern.

"I ain't goin' to make myself a target. But what the hell will I see out there in the dark?"

"You scan that barn till you know there ain't anybody in it," said Carter.

Benbow got up from his chair and walked to the stove and stood with his back to it. All the men had quit moving

137

while he made that change; they had stiffened, they had stopped thinking. Carter's hand had been nursing his pipe but it came away from the pipe and was poised thus, half dropped to his waist as though he were waiting to catch a ball, his fingers spread apart in that manner. Benbow grinned. He turned his head, letting his glance touch the window nearest the cabin's front door—let it briefly touch that window and come away.

Carter said with a little note of urgency: "Get outside, Turk."

Turk dragged his heels along the narrow hall. A full blast of wind slammed down the hall and crowded this room and the light of the lamp raveled to a thin and crazy streak that threw soot around the globe. Turk was wrestling with the doorway, cursing at it; and afterwards he had closed it. Looking up, Benbow saw the girl's face overhanging the attic opening. She was flat on her stomach up there, staring quietly down upon the lamp.

Carter said: "So what would a man be doing out there? You come alone, Benbow?"

The girl hooked herself through the attic hole and descended the ladder. Carter spoke to her. "You want Turk to knock your head off?"

She said dully: "It's cold up there."

The bearded one's attention divided itself with an impartial and scheming interest between the girl and the kid and Benbow. The light was dimmer than it had been, shining fitfully through the globe's soot. The girl came out of her corner and stopped at the table, her fingers wiggling the wick screw up and down. It seemed no better a light when she turned back and stopped near the kid. There was something here that called to his senses in a thin, vague way; something she had done that was meant as a message to him. He stepped away from the hard heat of the stove, not looking at the lamp again, but still thinking of the way she had moved the wick up and down.

138

13. "Let Them Die!"

Carter said, "Johnny, you watch Benbow," and then walked into the hall and opened the door of the single room beside it. He went into that room, leaving Johnny drawn to his full height and faintly white. Johnny's round eyes clung to Benbow and he muttered: "You stay still."

Carter's big body knocked over a chair in the adjoining room, which held no light. Johnny flinched a little at that unexpected sound and turned more squarely at Benbow. Benbow stared down the hall, but from the corner of his vision he was seeing his gun as it lay on the shelf near the door, its muzzle pointed away from the door, its butt ready to be grasped by an upreaching hand. Carter had quit moving around in the other room. Benbow let a long slow breath run softly out and spread his legs, his muscles beginning to press against his skin. He looked at Johnny and said, gently: "What's the matter with your feet, kid?" But the girl's head was shaking violently from side to side; she was behind Johnny, sending this signal across to Benbow with an outflung vehemence. Johnny looked obediently at his feet, which was all the chance Benbow had asked for. Yet the girl's warning had taken the drive out of his legs and he remained as he was—and then Johnny's head snapped up as he realized what trap he had fallen into. His face whitened and he ran his palm slowly up and down his pants legs, wiping away the sweat. Benbow let his eyes travel from the girl to the lamp and back to the girl again. Slowly and deliberately. She folded her arms and her head tipped in a short nod. And she was standing like that when Carter came into this room again.

He looked around him carefully and noticed Johnny's white surface; and that intimation of trouble so near to the surface wheeled his hard body about and he stood posed toward Benbow, shoulders thrust forward. His eyes flashed a swift look at the gun on its shelf. Somewhere below the bushy beard the heat of a smile worked its way outward and touched his eyes faintly.

"It might have been worth a try," he said. "I thought you'd do it. You ain't as tough as they told me." Then he was chuckling as though it were a joke on him. "I watched you, through that knothole."

Benbow said: "I thought there was a joker in the deck. There's plenty of time."

It was like the beat of a clock, that soft sentence spoken now as it had been spoken before. And it did something to the bearded Carter, breaking through the steel casing of his composure. He said gutturally: "Maybe I made a mistake."

"What's your idea of a mistake?"

"I ain't made one yet," said Carter grimly; and then stood perfectly still, his head cocked to hear the pound and furious slashing of that outside storm, to catch the wailing and the breakage and the squealing of boards coming through the wind's major tone. He retreated from the table until his back was near the wall. Then he did a strange thing, side-stepping and passing in front of Johnny and the girl; he was in the darkest corner of the room when he stopped.

Something snapped in Johnny's system. He turned his head from side to side, as though his neck muscles, strained from his taut watching, had cramped on him and he said in a high, shaken voice: "Carter, my gun ain't loaded."

140

Carter let the silence run on, the light catching his eyes as they turned toward Johnny and flashing wickedly. He said in a dry, dry way: "What'd you say that for?"

"Nothin'," said Johnny. But he stared at Benbow.

The girl moved out from the wall. "Where's Turk?"

"In the barn," growled Carter. "Where you going?"

She was in the hall, out of Carter's sight and out of Johnny's sight. She turned—Benbow was facing the mouth of that hall and saw her turn—and said, "I've got to see what's the matter—" and her arm lifted and caught Benbow's attention and pointed at the lamp. She wheeled and ran on to the door. Benbow lowered his head so that Carter couldn't see the change of his expression. He was a rigid shape by the stove, more rigid than Carter could know. The blood was aroar in him and his made-up mind telegraphed its messages into his arms, along his legs. He stood like that, with his eyes strictly lowered. But he heard the girl's hand touch the doorknob and he heard Carter suddenly call: "Rody, come back here!" Then the door was open and wind rushed in like a tidal wave, filling this room and swelling it; and then the lamp flame flared up, emitted one last yellow streak and went out.

Darkness whirled dismally around as Benbow made his long, low plunge for that little shelf containing the gun. Its shape and its position were printed in his mind; and he had reached it and seized it and had thrown himself forward before Carter's great yell split this blackness and Carter's revolver tore the room apart with its hard blast. The smash of the slug against the wall ripped a wicked echo over the smoky dark. Johnny's half scream lifted: "I'm out—I'm out!" And he heard the kid drop full-faced to the floor. The light of Carter's second shot licked its foot-long tongue from that dense corner and the stove and the stovepipe shed a dull-red silhouette. These were the things he saw, pulsing images in a dead-black cell aswirl with powder smoke, when he took his shot at Carter's corner—aiming it on the fading flash of Carter's gun. The roar of the shot washed back thunderously across him, but he heard the bullet tear its way through Carter and he heard a deep breath break out of the man and the fall of Carter's gun and then the slow collapse of the man's body along the floor.

Benbow yelled: "Rody!"

The girl's voice lifted out of the hall, her words flying back with the inpouring wind. "Turk—Turk!" The kid was crawling aimlessly around the room on his hands and knees, snuffling up his fear. Turk's heavy boots scudded down the hall and the girl was yelling up her warning for Benbow. "He's comin'!"

Benbow lifted his gun at the hall and remembered the girl at its end, and held his fire. A shadow sprang straight at him, which was Turk coming on with his slow-witted mind locked up and past changing now. Benbow brought the gun brutally down upon that shadow and struck nothing but the sheering point of a shoulder. A moment later he had been caught by Turk's two heavy arms, with Turk's head driving the breath out of him.

Carried back by that driving assault, Benbow's back struck the edge of the table. He tried for one more blow at Turk's head with the gun and failed; and then he fell over the table with Turk dropping fully on him and afterwards they were locked together, with the wreckage of the sudden-collapsing table all around them.

The weight of the fall knocked the breath half out of him and he lay there, his one free arm hooked around Turk's neck and holding it closely against his chest. He had this moment and used it to throw his gun away from him and to bring his other arm protectively to his face. Turk brought up his knees, one at a time, and began to smash them into Benbow's groin. Benbow rolled and released his grip. Turk's breath was a hot blast against his skin, and from his prone position Benbow looped over a short blow that struck Turk's mouth and slid away.

Turk's hand reached for him and got a hold on his coat. Benbow kicked out and reached his knees; and then they were two growling, heavy-breathing animals rolling

142

around this room savagely, striking and being struck, rising and falling and rising again. Turk was a wild and whirling shape in the stifling dark and his rocky fists burst Benbow's ribs, driving the deep wind from Benbow's lungs; and then they were on their feet, careening around the room, slamming in short and brutal blows. The edge of the stove clipped Benbow across the legs. Turk ran in and slammed him against a wall and smashed him with one straight punch across the eyes. It was as though a knife had slashed the tendon behind his knees, taking the sap out of him that suddenly. He dropped. Yet in dropping, he tripped the burly Turk and threw all his weight against the man. The heat of the stove rushed against Benbow's face and flamed against his eyes as he fell over it with Turk beneath him and cushioning him from its red-hot surface. It was Turk's body that lay on that dull-shining stove, with the smell of burning hair and flesh and clothes and rolling up its stench. Turk was screaming the way a woman would scream and Turk's great muscles bulged against Benbow. But his legs gave a mighty push and then the stove collapsed on its legs and the pipe fell down and smoke and flame lent its sulphurous light to the place and Benbow was rolling with Turk on the rough floor boards again.

He was half across Turk's body—and Turk lay there without fight, his breathing rushing in and out and a pure agony guttering up from his throat. There was no mercy in Benbow then. He reached down and found Turk's gun belt and ripped out the revolver and laid one sharp blow across Turk's head.

Afterwards he crawled away on his hands and knees. Blood ran freely through his lips. His legs were numb from that first sudden jackknifing of his spine against the table; his knuckles stung from the smashing against Turk's bony face, and from their contact with the stove. He pulled himself up along the wall and stood there, hearing somebody sigh across the room.

He said: "Johnny."

The kid's voice sailed back at him, ragged with fear. "I don't want to fight."

The girl was nearest Benbow. She had waited in this smoky dark until he had spoken; and her talk was cool and calm. "Johnny's no harm." Benbow heard her shuffle away. He turned a little, carefully listening, and his boot struck the yielding shape of Carter in the corner. A match flared and afterwards the girl lifted a lantern upward, its light showing the wild shine of her eyes. The shapes of Carter and Turk were curled and lifeless on the floor; and Johnny stood across the room with his hands slowly rising above a strained, sickened face. Smoke curled more thickly in the room; and fire licked up through the stove's pipe hole. The table's legs and top lay smashed. Kerosene from the broken lamp trailed its smell into the heavy smoke. The girl put the lantern on the floor and wheeled at Johnny and seized the gun from his belt. She came over to Benbow, handing the weapon to him and for a little while stared up at him. Her hair dropped irregularly across her forehead and her lips were softly parted and an accented breathing quickened the rise and fall of her breasts.

She murmured: "You got a wife?"

"See if Turk's alive, Rody."

She retorted, "Let him die." But a little of the strange shining left her eyes. She shrugged her shoulders and let them drop in a gesture of resignation and brought her lips together. Johnny crossed the room and bent above Turk. He said after a while: "Breathin'." It was the fire shooting out of the stove that bothered him most. "Damn place is goin' to burn up if we don't stop that."

"Let it burn," breathed the girl.

"We got to do somethin'," insisted Johnny.

"Let them die—and let the house burn."

Benbow stood there against the wall, the bruises of his body pounding with the rhythm of his heart's beating. The taste of blood soured his mouth. Feeling crept back into his legs, but their long muscles were still unsteady.

They were watching him—Rody and the kid—and waiting for him to speak. The kid was afraid, but the girl had no fear in her. It seemed to Benbow that a long-concealed hatred was having its way now, stripping her of all sympathy, making the tone of her voice thoroughly cold, altogether pitiless.

He opened Johnny's gun and slipped its shells into his pocket and dropped the gun on the floor, Johnny's round eyes following all this in frightened silence. He said: "Which way is the badlands trail from the house?"

The girl's arm lifted, pointing past the stove. "There."

"Not in this weather," said Johnny.

Benbow said: "The bluff wall will keep us from strayin'. Not you, Johnny. You're staying here."

"I'm not stayin'," said Rody.

Benbow bent over and retrieved his own revolver, the muscles of his back seeming to rip loose from their moorings at the effort. He got down on one knee and hauled Turk across his shoulder, and stood up. They were watching him with a narrowing attention as he went down the hall. He said: "Bring Carter out, Johnny." Rody snatched the lantern and squeezed by him, opening the back door. Wind beat him away from that opening and he had to brace himself and gather momentum to step forward into the foot-deep snow. There was a rope stretched from the house over to the barn, with the barn buried somewhere yonder in a howling universe. He paced on carefully, the guide rope rubbing against his hip. The air was hard to breathe, and snow kept stinging his face and crawling up his nostrils. Rody was behind him with the lantern, yet its light had no effect. And when he came against the stable wall he had to search for the door. Afterwards he stumbled through the opening.

Rody's lantern shot little lanes of fractured light into this gloom. He let Turk drop. His black mare stamped in an adjoining stall, softly whinnying; and four other horses stood behind. Hay covered the rest of the barn, up

to its joists. Benbow went into the black mare's stall an
saw it standing three-footed to favor the fourth leg. H
ran his hand down along that leg and felt the swell of th
knee; and came back. Johnny staggered in with the dea
Carter, and fell with Carter. He panted: "What's the us
of it?"

"Put my saddle on a good horse, Johnny. And fix u
another one for Rody."

The girl lifted the lantern, throwing its glow agains
Benbow's face, saying with a terrible and eager swiftness
"Goin' to burn the house?"

He went back along the rope, Rody following closely
The house was filling with smoke and it was hard t
breathe, with the smell of scorched wood growin
greater. The girl stood obediently before him, all th
while watching with that eager wildness in her eyes.

He said: "If you've got anything to take away, get it."

She left the lamp on the floor and climbed into th
attic. Smoke was thickest up there and he could hear he
sudden coughing; when she came down she had all he
possessions knotted up inside the torn section of a skirt
And then she was standing by him again, the sense o
hatred strongly rising from her. She said:

"Goin' to burn the house?"

"That's all you've got?"

"I ain't seen the inside of a store for two years. Bur
this dam' house down!"

But her eyes ran along the wall and she went over an
took Turk's huge buffalo coat from the wall, and brough
it to Benbow, lifting it up to him.

"You use it," he said.

"There's another coat," she said, and held it ther
until he stuck his arms into its sleeves. Afterwards sh
turned through the hall into Carter's room and thing
began to smash on the floor. The light in the room go
worse and worse and the smoke was hard to stand
He went over by the stove and picked up a handful o
wood, and stood still a little while thinking ahead o

him carefully.

This was the end of Carter's ranch, and the end of Carter. There wouldn't be any more Hat beef coming this way. Yet Gore remained untouched in the Yellows and Gore's power was still strong—as strong as it had ever been. He knew now how it would be. As long as there was life in the man, Gore would fight. He would stick to Running M until he was driven from it; and then he would lift himself higher in the hills and keep on fighting. There wasn't any fear in that rust-haired man and there wasn't any surrender or mercy in him. All the peace was gone from Two Dance now; and nothing but trouble lay ahead.

The girl came out of the other room wearing a long blue army overcoat. She caught up her bundle and the lantern—and stood passively by, waiting for him to be through with his thoughts. Benbow said: "How long you been here, Rody?"

"Two years."

He looked down at her, gently shaking his head. "Too bad you can't burn those two years like we're burning this house." Then he went to the stove still carrying the wood in the crook of his arm, and reached down with his free hand, heaving the stove over in one swift crash. The lids fell off and all the live coals poured out and fire began to run up the room's tinder-dry walls. He waited only a moment, until he was sure those flames had bitten in. When he knew the place was afire he went down the hall and bucked the storm back to the barn, Rody following.

Johnny waited there with two horses ready. Benbow found a feed sack to hold the wood, and tied it on his horn. He motioned to the girl, and watched her climb into her saddle noticing then that she had wrapped a bandanna around her head and ears. Wind beat its tremendous blows against the barn and the horses stepped impatiently back and forth, smelling something they didn't like. Johnny's face was hungry and pale.

Benbow said: "The wind will blow the fire the other

way. You're safe, Kid. Stay put till the weather clears
Then let the cows out of that pen—and don't waste an
time leavin' here."

Out in that dense wall of snow a fugitive light showe
a faint and growing spot. It was the open door of th
house that fed a draft into the fire. He had his look a
the dead Carter and at the motionless shape of the gian
Turk; and went over to his own horse, stepping up.

Johnny said: "Well, you could of put a bullet in me."

"Something to consider," murmured Benbow. "Mayb
you'll die like this some day. Maybe you won't. Depend
on what you think about the rest of this night. I wouldn'
lay a bet on you, Johnny—but I'll wish you luck."

He walked his horse as far as the door, seeing the ligh
spread its higher and higher stain against the curdled
oppressed black. The girl said something he didn't hea
and he turned in the saddle to see her look down o
Johnny in a woman's strange way. The kid put his hand t
her, but she shook her head, and crowded her pony u
beside Benbow.

Benbow shook out a few feet of his lariat, passing th
free end back to her. "Tie it to your horn," and thus
having taken the precaution not to lose her in th
smothered world ahead, he put his horse through th
door and rode straight toward the growing light.

He reached the back porch, and swung and went alon
the house's side. There was no substance to that house
though it lay no more than three paces from his elbows
yet the firelight spread its wider, higher glow and by thi
glow he saw how thick was the onracing wall of snow
With the light as a beacon, he passed on, put the win
squarely at his back and struck out for the badlands trai
which lay somewhere ahead.

14. Through the Blizzard

As he remembered it, the mouth of the badlands trail was about three hundred yards due north of the house. He let his sense of direction carry him along, with the fullness of the wind at his back for a guide. Rody's horse, three feet behind the tail of his own horse, now and then pulled on the rope but when he turned he could see nothing of either girl or animal. The fire had caught hold of the house, that light spreading hugely beyond the solid wall of snow. He could see the light but not the fire.

He thought he had set a straight course, yet when his horse brought up suddenly he knew he had missed the way. He got down and pulled the pony on until his reaching hand struck the bluff's solid face; and stood there a moment to consider which way he had drifted. In the end he turned to his right and crept on one foot at a time beside the bluff, stumbling over the heavy cakes of clay fallen down from the rim. It was as though he walked with a hangman's hood dropped over his head; the blackness was that absolute, without shadow, without form, without point. Going this way, he at last felt the wall withdraw from his reaching fingers and thus entered the mouth of the trail. After he was certain of the trail, he got back into the saddle and pushed forward.

Presently he looked back and discovered that the glow of the burning house had disappeared, shut out by the sudden curves of the gully. The wind had quit pounding at him; its reports boomed and rushed by overhead and its echoes now and then dropped into the gully and rolled hollow reverberations along it. The snow fell straight down, the blackness of the night took on an inkier, thicker tone. Traveling steadily through the deeper footing of the snow, he felt his horse winding to left and to right. After an hour of this he remembered the girl had said nothing. It stopped him long enough to throw his call back, high-voiced against the overhead shrilling of the blizzard.

"All right?"

Her answer was brief and faint. "I'm all right."

He went on, with the sense of time's passage sharpening up his attention. It had taken him six hours to get from the tunnel to Carter's ranch, but this had been because of the constant detours he had made away from the main trail. By the direct way he now took, half that time was enough, if the pony didn't get lost. He had no hope of locating the cavern by any ordinary sight; yet he remembered one thing and on this one thing he based his faith. The tunnel was in the gully's west wall just beyond a point where a straight clay chimney reared up and split the trail two ways. Rubble from the disintegrating chimney had made a definite hump on the trail and this he knew he would recognize as soon as his horse passed over it. . . .

When he came to that hump, he had been riding far beyond his allotted time and it was with a sudden let-down of nerves that he pulled himself stiffly from the saddle, and stood a moment stamping life into his legs. Crawling carefully to the left of the chimney, he followed the gully's wall until it gave way before him. Snow had drifted into the first part of the cavern, making a high, soft barrier. He broke through this, leading his own horse and Rody's horse.

He said: "Climb down."

He heard her saddle leather creak; and a kind of thin groan came out of her when her feet, no doubt as numb as

150

his own, struck the ground. But that was all. He untied the feed sack which held the wood, and got out his knife and crouched there in the crackling cold darkness, shaving off splinters and silently admiring this girl. There was nerve in her. He got his bits of wood together, making a loose pile of them with his hand, and struck a match. That sudden break in the blackness was as startling as the crack of a bullet. As explosive. He hovered over the ignited shavings, nursing up the blaze and adding other pieces of wood. There was a little draft running in from the cavern's mouth and being sucked backward to some thin crevice at the rear. He waited until he had his fire freely burning before rising from it. The girl stood in the shadows, quite motionless.

He said, "Come up and get warm," and saw her move forward with a half stumbling stiffness. She dropped to her knees and pulled off her gloves; and bowed over the fire with her hands against the heat and her face against it. No expression showed through that stolid composure. She was like an Indian, troubling nobody with her feelings, yet he remembered how bitter and hating she had been for one brief instant in Carter's house, which was two years of misery coming out of her in a fierce wish to see Turk dead.

He pulled the horses around and unsaddled them, and rolled out the blankets by the fire. Heat lifted up, thawing his frigid blood; and the heat and the fire's light was a small, round cell, within which they crouched and against which the blank, bitter world vainly howled.

He said: "Feel better?" And watched her head lift and fall. The heat turned her cheeks red; it loosened the tight line of her lips and took some of the stony composure from her eyes. She wasn't more than twenty-five, and good-looking in a sharp, hard way; but somewhere along her life she had forgotten how to smile. It wasn't, he guessed, a pretty life. She had been Turk's woman and before that probably somebody else's woman, and in time would find another man. Indifference seemed ground into her and her eyes were odd and old in the way they

151

judged him. But he admired her for that silence which held so much courage.

He said: "How'd you get on Carter's ranch?"

Her eyes dropped to her hands. After a while she said: "I went there of my own will. That was a mistake."

"Where'd you live before that?"

Her glance came up and showed him a guarded interest. "No place that matters."

"Roll up in the blankets. We'll be leaving here early."

She said: "You married?" And watched him shake his head. She sat like that, very quietly, searching his face with her dark shrewd eyes. Something seemed to occur to her then. Casually. "You wouldn't want me anyhow," she reflected, and sank down, drawing the blanket around her. But she was still watching him. "What you think will happen to Johnny?"

"Nothing good."

She said, without interest: "He'd been glad to have me. I could have made something out of him."

"That's an idea, Rody."

Her answer held a fatalism hard to hear. "What's it worth? Too late for me."

He poked the edges of the fire, feeding in the wood with a husbanding care. His thoughts swung away from the girl, back to the cabin which was cold ashes now under the deepening snow. The spring wind and rain would dissolve the ashes, leaving only a few twisted relics on the ground; and grass would grow up over the relics and in time nobody'd remember the house that once had stood there.

Yet his own memory would hold that house forever intact. It was cut in his mind with acid and steel. All the edges of that picture were clear—the flaming, sawed-off expanse of Carter's beard, the sound of his bullet tearing the life out of that man, the smoke raveling up the lamp chimney that moment before it died out, and Turk's breath against his face and the smell of burned flesh against the stove's redhot surface.

The girl sat up from the blanket. Her voice was gentler

than it had been. "Don't look like that."

"What?"

"Don't ever think back. I can remember I used to think back—and cry. It's been a long time ago. Don't you think back—it hurts too damned much." She lifted the edge of the blanket, her arms open for him and her expression all soft and wistful. "You come and sleep."

He said, quietly: "Wrap up, Rody. Mornin's soon here."

Her shoulders lifted and fell and that odd resignation caught her features into its stillness. She fell back on the blanket again, her eyes studying him. After a while she said: "There was a yellow-haired man who rode up to the cabin once in a while. He and Carter used to talk a long time after I went to bed. Then he'd go away."

"What was his name?"

"Never knew it. He looked at me one night. Turk saw him. He laughed at Turk—he was always laughin'. They went outside and had a fight. Turk licked him. He never came back any more."

He could see her lips show the pleasure of that memory—of men fighting over her. It was a little fire brightening her life. He sat there and watched her fall asleep, and suddenly she had lost all her hardness and was just a slim-faced girl with black hair falling down across her forehead. The places on his body bruised by Turk's fists began to thump and burn; the taste of blood still remained in his mouth. Lying by the fire, he alternately slept and woke to feed the blaze, and slept again.

It was full daylight when they resumed the trail. The wind howled above them without abatement but the snow whirled less solidly through the air and the way was reasonably clear. After bucking the three-foot drifts most of the morning they came out of the badlands at the same spot Benbow had entered them two nights before, and crossed over the open plain to the timber. At this point the girl stopped.

She said: "Good-bye."

153

Benbow pulled his horse about. "Where are you going?"

Her face was framed inside the protection of Carter's lifted overcoat collar; stolid again and showing him nothing. "Down there," she said, pointing to the broad plain sweeping southward.

"Bad traveling," he said. "Better come along to Hat with me."

"Women on your ranch?"

"Sure."

She shook her head. "No. I'll find a place. Always have." She considered him for a moment and he saw the oldness of her eyes once more. "Men," she murmured, "ain't hard to please." She reached out and caught his hand and held it with a tight grip. "I wish," she began, and afterwards dropped her arm and whirled her pony and put it through the snow as hard as it would run.

He watched her aim straight for the blur of a house a mile or so in the yonder mist; and not until she was a small shape on the plain did he resume his own course, stirred and made sad. She had come before his vision casually, she was leaving it casually—yet in that brief contact some strange part of her personality brushed his emotions and left an indelible print on his mind. It went with him, this feeling, as far as the swing of the trail; and then, going up toward Cherokee, he put the thought of her away by necessity. He did not wish to appear in Cherokee, and so laboriously detoured the town, slogging through the heavy drifts. It was late afternoon when he came down the Ramparts and struck out for Hat, slashed by the wind racing the length of the valley. At dark he rounded into the yard and entered Hat's big living-room to find Connie there with Doc Payson from Two Dance, and Izee and Price and Gordon Howland and Nelson McGinnis.

Connie made one swift turn. She said, "Jim!" And that tone was heartfelt and near to breaking, affecting him in a deep and powerful way—taking the grayness out of his mind and thawing the coldness from his bones. She came directly against him and caught his arms and looked up, her eyes dark and near to tears. She murmured: "What have you been through?" Then, looking over the top of her shining head, he saw Clay Rand turn slowly from the room's far corner and stare at him with an expression half relieved and half resenting.

He said: "Hello, Clay."

Clay didn't answer. None of the other men spoke. Something pressed down upon the room. Benbow said: "What's up, Connie?"

"Go see Dad."

He knew what it was then and turned to the stairs. Rising a step at a time he felt the accumulating effect of his long ride. His leg muscles were slow in pushing his body up and all the snap had gone out of him. Paused in front of Old Jack's bedroom door, he put his hands against it and rested like that, staring at the floor. Something in his chest had the weight of lead. He tried to erase his feelings from his face; and then entered and saw Jack Dale shift his head on the pillows.

Dale said in a small, small voice: "Glad you got here."

Benbow crossed to the bed's side and stared down at the old man, trying to hide his shock. Hat's owner, who had been so proud and bully a man, lay helplessly here and waited for the ebb tide. He wasn't in any pain and he wasn't afraid, but it was that sense of resignation that hit Benbow so hard, for Old Jack had never been one to quit fighting. Seeing him thus, all his combative instincts quenched, Benbow knew the end wasn't far away.

"Kind of a long wait," whispered Dale. "Didn't know whether I could hang on—but I knew you'd get back." He quit talking to catch his breath and his eyes studied Benbow shrewdly, reading the story on his foreman's face. He said: "What happened, Jim?"

"I followed the beef. You know a place called Carter's ranch, about sixty miles down the badlands?"

"Used to be headquarters for the Mallon boys. We cleaned 'em out, ten years ago. Ain't been there since."

"That's where Gore sends the beef. I saw our brand in

155

Carter's corral. He'd started running his own brand on—"

Dale shook his head, whispering: "Don't waste time, son. What happened?"

"There were three men. One was just a kid and didn't count. I let him go. They had a girl. She came off with me. We burned the house."

Silence settled. The color of Dale's cheeks was bad, but one remaining spark of vitality put a little heat into his eyes. "It's a thing I saw in you when you was a fresh kid come to this place."

"What's that, Jack?"

"You can fight. It's born in you to take punishment and still plug ahead. I observe somethin' in your eyes. It ain't pretty, for you been down into the hell every man reaches when he kills another man. Still, you'll close your mouth and keep goin'. And now it's Cash Gore."

"Yes," said Benbow, "I guess we've come to Cash finally."

Dale whispered: "You're up against somethin' tough. Listen. When the wolves start howlin' it's time for you to remember no man's to be trusted. The ones you figure for your friends may not be your friends. That's the way it goes when you spill blood. From this time on—until the valley's cleaned up—you'll be the loneliest man in the world. Written that way in the book. I wish I could watch you go through it."

"Jack," said Benbow, "what's in the back of your head? You've come close to tellin' me twice lately."

Dale shut his eyes and for a moment Benbow thought he was slipping out. Long afterwards Dale murmured: "Was you a weaker man I might tell you. But you're tough enough to take the thing that's goin' to tear your heart out—and see the end of it your own way. Jim— stick by Connie till things are settled down."

"Sure—sure," muttered Benbow.

Dale lifted his hand feebly from the bed. He made a faint circle with his finger. "I've had fun. I've tried to keep away from little sins. The big ones have been plenty,

156

but I did 'em with reason, though maybe Gabriel will have some little trouble readin' my account book. I been proud of you a long time, Jim. God hates a piker. Do what you got to do, and to hell with the reasons."

"All right, Jack."

Dale rolled his head away from Benbow and gasped: "Tell Connie I want to see her."

Benbow wheeled out, going quickly down the stairs. He nodded toward Connie, instantly sending her up to Old Jack's room—with the doctor following at once. McGinnis and Howland and Price and Izee made a loose group by the room's fireplace; Clay Rand stood at the other end of the room, alone and high-drawn and with a sharp discontent on his ruddy features. Benbow saw this scene and didn't understand it. Something lay here strangely, a feeling that dropped a partition between Clay and the rest of the crowd. He went over to the window and jammed his fists into his pockets, watching the wind rip long clouds of snow across the yard.

Nelson McGinnis said: "Jack and me came up the trail together. Connie was just a leggy kid straddlin' a paint pony. The Indians were bad that year. Jack's wife was a beautiful woman but the country was too tough for her. I remember her sitting by the piano in this room, singing. Half of Jack died when she died."

Howland spoke across the room. "Find out anything, Jim?"

"Yes."

He had his back to them. He heard their boots scrape the floor as they swung. McGinnis said in a quick, rapping voice: "You ready yet?"

"I guess so," said Benbow, and then the stretching stillness pivoted him on his heels. Clay Rand's eyes burned against him with a pale, hot light; all the others were stonegrave. Price Peters suddenly shook his head.

"Don't let anybody pull you into this, Jim."

"For God's sake, Price!" snapped McGinnis. "What's eatin' you?"

"I'd sooner cut off my hand than see you lead a bunch

157

against Gore," insisted Peters bitterly. "Let Nelson do it. Let anybody do it. But not you."

They were waiting for him to speak. Izee turned from the group and walked over beside Benbow and took his station there. It was his declaration. They could see for themselves how he felt about it. Price understood that gesture immediately. "Sure," he said with the same deep dissatisfaction. "If Jim leads off we'll all string along. But I don't want him to lead off."

"Why?" said Benbow.

Peters shook his head, not speaking. Clay Rand, so definitely apart from these men, let his head drop until the strange set of his face was half hidden.

Benbow shrugged his shoulders. "This mysterious talk doesn't get anywhere. I'm already in it, Price. I found where Gore drives Hat's beef. I went down the trail and ran into the place. There were three men there."

He didn't add to that. It wasn't necessary. They knew the way the country was, and what that meeting had to be like. So he let the silence go on while they drew their own conclusions.

McGinnis slapped his hands together. "Gore'll know about that soon enough. We got no time to waste."

"Don't worry," said Benbow. "Gore won't run."

"Run?" echoed Price. "Of course not. Why should he run? He'll draw back into the Yellows and shoot hell out of anything that comes his way."

"He ain't that strong," contradicted Gordon Howland.

Izee, not a talkative man, broke in. "Wrong there, Gordon. You try to ride up Granite Canyon some night and see how far you get."

"As good a time as ever to have it done with," murmured McGinnis. "When you want us, Jim?"

"I'll let you know."

Price Peters said, "Jim," in an altered voice. Everybody looked at him, even Clay Rand. Price's educated and half-disillusioned face showed a greater gravity than before. "I'd like to get something straight. You're going to lead the boys into this business?"

158

"That's the way it has to be."

"Supposin'," said Peters, "you catch somebody in this roundup you didn't expect to find. What then?"

"More mystery," said Benbow irritably. Weariness kept pushing at his shoulders. His eyes burned with the need of sleep. Even with the light shining on the group he saw them through a bluish film of fatigue.

"Supposing you do?" insisted Peters, that same determined care in his tone. "And supposing it's somebody you considered a friend?"

And then he understood they were all a part of that mystery. Price had expressed something all of them felt. For the silence following was so complete that he could hear the lift and fall of their breathing. Nobody moved except Rand who raised a hand and passed it across his face, as though to shade away the glare of lamplight.

Benbow spoke slowly: "How could a man be my friend if he strung along with Cash? You're spooky, Price. But I'll tell you something. Jack Dale put Hat into my hands six years ago." He stopped talking and reached for his tobacco. Standing like that, his heavy-planed face bent over the cigarette shaping up in his tough fingers, he made a hard and solid shape in this room. Three days' beard darkened his cheeks and a raw scar slanted across a corner of his mouth. He looked up from his fingers and his eyes were blacker and colder than any man's eyes at that instant. "Hat comes first," he said gently. "I want—"

Connie descended the stairs, her hands hanging stiffly down. She reached the living-room's level and looked around her, her cheeks whitened and strained. Clay Rand started across toward her and then she turned from him and saw Benbow nearby and stepped against him. The moment he put his heavy arms around her waist he felt her let go in a silent, terrible way. Doc Payson came down and made only a gesture with his hands. That was all.

15. Fire Goes Out

McGinnis drew out a handkerchief and blew his nose.
Izee whirled suddenly from the room; and afterward
these other valley men followed him. Clay Ran
remained, staring at Benbow and Connie with a quick
pale light freshening his eyes. He said, "Connie, I'r
sorry," and then, having no answer, he jerked himsel
away from the wall and walked into the office.

Benbow remained wholly still, feeling the grief of thi
girl shake its way through her, even while his ow
thoughts went spinning down into farther blackness. Ol
Jack had been a mighty pillar of strength. Even in his las
days when silence came upon him, his presence had fed
faith into Benbow. Thinking of that now, Benbow
recalled the old man's shouting laughter of earlier times
it was an echo that remained with him, like the sound of
bell's rolling stroke coming out of a far distance.

He heard Connie whispering against his chest. "Don'
go, Jim. Not for a while."

He said, quietly: "I'm right here, Connie."

She said: "I don't mean that. Don't leave Hat. It's hal
yours now."

He said: "Your dad was one of the few white men lef
in the world. I'll finish my job, which he expected me to do
Then I've got to pull out, Connie. You've got your man."

Her hands were on his shoulders, gripping him fast
She lifted her face to him and he saw its wetness
160

Fragrance rose from her hair. There was no reservation in her eyes and for one moment he looked far down and saw something there that whipped up his own wildness and made him forget the dull ache of his body. It was soon gone. She had remembered Clay Rand; and then there was nothing for Benbow to see. She stepped back, murmuring: "Nothing changes you, Jim."

"I can remember when we were just a couple of kids, having fun. But we've grown up—and nothing like that can come again."

He went out of the house quickly.

Connie walked into the office and found Clay standing by the window. He wheeled around, high and stiff-shaped and showing her the sultry edges of his strange temper. He had been smoking. He dropped the cigarette and seemed to wait there for her to cross to him. It was only a little incident, this way he had of waiting for her to come to him, and yet it served to stir up her memories of the man so clearly, so strongly. She remained by the office door, the point of her shoulder resting against the casing, and was shocked by the turn of her thoughts. She was in love with Clay and every wayward episode of his life left its scar in her heart even though the teasing lazy smile of this man softened the hurt and made her temporarily forget his lapses. Well, she had no command over her heart. Or so she had thought all this while. Yet something had happened this night to hold her at the office doorway while her reasoning turned more and more honest and a light seemed to shine down on Clay with a force that was almost unmerciful. Always she had found excuses for him; always she had crossed the space between, to accept his smiling kiss. What bound her to this man? Not the need for strength. When she had needed strength it was to Jim Benbow she had turned, without a moment's hesitation.

He said in almost a curt voice: "I'll repeat what you didn't hear me say before. I'm sorry, Connie."

"He tried not to show it, but I've long known he was very sick." Afterwards another stray thought came out of her and made her proud. "He hated crying and he hated

161

foolish talk."

He said: "Connie, you've got little to hold you here now. Let's put the country behind us."

She drew a long, long breath. The way of her mind was strange; it wouldn't let her alone. She was seeing Clay so plainly. "Clay, I want to know something."

He lifted his head and a guarded expression tightened the lines of his ruddy face.

She said: "You and Jim and Izee and Price have always been so close together. I've noticed that Price and Izee don't say much to you any more. Only Jim sticks. What have you done?"

He said easily: "What would you figure?"

She murmured: "Men like Price and Izee don't come to snap judgments, Clay. I trust them. Why don't they trust you?"

He said, half in anger: "Ask them."

She said, "No," in a small voice. "I don't ask questions. My father taught me better manners. I trust you because Jim does. If the time ever comes when he—"

He stopped her brusquely, coming across the room. "You had better make up your mind whether it's Benbow you want, or me." His ruddy cheek showed a deeper flush and a pale rage sparkled in his eyes. "Maybe it's me that has reason to figure whether I ought to trust Price and Izee. Or whether I ought to trust you and Benbow—"

She pulled up her chin and said: "You'd better go."

He put his hands on her shoulders and there was a checked pressure in them that she could feel. He was that near to hurting her physically. But it was for only a moment, and then his unstable temper snapped and he was speaking in a rapid, groaning way: "Connie— Connie, what in God's name are we quarreling for?" He left it like that, rushing across the living-room, slamming its door behind him.

Once, she thought, her heart would have gone crying after him. Tonight she let him go, and seemed not to care. She walked over to the big desk and put her hands on it, thinking of her father whose heavy arms had worn grooves

162

at the desk's edge; thinking of Benbow whose own big arms fitted into those grooves. He had held her and said nothing while she cried, and the rough surface of his coat, smelling of tobacco and leather and all the ingrained articles of a man's being, had cut the edge of her grief.

Benbow and the others were standing on the porch when Rand came out. Nelson McGinnis quit talking, obviously leaving his thought unfinished, and silence came upon them, uncomfortably. There was a little light shining out of the house, to show Benbow how swiftly his friends reacted to Clay's presence. Even Price looked away from Clay, and Izee went down to the foot of the steps, and stood half turned. Wind raced around the edge of the house, throwing up the loose snow. Benbow put his long arm on Clay's shoulder and let it lie there so that McGinnis and the rest of them might see how he felt.

McGinnis went out to his horse, with Gordon Howland and Price at once following suit. McGinnis settled himself in the leather. He said: "I'll notify the valley, Jim. You'll bury him here?"

"Tomorrow."

McGinnis said: "He was a man that liked his fun. Somewhere, this minute, he's gettin' his friends around a fire and tellin' all the old stories. He was a great hand for that. Well, we'll be back tomorrow."

They trotted out into the yonder darkness, soon disappearing. Izee walked on toward the bunkhouse. Benbow pulled his arm away from Clay's shoulder, feeling his partner's restless stirring.

"Kid," said Benbow, "I've got to tell you something. Take it right."

Rand's head swung around until the outshining lamplight hit his eyes and showed their glitter. He stood very still, his long body lifted and held alert.

"You've had your fun foolin' along," said Benbow. "I'm not laying any blame against you. A man can't get around his nature. But you've had the fun and now's time to buckle on the harness. You're beginning to get a reputation for wasting your time. Hat's a big outfit and you'll be running Hat when I pull out."

Clay said suddenly: "When?"

"Soon as I clean up my chores."

Rand said: "Stay away from Gore, Jim. He's after you skin."

Benbow went gravely on. "You've been God's wors fool with women. Connie deserves better than that. You ought to know it. But it's your affair—and Connie's. No mine. I wish you'd thresh that out with her, and do i soon. Spring will roll around quick enough and Hat wait for no man. You're through playin' poker at Far Charley's and you're through with Eileen Gannon."

Rand spoke with remote irony. "Layin' out my life fo me, I see."

Benbow turned squarely on Rand and let his talk strik Clay without softness. "I'll let nobody neglect Hat, Clay And I'll let nobody hurt Connie. Grow up—and grow u damned sudden."

"All right," grumbled Rand. "But listen. I wish you' stay clear of the Yellows. Price is right. Let McGinnis g in there."

"It's Hat he's stealin' from." Then Benbow, weary t the bone and rubbed raw by his partner's strang indifference, let go. "God damn you, Clay. Wake up! Jac Dale never let any man do his dirty work, and neither wi I. And if you're coming in here, neither should you. Ha comes first."

Rand said nothing. He whirled down the steps, got int his saddle and cantered out of the yard. Izee suddenl appeared around the corner of the house. He cam forward, saying nothing. Benbow grunted: "What yo been standin' there for?"

"Nothin'," answered Izee.

Benbow returned to the office. Connie had gone int another part of the house. He stoked up the stove an moved around the room, too tired to think and yet strun up to an odd restlessness. After a while he stretched ou on Jack Dale's old leather couch in the corner. Slee simply struck him across the forehead like a maul; and h

ay there like that, sunken to exhausted slumber when
Connie returned. She stood over him awhile, watching
he corners of his big lips slowly relax. One hand hung
ut from the couch, the square fingers limp. She brought
p a chair beside the couch and sat down and held that
and in her lap.

A mile from Hat, Price Peters stopped. McGinnis and
Rowland instantly followed suit, thinking he had spotted
omething in the heavy night. But he said, "I'm going
ack," and left them there. Coming again into Hat's yard
e saw Izee's short and solid body rise up from the porch
f the main house. Izee said instantly: "Who's that?"

"All right," answered Price, and got down.

Izee drifted forward, grumbling: "I'm just tuned a
ittle high, I guess."

"Jim inside?"

"Sleepin' like a log."

"I think I'll bunk here tonight."

He led his horse to Hat's long horse barn, stabling it
here. Izee followed him and the two of them stood
eneath the lantern hung to the runway ceiling, its frosty
one of light slanting over them. Izee said: "Anything on
our mind?"

"No."

Price sought his tobacco and rolled up a smoke. Izee
hoved his back against the inside wall of the stable and
onsidered Price with a long, taciturn attention. It went
his way while the time dragged on—two men thoroughly
understanding each other's thoughts and hating to give
oice to those thoughts.

"Clay," murmured Izee, "went home. What we goin'
o do about him, Price?"

"Nothing."

"The hell." Izee pushed himself away from the wall.
"Think of it, Price. There's the man who'll be boss of
Hat. Why, my God—!"

"He'll never get that far."

165

"Why not? He's workin' with Cash Gore and no ma[n] ever gets free of Cash. Cash will tell him what to do. Righ[t] now, with Benbow ridin' for Cash, it's Clay that's her[e] listenin' for what he can carry back. Think of that, Price![o]

Price repeated gently: "He'll never get that far." Cigarette smoke clouded his sharp features, for a momen[t] dimming the arrogance and the disbelief so habitual[ly] established in them. "Sometimes," he went on in th[e] same resigned voice, "I wonder what a man lives for. [I] had all the future anybody could ask. Money and plac[e] and pride. The pride went out first. Don't ever regr[et] your lack of learning, Izee. It's done nothing for m[e] except to keep me awake at nights wondering what might have been. Here I am, of no use to a single sou[l] except as a bad example. Once in a while somebody of m[y] earlier days probably stops to think: 'Now there wa[s] Price. Whatever happened to Price?' But that's all."

Izee grumbled: "You give a man the fidgets."

"There were four of us," mused Price. "You and Ji[m] and me and Clay. Now it's just Jim and you and me. I hav[e] no other ties on this earth. As for Jim, I don't want hi[m] hurt. When he rides after Cash Gore he'll soon enoug[h] find out the truth about Clay. It's a thing that won't sta[y] hidden. Then he'll have to make up his mind what to d[o.] Whether to hunt Clay like the rest of the wild bunch. O[r] let Clay go. It'll tear his heart out, Izee. Because that's th[e] way he feels about his friends. I don't want it to happen.[o]

Izee said after a long silence, "It'll happen. When h[e] starts for the Yellows, Price, he'll cut it clean an[d] complete. I know that fellow."

"That," said Price, "is why I didn't want him headin[g] up a posse. Well, never mind. It won't come to that. Fin[d] me a bunk."

He slept that night in Hat's bunkhouse; and was u[p] before daylight, ready to go, when Izee stumbled sleepy[-] eyed into the windy, snow-laced air. Izee said: "Wher[e] you travelin'?"

"I'll be back for the funeral," said Price.

"Better wait for some breakfast."

Price started off, and then seemed to think of something. He rode back to where Izee stood and held out his hand. Izee, displaying a sleepy puzzlement, took it and held it. He said: "What for, Price?"

Price showed Izee one of his rare, half-sad and half-insolent smiles. "So long, Izee," he drawled, and then put Hat's yard quickly behind him. Just before he turned around the barn Izee noticed that he had buckled his revolver outside his overcoat. Long afterwards Izee kept thinking of that. Being a thoroughly still-tongued man it never occurred to him to mention it to Benbow at the breakfast table. But, helping to dig Old Jack's grave in the ranch cemetery that bitter morning, he kept recalling that gun strapped outside Price's coat; kept turning it over and over in his head.

Price bucked his way across the Two Dance and by eight o'clock had reached the Ramparts south of Gannon's ranch. He pushed his way up through the heavy drifts of snow caught in the trees, arrived at the main trail on the Ramparts' rim and found an easier path here where earlier travelers had beaten a way. Gannon's chimney smoke twined the windy air below him and down one alley of the pines he saw Eileen chopping wood in the yard. Later he dropped into Granite Canyon and climbed the far side, seeing the road along the canyon's bottom well marked by traffic between Running M and Riley's settlement higher up. On top of the rim again he rode his steady way northward until, two miles from the canyon, he sighted Clay Rand's long low cabin to the fore, its barn and sheds leading back into timber, its front porch facing out upon the sweep of the prairie.

It had been his intention to ride directly into the yard, but he didn't do it. For, while he was yet two hundred yards from the place, Clay swung around the house and advanced on him.

Stopped there, Price knew that Clay wasn't quite sure. The day was dull, with the trees casting heavy shadows across the trail, with the snow clouding the air. He watched Clay stiffen in the saddle and he watched Clay's right arm drop and swing loosely back and forth brushing the gun butt at each passing. Fifty yards off Clay suddenly sent his call on: "That you, Price?" And came ahead until only a yard separated the horses. Clay was smiling. Yet—and this detail Price's quick eyes instantly saw—the big blond man's muscles didn' loosen. Behind that smile lay a risen suspicion.

"Goin' to the funeral?" asked Clay.

"Yes."

"We'll go together."

"Hold it, Clay."

The smile went away and the intimation of trouble was between them even then. Clay's lips lengthened, tha' pressure streaking straight lines out from them. Price sa' still and saw this one-time comrade change and become another man. A quick fire began to burn in Clay's changeable eyes and in the space of a spoken word he had lifted his nerves to a readiness. Price felt the weight of an antagonism push against him, like the weight of a hand and he knew that the story was half told before he opened his mouth.

Clay spoke out, violence having its unsteady way with his words. "Well, what's up?"

"You've got no warning coming, but I'd be the last man to shut the door in your face. Get out of the country."

Rand eased his body in the saddle. "Kid," he said turned stony-quiet, "what do you know?"

"You're a miserable dog, Rand. That's what I know— and too much for any man to know."

He kept his voice down, his feeling for Rand entirely dead; yet his recollections of their past fun held his anger low. The hearty color was ebbing from Rand's cheeks leaving them yellow-pale; and his light-colored eyes were sprung wide. In that instant some of his hope and some of his assurance and some of his pride fell in ruin around him. It must have been that, Price thought distantly, for Clay grabbed the horn of the saddle with his gun arm and let a long, long breath fall out. He asked his question again with a kind of desperate anxiety.

168

"What do you know?"

"What did Gore tell you to do—in Two Dance the night he tried to get Jim?"

Rand shook his head, muttering. "That's too much for you to know, kid. I wish to God you didn't."

"You can turn and ride out. I'm not stopping you."

Rand said dully: "I can't do it, Price. I'd keep remembering you still knew that."

"I don't give a damn about you!" snapped Price. "It's Jim I call to mind." He had his moment of cruelty, and used it. "How well does a man sleep, Clay, for knowin' he's leadin' his best friend into a trap?"

"Wait," said Rand. "I had nothing to do with that shooting. Neither did Gore. It was Kell's idea." But he kept staring at Price, the yellow tinge more and more distinct in his eyes. It turned them queer, it stained them with unreason. He said hoarsely: "Who else saw that?"

Price thought of Izee, and then lied. "Nobody." And afterwards the thought in Clay's head was as apparent as a shouted word, and all hope of a gentle ending left Price's mind. He knew what strange and abysmal and hopeless phantoms danced beyond those yellowing eyes. He knew, because his own life had been as twisted and as futile and he had been tortured with thoughts that ran like hot irons across his sanity. He had that insight, cruel and bitter-clear. And so he waited, noting the way Clay's arm fell down from the saddle horn and hung beside the gun. He could trace each added wave of despair that swept Clay's impulses to a higher and higher peak. Detached, without feeling and without much interest, he sat there watching a man head for murder. Like a scientist watching a test tube's froth boil toward the spilling point.

"I think," he said coolly, "you're past turning. But turn and ride out of the Two Dance."

Rand said: "All right, Price. Go on back and let me alone."

Price lifted his reins and turned his horse partly around. And stopped, making a broadside target. He was

169

smiling gently at the thin and bloodless and suddenly cunning shape of Rand's face. He was smiling sadly and speaking sadly: "I gave you credit for having one thing left in you, kid. Guess I was wrong. You'd shoot a man in the back."

It reached Clay. It broke him apart as no other thing could have done. He cried out in a long, wild voice: "You know what I've got to do!" And as he yelled, he ripped his gun from its holster and took a snap aim and fired. Price Peters had matched that sweep of Rand's gun; and then the hammer of the rising weapon caught in the folds of his coat which overlapped the belt. He never lifted it higher. Rand's bullet tore through his body. With the faint shadow of a smile still remaining, Price slowly fell from the horse, sprawling in the snow on his hands and knees, and turned over. He had a last spark of strength, his eyes turned up to Rand and his lips framed a word that never came out. That was all.

Rand jerked his eyes from the ground and opened the cylinder of the gun. He pulled out the exploded shell, threw it far into the brush and fed a fresh cartridge into the vacant cylinder. He had trouble doing this, his hands shaking terribly, and he had trouble returning the gun to its holster. For a short time he stared around him, the yellow gone from his face and a marble whiteness showing. He dismounted, pulled Price's body into the brush and mounted again. Afterwards he sat there, collecting his thoughts. Snow thickened around him and the light of day got worse. Presently he herded Price's pony down the trail the full two miles to the canyon and watched it go riderless along the road toward Running M. It was what he wanted. He descended into the canyon, rose to the far side and raced on along the Ramparts trail as fast as the footing would permit. Beyond Gannon's place he dropped into the open country and headed for Hat to attend Jack Dale's funeral.

16. A Showdown

Benbow stood on the porch with Connie, saying goodbye to those who were leaving. There wasn't much light left in the day and the snow still whirled before a strong wind. Everybody in the valley had attended Jack Dale's funeral and half the folks from Two Dance town had made the hard trip over. It was a way of showing the kind of a man Old Jack had been. He was the valley's first settler, his houses first breaking the monotony of the sage and his own personality standing like a landmark throughout the country. And now that landmark had fallen, to remind many of these folks of time's swift passage, to touch them with the faint intimations of life's brevity.

Bill Best, Hat's cook, had opened up the dining-room to feed the crowd against the cold homeward ride. Except for Running M, all the valley outfits were here in solid force. From Running M only Jubal Frick had ventured to put in appearance. Jubal was in the house now, his present station forgotten for a little while as he paid his respects to the man who had once been so sound a friend. Mauvaise Valley men rode out, lifting their hats to Connie. Square Madge came up to shake Benbow's hand and nod at Connie, and depart in a rig driven by Faro Charley. A group of reservation Indians trotted away. Shad Povy came up and said: "Missy, I've thrun many a loop for Old Jack. A man's got his time. We'll all come to that, but none of us are a-goin' to leave tracks as plumb deep as him."

They had all been here. Folks he had loved and folks he had fought. Good ones and bad ones. It was the way Jack Dale had looked at life, with a gusto for all its fun and all its wickedness; with a laughter that shattered meanness and a courage that struck like thunder. The news had got to all these people, and they had come.

Group by group, they pulled away from Hat, and presently there was left in the yard only the riders of the neighboring outfits—Block T and Diamond-and-a-Half and Crescent. Connie was shivering from cold and letdown. Something had gone from the day and something had gone from Hat—leaving a terrible emptiness behind. Benbow said gently, "I guess that's all, Connie," and took her inside.

McGinnis and Howland and Gray and Jubal Frick and Joe Gannon stood in a loose group around the fireplace. Clay had been in here but was somewhere outside now. McGinnis and Frick were talking, as though nothing lay between them. For this little while the valley men were scrupulously forgetting what Jubal had become. They were only remembering what he had been. Mrs. Gray and Karen Sanderson and Eileen Gannon were upstairs. Connie stopped, turning to Benbow. Her voice was quiet and what she said carried only to his ears.

"Hat's empty enough. Don't go."

He looked down at her, proud of the way she held herself. She wasn't crying, and her grief was something she would keep to herself. It was a far stretch of memory back to the time when she had been a leggy kid all fire and fury. Short as the interval of time had been, it seemed long ago. She had grown up—a still girl who could show the world a poker face, who could look on a man and hold him with the power of her thoughts.

Karen came down the stairs. Connie went across the room and touched Jubal Frick's arm and smiled at him; and afterwards both women went up to the second floor.

McGinnis cleared his throat and stooped over the fire, poking it up with his boot. Talk didn't come, but the feel

172

of talk was in the air, held back by something. Jubal Frick lifted his old eyes around the circle and knew what kept them that way. His face changed; it settled and showed his sudden age. He had been one of them for a little while and was no longer so. He said quietly: "I better be trackin' for home."

"Have supper before you go," suggested Benbow.

"I believe I will, thank you," said Frick, and went out of the house.

McGinnis said: "Never a bad sort. It's Gore that's got him afraid of his life."

Benbow said: "He stays here tonight."

They had been more or less occupied by their own thoughts. But when he said that all of them swung and looked at him, turning over his words and weighing what he hadn't said. McGinnis drawled: "He doesn't know anything."

"I don't want him to be around Running M in the morning."

McGinnis let a long breath out of his lungs. Beneath the grizzled silver eyebrows a quick light started up. Howland's broad jaws tightened and George Gray stared at Benbow and found nothing there to change the rather sad gravity he always maintained. Joe Gannon looked around him, somehow ill at ease in this company. He said: "Maybe I'd better get out."

Gray said sharply: "Stay here." And then asked Benbow his quiet question: "What is it, Jim?"

"We'll meet at Gannon's before daylight."

"All of us?"

"The more we have the sooner it's over."

McGinnis said: "Gore?"

"If he's there."

"It's high time," stated McGinnis. That was all. They stood there considering it, the talk gone out of them and the grayness of their thoughts staining the room. McGinnis presently nodded at Gordon Howland. They went out together and in a little while those two outfits left Hat. Gray and Gannon waited for their womenfolk, neither man particularly comfortable in the other's presence. Benbow could see it. Gray wasn't fond of his son-in-law; and Gannon, a gaunt and somber man with little grace in him, felt that dislike and had no way of overcoming it.

Gannon said, in a half-humble manner: "I'll do what you want, Jim."

"You better stick to your house as long as Eileen's in it," said Gray gruffly.

Gannon's face showed a quick flush. All of them understood what that meant and the silence was painful. Gannon brought his glance up from the floor and stared at Gray. "George," he said, "I trust my wife."

"News to me," growled Gray.

"I know," assented Gannon, strangely without anger. "But maybe a man can change."

Benbow turned from the house and met Izee in the middle of the yard. "I'm talkin' to Jubal," he said. "But just to make certain, don't let him out of your sight. He stays here tonight and maybe he won't like the idea."

Izee stolidly digested that information. He said: "All right." Clay Rand came out of the mess hall and Izee suddenly said in a lower voice: "Where's Price?"

"I don't know."

"He said he'd be back," grumbled Izee and then swung away as Rand arrived. Rand's glance went after Izee with a pale, swift questing. Benbow observed that and observed also the strung-up condition of Rand's nerves. They kept jerking at his muscles, they kept shaping and reshaping his lips. His eyes were red from a lack of sleep.

"Haven't seen Price?" asked Benbow.

"No."

Benbow stared irritably at his partner. "You fiddle around like you was standing on hot bricks. Been drinking again?"

"I wish to God I was," growled Rand. "I think I'll run into town."

"Not tonight, Clay. We're pulling out before daylight."

Rand jerked up his chin. "What?"

174

"It might help if you went in and talked to Connie," said Benbow and went into the mess hall. He sat down beside Frick. "Jubal," he said, "I'm sorry about this. You'll stay here tonight."

Frick laid down his knife and pushed his plate away. He was bald and fat and his spirit was broken; and Benbow observed how the man's hands began to shake. It was queer to look into Jubal's eyes and see the dead hopelessness there. All at once Frick dropped his head on his hands and began to cry before Benbow's shocked gaze. Benbow got up and left the mess hall as fast as his legs would take him.

George Gray's voice ran up the stairs into the big sittingroom Old Jack Dale had built particularly for his wife. Mrs. Gray said, "Well, I guess George won't wait any longer," and went out, leaving Karen Sanderson and Eileen with Connie.

Connie said: "You're staying here tonight, Karen."

"Thank you," said Karen and watched Eileen Gannon walk restlessly around the room, lighting up the lamps. Darkness had begun to blank out the windows; the wind had lifted. Connie stopped to listen to that wind, her quick features registering all the changes of her mind. Karen said calmly: "What bothers you, Eileen?"

Eileen said: "Nothing."

"Yes," said Karen, her voice resonant and yet soft, "I know how that goes." She got up. "I will go down," she said, and went out of the room.

Eileen said: "How does she know so much? She makes me feel like a kid." Her breasts stirred to the odd agitation of her breath. She came around Connie and stood before her, pale and black-eyed.

"Connie, I've got to tell you something." It took all her breath to say that. She stopped, and blurted out: "About Clay."

Connie rose from the chair. She went over toward a window, not wanting Eileen to face her like that—so

175

upset, so dismally wise in what she knew. She said: "I know it, Eileen."

"What?"

Connie said: "You're not meeting him any more, are you?"

"Oh, that," said Eileen, dully. "No, not any more. But he's been to see me."

"After you married Joe?" asked Connie, half disbelieving.

"It's all right. I sent him away. I guess I was in love with him. I guess I had to be. But the last time he came to the house I got to thinking how he waited in the trees for Joe to go away. Well, you can't love a man who sneaks. I guess I despise him. You know something about him? It's what he can't get that he wants."

Connie said in a half-whispered, indrawn tone: "Yes."

"You know all about that—I knew you did. I guess you just couldn't help making allowance for him. If I thought you didn't know I'd of told you long ago. Because I can't stand seeing you tricked."

"Then what—?"

"He's a crook, Connie!"

"Eileen!"

"I talked it over with Joe. I've told him everything." Afterwards her tone was very quiet and very proud. "I wish folks knew Joe better. He's been dam' good to me. He said it was something you'd better find out for yourself. That it would come out soon enough anyhow. Everybody knows it, except you and Jim. But I can't let you make a mistake, Connie. I can't. He's crooked."

"Eileen—Eileen," said Connie in a falling, begging voice.

"The day after Jim left here for the Yellows I was up in the trees near our place. Clay came into a little clearing and then Gore came up and they talked about Jim. He told Gore that Jim had ridden away from Hat. Gore had sent him to Hat to find that out. I could tell that from the way Gore was speaking."

Connie had stepped away from the lamp. She was in the far shadows of the room, showing a stony composure

176

to Eileen.

Eileen said, in a muffled voice: "You'll hate me now. I can't help it."

"No, Eileen. No."

"He's had his way with me," Eileen said dully. "But I'd kill him before I'd see him hurt you. Connie—do you see? What can a man be like to sell out his best friend?"

"You're sure?" murmured Connie, faintly whispering that question.

"I heard it all. I was so near." Then Eileen lifted her eyes and showed Connie the misery in them. "I think I'd shot him if I'd had a gun. You see, Connie, I still couldn't get him out of my heart. I know I'm small. But I still loved him. And then, after that, I didn't. You can make excuses for a man for a long while. Then you can't make any more excuses."

There was a quietness about Connie hard for Eileen to understand. A quietness, a faraway thinking, a stilled and unreadable expression. Wind pounded at the houses and men's voices ran down the yard and a door slammed below. Connie said: "Then that's why Izee and Price have turned from him."

"They don't know all that I know, but everybody's been talking about Clay. How could he get his money from that little ranch he runs? He's never on it."

"What could be in his heart?" whispered Connie. "What could be?"

"Nothing," said Eileen bitterly. "Nothing!"

Connie came out of the shadows. She touched Eileen's shoulder. She said: "Jim mustn't know."

"How can he help from finding out?"

"He mustn't know," repeated Connie. "He's stuck by Clay so long. There's got to be some way out of it."

She left the room and went downstairs. Joe Gannon stood with his back to the fireplace, his heavy and work-worn frame bent faintly. He watched Connie with his strange, inexpressive face. "My girl about ready to go?"

"Joe," said Connie, "I like you better."

It did something to him. It made a powerful change. He

put his arms behind him and met her glance with a terrible soberness. "Thanks," he muttered. "It's been kind of hard, but I think it's all right now. Maybe—"

The front door opened and Clay Rand walked in quickly, and kicked the door shut with his heel. His eyes, pale and excited, raked both these other people with a sharpness that had a quick, deep suspicion behind it. Gannon's long lips closed together and a blackness rushed over his face and then he turned and put his back to Rand and stood that way.

Connie nodded at the office. Clay turned in there, Connie following him, closing the door. He wheeled around, the paleness of his eyes so bright and so attentive, and all the points of his slim face sharp-whetted. He said: "I'm going back to the ranch, Connie. I'll see you tomorrow."

She said: "You'll never see me again, Clay."

He said: "What?"

She was quietly shaking her head, looking at him and looking through him. Almost impersonally, with neither anger nor pity, with nothing in her eyes for him and nothing on her lips for him. He said again, "What?" And then he was a thin, yellow-haired stranger who stood with his ears turned to the wind, like an animal listening for pursuit and ready to run. Predatory and ungovernably wild, his shallow emotions lifting the bitter-bright flash of his eyes. He said: "What do you know, Connie?"

Her tone was controlled and distant. "How much misery you have left behind. Is there nothing you believe in, Clay?"

He asked his question with an eagerness that showed the cruelty behind. "Gannon tell you anything?"

"No."

He said, more and more aroused: "Who told you? By God, Connie, I've got to know!"

She shook her head, still holding up to him an expressionless face, yet shocked by the plainer and plainer appearance of an ugliness of an actual savagery he no longer bothered to conceal.

178

He said, "Connie," in a demanding tone, and afterwards the silence ran on and they stood opposed like two strangers who had no trust. It went that way, her skin cold with his presence. Fear touched her. He was smiling so heartlessly. "Why should I go away?"

"Do you want Jim to know?"

It was like the point of a knife driving into him. He quit smiling. "That good and great man," he growled. But she could see how it all came back to him and tortured the little decency he had left. "You never would have left Hat," he said. "I knew that. You'd never leave it as long as Benbow was here. If it hadn't been for him things might have been different."

"You had your chance, Clay. But it was all too easy. Nothing holds your interest—except the things you can't have."

He said shrewdly: "I've heard that before." And afterwards his anger shoved its way forward. "What do I owe Benbow? He played his cards well—and you're turned against me. All right, Connie. I don't give up anything, unless I'm tired of it. Now let's see what the good and great man will do."

"Clay—don't ever let him find you with Gore."

"He'll find me, but it won't be with Gore." He crossed the little distance between them and threw his arm around her waist, pulling her up until she winced; and kissed her. He was smiling out his bitter amusement and his pride was a stung, vindictive thing in her eyes. "You never fooled me much, Connie. Benbow was always in the corner of your mind. I knew that even when you didn't. I blame Benbow for it—and I'll make him answer for it."

Gannon called through the door. "You say something, Connie?" Rand opened the door in Gannon's face and pushed him aside—striding across the room as fast as he could go and slamming his way out of the house. Gannon's slow-changing face began to stir up a wicked expression. He said: "You want me to do anything, Connie?" She shook her head, listening into the night

179

and its wind. There was a shout, and afterwards a silence. Rand had left Hat.

Benbow came in a few minutes later. He said: "Where'd Clay go?"

"Home," said Connie.

"He was to have ridden with me."

Gannon said: "He knew you were ridin' tonight?"

"Sure. Why?"

"Nothing," said Gannon. But he wheeled across the room, calling up the stairs. "Eileen. It's time to travel."

Rand plunged into the teeth of the night, the storm inside his head as great as the storm whirling around him. Two hours later, with his horse exhausted by the spurring it had received, he came into his own Anvil yard and saw lamplight burning. He got down and crossed the porch on his toes, his gun drawn out; and weaved aside as he kicked the door open. Gore sat over by the fireplace waiting for him.

Gore said: "Where you been?"

Rand pushed the door shut and laid his back against it; and put away his gun. Gore's tight, searching eyes considered that with an obscure attention. "Dale's funeral," said Rand.

"What you afraid of?"

"Nothing."

"Men don't yank out the smoke-blowers without some reason," said Gore. He sat very still, raking Rand's face with a plainer and plainer watchfulness. "I let Jubal go to the funeral. He ain't home. You see him?"

"Still there when I left."

"Was he?" intoned Gore. One hand idly turned on his knee, the fingers loosening. His hair and his mustache showed a raw-red glinting under the light. He had his hat tipped down and Rand, increasingly warned, saw only the faint gleaming of his eyes. They held an unreadable expression.

"All the outfits there?"

180

"Sure."

"Any talk?"

"The owners got together. I didn't hear what was said."

"And then they all rode home?" suggested Gore in a soft, sliding voice.

"Yeah."

Gore got up slowly. "That all? You didn't catch anything Benbow said?"

Rand pulled off his gloves and looked down at them. He grumbled, "No." But afterwards he lifted his head. The silence was like that—and Gore's thin body had turned fractionally aside. It brought a dry, slow warning from Rand: "Be careful, Cash."

"Something's made you spooky," observed Gore. "I been waitin' here a hell of a long time—and I don't get any news. Where's your ears?"

"Cash—the valley's got my number."

"Didn't you know that would happen?" asked Gore dryly. "I could have told you."

"To hell with it."

"Sure," said Gore. He passed Rand and put his hand to the doorknob. "I've got a job for you tomorrow."

"No," said Rand. "I've got a job of my own."

But Gore's red-rimmed eyes drilled a glance completely through Rand. His voice didn't change. "You'll do as I say, kid. The jobs you do ain't well done. Like Peters."

Rand whipped his shoulders about, squarely facing Gore. "Cash," he said, unsteadily, "you know too much."

"Enough," said Gore evenly. "You stay on this place tomorrow till I see you." He went through the doorway with one unhurried yet complete motion.

Rand listened to the Running M foreman's boots strike across the porch and drop into the snow. All at once he whipped himself away from the door and drew himself rigid, a flash of anxiety showing in his eyes; and then he crossed the room almost on the run, whipped out the light and stood back against a wall, his breath springing fully from his chest.

181

17. Attack

The lights of Hat's mess hall drove narrow streamer across the mealy blackness of the yard. Hat's riders wer in saddle and waiting to go, heavy-shaped in thei overcoats and a little sullen and stiff for want of sleep. I was near three o'clock of a dismal night. Izee slogge through this weather, swinging a lantern upward as h passed each man. The horses were stirring the snow witl their feet. Gippy Collins called: "Where we goin', Izee?" And afterwards Rho Beam growled: "You talk too damn much, Gippy." There were eleven men in this party.

Benbow went back through the mess hall to the mair house and found Connie waiting in the office. She hel her heavy robe tightly together, against the room' cutting cold. Her hair lay loosened along her head and h could tell by her eyes that she hadn't been sleeping. Bu she was, he thought gently, like Old Jack Dale understanding what had to be done and saying nothin, unnecessary. She held herself straight for him, showin, him a pride and a will.

He said: "Price was supposed to be here. Tell hin we're heading for Gannon's ranch."

She said, "Jim," on a sudden impulse, and then put he lips together. They were long and soft—and pale tonight

"What?"

"No. I'll make no scene. You have troubles enough."

He said: "I think part of the crew will be back here late

182

in the afternoon, if things go right. Otherwise I can't tell."

"Jim," she said again, and stood quite still, faint color touching her cheeks; her shoulders were small and square and the darkness across her eyes was breaking before a deep warmth that he couldn't understand. Once he had known this girl better than she had known herself. But she had grown up and he had lost all touch with her thinking. He stepped nearer, trying to make out what her glance seemed to be telling him, trying to understand what that poised stillness of her body meant. It helped him none. Izee's voice called through the wind.

"Benbow."

He said, quick and blunt, "You make a man want you, Connie," and wheeled back through the mess hall and out into the yard. He swung to the saddle and led off. This column crossed the river's bridge and sunk into the shapeless, pointless night. Nothing showed substance ahead; behind him Hat's lights grew dimmer and dimmer behind the snowfall.

At a quarter of five, after two hours of steady, speechless riding, the peaked shape of Gannon's house lifted vaguely through the whirling, snow-laced black. A rider slid across the path ahead, and turned and came nearer. He called, "Benbow," and then came on up to make sure.

The yard was filled with the shapes of waiting men and horses. The point of a cigarette glinted somewhere and afterwards a quick voice said: "Pinch out that smoke." Benbow left his men and crossed to the house, noting how Gannon had pulled the window shades and blocked the windows' edges to conceal the inner lights. Benbow opened the door and went through and shut it. McGinnis and Gordon Howland and Gray were waiting here for him, with Gannon in the background. They hadn't built a fire and the lamp's glow was dim; and all of them stood glum and cold inside their coats. But it wasn't only the cold. It was what they were about to do that made them show Benbow the taciturn edge of their features. Nelson

McGinnis' eyes were narrowly set, with a little glitter coming through. Howland was without much expression. George Gray shook his head, more fully aware of the way the night might go and saddened visibly by that thought.

McGinnis said: "How many men you bring, Jim?"

"Twelve, with me."

"That's thirty-two of us altogether. It will be enough. Running M's crew and Riley's boys won't size up more than twenty-odd, unless they got recruits."

"Where's Price?"

"I ain't seen him."

George Gray said: "He knew about this. He'll show up."

"We won't wait," said Benbow. "It'll be daylight in an hour."

"It's your say," murmured McGinnis.

"George, take your boys—and Gordy's—and follow the Ramparts trail into the canyon. Plug it up so no one from Running M gets through to Riley's camp. Nelson and I'll reach Running M by the front door. I guess that's all there's to it."

Gannon said: "What'll I do?"

"Stay here. You've got Eileen—and I wouldn't guess what might come back along this way durin' the day."

There was a silence, the room turning colder and colder. Benbow said: "Well, come on."

But Howland spoke up then. "I want to get this clear. What's the limit on this thing?"

They had all been considering it; Benbow could see that. They had been turning it over in their minds. It surprised him a little, for he knew how they felt about Gore. They had their minds made up and he couldn't see the sense of the question. He said: "We're breaking something up. How do you break a thing? That's your answer, isn't it? I want Gore and Riley and Kell. If any of the others get away that's their luck. They won't come back. But they've got to make their own chances. You understand? They get no chances from us. It has to be that way."

Howland said: "No exceptions?" His voice was down-bearing and insistent. Benbow stared at him. Here was something else. He didn't know what it was, but all of them wanted to know. He could see it in the manner in which they watched him.

"No," he murmured. "No exceptions."

"I guess," said McGinnis, not looking directly at Benbow, "we better be on our way."

"The trip by the rim is the longest," said Benbow. "We'll give George a ten-minute start."

Gannon turned down the lamp wick and under cover of this semidarkness Benbow opened the door and led his party back to the yard. Gray and Howland were calling up their men; and he climbed into the saddle and waited while Crescent and Block T assembled and filed away in single column, up through the trees to the Ramparts trail. They were soon lost in this driving dark.

His own men and those of McGinnis' Diamond-and-a-Half were grouped around him, all bowed vaguely against the weather and nobody speaking. But they were considering what waited for them in front of Running M at daylight. He could feel the force of that thoughtfulness press against him, even as his own mind kept sliding away from this night and its cold wind and from this night's gray business. There were strange memories in his head, each laying before his eyes a picture bright and clear. Of roundup time in the valley, with campfires burning high against the Indian summer haze and men's voices low and lazy in that pleasant dusk. Of Price and Izee and Clay standing by Faro Charley's bar, all smiling at something said. Of Jack Dale seated in the office chair and wistfully watching the far valley. Of Connie standing before him in the office, the shapeliness of her body only half-concealed by the old woolly robe she liked to wear—and looking up to him with her eyes mirroring something he couldn't understand.

McGinnis said: "The ten minutes is up."

He turned his horse and McGinnis came beside him, and Hat's crew and the Diamond-and-a-Half crew fell into a following column. They walked away from Gannon's, keeping the heavy shadow of the Ramparts close by their right flank. The wind was at their backs, setting up half a roar in their ears and wildly driving the snow before it. The horses made heavy going in these drifts.

The world was still lightless and there was no warmth in him; at this dreary hour he saw himself more clearly and less mercifully than at any time in his life. Jack Dale had said he was a fighter. It had seemed a compliment, coming from that hard and heady old man. But now he understood how much more Jack had left unsaid. It wasn't just the ability to fight that Jack had marked. It was also the ability to kill. This was why McGinnis and the others had wanted him to lead the way. They trusted him because he was honest, yet they had pegged him in their minds as having no more conscience than Gore or Riley when it came to using a gun. They figured him a killer. They put the responsibility on him, not wanting it on their minds afterwards.

The thought led him down into the gray bottom of his mind. He saw all his pleasant days behind, he saw all his hope behind, and then he had that picture of Connie again, gently smiling at him and holding her real thoughts away from him—too kind to tell him of that hardness that she also saw in him. It was Clay's laughter and Clay's way of life she wanted.

This was the end of his thinking. It had led him to a blind end, and now with the day beginning to send a first gray stain through the half-blizzard, he closed his mind completely. Nelson's voice seemed muffled.

"There it is. No lights showin' yet."

The mouth of Granite Canyon opened vaguely. Running M's house and sheds crouched before them, barely visible behind the streaky film of the wind-rushed snow. Benbow swung directly in toward the place, the column breaking without order and coming up into a single loose line abreast, the heavy drifts absorbing all sound. Running M's house became distinct and black.

"Chance for trouble here," said McGinnis in a trigger-set voice.

They were in the yard, and stopped. Benbow said: "Spread up against the walls of the house—and the bunkhouse."

He got down and went forward. Nelson had disappeared but Izee tramped forward and stood beside Benbow. Men were ducking around the house, merging with the shadows. Benbow said, "Well, let's get it over with," and walked directly to the porch. Izee grumbled: "Watch that door." Benbow crossed the porch and put his hand to the door. It gave way before him, the wind throwing it around and slamming it against the wall. Flattened beside the casing, Benbow heard that echo rattle back into the house's rear rooms. Heat came out of the door and coals began to sparkle in the fireplace at the room's end—fanned by the sudden draught.

Men were running back from the bunkhouse. Boots hit the porch and broke the long quiet. Benbow said: "Stop that!" But a man called urgently: "Nobody in the bunkhouse."

Benbow thrust himself into the room. Izee came after him and the rest of the party, turned nervous and impatient by waiting, followed. Benbow strode across the floor, remembering the layout of this place. There was a kitchen behind the living-room and a couple of bedrooms adjoining this main room. No upstairs. He reached one of the bedrooms and found its door standing open. Paused again beside that opening he thought he saw a shape lying on the bed; and lifted his gun on that shape. "Cash," he said gently. "Cash."

There wasn't any answer. Two windows began to show their gray squares against the dull dark of the room. He braced himself against the casing and jumped in, and came beside the bed, his hand ripping at the quilts. It was the quilts, thrown carelessly on the bed, that had lent the illusion of a man lying there. Izee called across the house, from the other bedroom. "Nobody here."

Men were running down the porch, returning from the

farther sheds. McGinnis spoke from the front door. "Jim."

Benbow turned into the living-room and found it filling with the rest of the crew. They were restlessly scraping the floor with their boots—dissatisfied and keyed up. "Jim," said McGinnis, "they ain't here."

"How about the barn?"

"Nobody on this place."

Somebody growled, "Sold," and began to swear.

Benbow wheeled over to the fireplace. His foot struck a wood box and, reaching down, he touched a layer of paper lying on it. He put away his gun and crushed the paper into loose balls.

"What next?" said McGinnis.

Benbow put the paper into the fireplace, dismally crouched by it. Somebody suddenly smashed one of the room's windows. The paper caught fire and Benbow got up and carried it to a corner of the room and dropped it against the wall. There was a quick rise of light in the room, shining against the wind-whipped surface of these men's watching faces. One of them said, "It won't catch," and ran out of the place and afterwards the flame died and the charred paper turned dull.

"Somebody," said Nelson McGinnis, "talked."

"Cash always had long ears," answered Benbow, evenly.

"If they're gone from here they'll be gone from Riley's," fretted McGinnis.

"They won't go far," replied Benbow.

"You take it easy enough," said McGinnis brusquely. The night wore on his nerves.

"There's plenty of time," observed Benbow. "I know Cash. He won't run away."

"He's got the jump on us now."

Benbow's long interval of calmness came to an ending; his voice bit into McGinnis.

"What the hell do you expect, Nelson? A summer's vacation? You'd better make up your mind to take home some empty saddles."

A man ran in. He said: "I got some hay from the barn." There was a moment's silence, until he struck a match and dropped it on the hay he had dumped in the corner. A quick pale curl of fire licked up.

Benbow said: "We'll go up the canyon—" And bit off that sentence between his teeth and wheeled and rushed for the door, throwing aside other men standing near it. Down the canyon, twisted and stretched thin by the wind, came the echoing bursts of a sudden-started fusillade.

He was across the snow and in the saddle, the rest of the party pouring after him. He heard Izee shout, "Wait a minute, Jim," and wheeled into the canyon without delay. The Ramparts trail dropped into the canyon only a quarter mile ahead, which was where he had sent Gray and Howland. And from that spot the firing had originated.

There was a ragged aftervolley and no more. Silence settled down and the thick shadows of the canyon walls blocked out the pale stain of a daylight ineffectually filtering through the dense stain of snow overhanging the Yellows. The drifts in here were thicker and his pony labored against them at a half-bucking run. A shape drifted down the canyon toward him and stopped. A yelling shout sailed on.

"Benbow! They're all up the canyon!"

He caught up with this rider and went past. He heard Gray's voice sing out, loud yet unexcited; and in another minute he struck Gray's outfit head on. They were all grouped together and some of them were kneeling in the snow. A match flared and soon died, but by its brief light he had seen a man lying there, face upward.

Gray was saying: "Who's down?"

It was Howland who answered from the kneeling bunch. "Harry Train."

"Harry," called Gray, "you hurt?"

Benbow's outfit was crowding forward. He listened for Harry Train to speak, even as all these other silent men listened. There wasn't any answer and a little later

189

Howland stood straight. It was a sufficient verdict; Train was dead. Benbow pushed his horse by them. He said, "Come on—come on," and led the way. The snow here had been broken down and the footing made easier by Gore's men running before them. George Gray followed closely at his heels, his voice very calm in this wild night. "They were drifting down and we opened up. I guess they figured on joinin' Cash at Running M. They'll be at Riley's. The light's getting bad—for us. If I were you, Jim, I'd take it a little slow from here on in."

"It was the whole bunch you ran into. Cash pulled out of the ranch."

"God bless us," called Gray. "I guess it's a fight. There's no doubt in my mind but what he's waitin' for us now."

They were traveling freely through the tramped snow. Gray pulled abreast and the rest of the riders had closed up. It was still definitely dark, yet here and there little sprays of dismal light broke down from the canyon walls, like waterfalls frozen to the rock. A horse stood crosswise in the trail ahead and Benbow lifted his gun at it, seeing no rider's shadow sitting above. Before he had quite made up his mind the horse wheeled and stampeded away. Riderless.

"One of 'em anyhow," grumbled George Gray.

The canyon trail broadened. They ran around a long bend. Wind came at them, driving denser gusts of snow from the hills and at the end of that bend's wide sweep Indian Riley's house lights flashed out quick signals. Benbow drew up—scanning the foreground and seeing nothing definite through this mealy air except the shine of the lights. His men were spreading beside him, breathing a little from the long run.

Izee said: "They'll make a stand."

Gray said: "I been in those shacks. Just inch lumber covered over with paper. A bullet would cut through easy."

"Drag out the rifles," said Benbow. "We walk the rest of the way. Gippy, you and Bill Best stick with the

190

horses." He was down in the snow, slipping out his Winchester.

McGinnis said: "I don't like the idea of those lights. Looks funny."

"We'll throw a circle around the settlement," declared Benbow. "Come on." He led the way, sticking to the road until at the end of three hundred feet he began to see the house walls take definite form through the snow. At this point he wheeled and led his crew into the deep drifts, meaning to make a circle. All the front windows showed their lights and he was abreast the farthest house and on the point of turning again to draw his loop more securely around Riley's camp when abruptly a yonder voice rose to some kind of a shout and all the lights died.

He reared around, calling back, "Go ahead!" And flung up his Winchester and fired at the vague square of the nearest house wall. The sound of the gun flattened out through the windy air and was whipped away; and hard on the heels of that report all the guns of the crew let go. McGinnis was far back along the line and McGinnis' yell sailed above the crackling noise. "Come on—come on!" The yell seemed to suck the whole outfit back toward the house farthest from Benbow. He could see the men nearest him plunge through the drifts toward that house; and afterwards he lost sight of them completely. Light flickered up in the window of the shack straight ahead— the quick, heatless light of a gun pumping out its fast shots. In the general melee he didn't hear the gun's individual report, yet he felt its bullets whip by.

It was that flash which pulled him forward. He fought out of the waist-high drifts and reached the road, swinging away from the window as he ran up. It was ten yards to the shanty's wall and he had at last, he realized, come into the marksman's definite survey. The gun went off again, the whole shack booming out that crowded report. The flash of its muzzle light leaped toward him. A long, low dive carried him against the base of the shanty wall. Crouched there he lifted his gun at a sharp angle, threw a bullet at the window and ran past the nearest

191

corner, down the shanty's blind side wall and around to the house's other face in time to see a shape make a turning jump out of an open door, strike the ground and come to his feet on the run. Benbow took a snap shot and missed; and afterwards he lost the man in the farther dark. But he rested where he was, hearing somebody else creep across the floor of the shanty.

The fight whirled around the far end of the settlement, the guns snarling up a higher and higher anger there. Horses stood a few yards back from the settlement, snorting out their fear. Stray lead slapped the wall of the middle house, producing drumlike echoes. The man in this nearest shanty moved again, his boots audibly scraping. Benbow lifted the weight off his knee and saw the black outline of the door; and went through it in one straight rush. A man here yelled: "Who's that?" And then let go without answer. The room roared and powder smoke stung Benbow's eyes. He swung and fired, and made one wild leap aside—and heard the fellow go down with a sweeping crash, carrying over a chair as he fell.

Men were rushing up from the lower end of the settlement. The firing hauled around and lead began to bite more freely through the boards of the shack, the sound like that of the sharp strike of a finger against a taut sheet of paper. It dropped Benbow to his knees; and in this manner he reached the door and saw the vague whirling of men and horses beyond. The pressure McGinnis had brought to bear upon Gore's men had dislodged them from the first shack. They were giving way. They were running. He heard a voice sail high above the other voices—the sonorous, wide-lunged tone of Indian Riley. "Kell—stick close! Kell!"

Benbow came to his knees and cradled the Winchester against his shoulder. It was point-blank range at the heaviest mass shadow made by Gore's men as they fought to reach their horses. He let go on that general shadow, firing with the cold method of a marksman. He heard men cry above all this sound and all this terror. A horse bolted by. Riders rushed away. A shape staggered forward and

192

dropped and a furious gust of lead began to slap the front of the house—pot shots taken by men caught in their own confusion. They were racing away, headed for the deeper Yellows in a streaming line. He kept firing until his hammer snapped down on an empty chamber.

The rest of the outfit swept forward. McGinnis was howling out Benbow's name at one breath and using another to cry up Gippy Collins with the horses.

Benbow called, "Stop the shootin'," and walked away from the shack. His foot struck something that rolled and groaned. He could hear his outfit beating through all the shacks. He knelt down searching for a match. The man on the ground said, "Never mind," faintly. Benbow found his match and lighted it and had his one quick look. He got up then and went on to where Izee and McGinnis stood. Izee came close by until he could see Benbow's long face in the muddy gloom. He said, gruffly: "Where the hell you been?"

The horses were coming up. Men were moving in and out of the shacks; somebody had lighted a lamp in that shack around which the fighting had centered. The rest of them made a group here, waiting for Benbow to talk.

McGinnis said: "Damn the luck!"

Benbow called out: "Set 'em afire." He stood there, the network of trails through the Yellows unrolling before his mind's eye. The main road cut through the hills and passed on to the reservation, but it wasn't the trail Gore would take. He knew Gore too well. As long as Gore's men hung together, he would stick to the hills; and even if the outfit fell apart Gore would stay behind until he had left his mark in somebody's hide. The Running M foreman had no fear in him, and no forgiveness.

He said, as an afterthought: "How do we stand?"

"Your cook," said McGinnis, "got shot in the leg. Otherwise we were out in the dark and they couldn't hit us."

"I told him to stay with the horses."

"He forgot he was a cook, I guess."

193

"Izee—send Gippy and Rho Beam back with Best."

Light began to flicker inside the shacks. Izee went away. Gippy Collins, over by the horses, suddenly took to complaining about his luck. Day definitely crawled through the thick, snow-laced air and men's faces appeared more distinctly before him.

"Let's go," said Benbow.

"Go where?" McGinnis asked. "They're scattered all over the hills by now. This snow's hard to get through."

"Hard for them, too," said Benbow.

"They'll scatter."

"As long as there's tracks to follow, we'll follow. What did we come up here for?"

"You're the boss," said McGinnis.

He went back to his horse. Fire threw spirals of smoke out of the shack doors and began to brighten the broken windows. His outfit collected slowly; and he said, "If you boys are too tired to ride, I'll go on alone," and spurred away.

"That's a little bit hard," called Howland. But they came on, closing the gap. The tracks of Gore's outfit made a churned trail all up the shallowing canyon and this trail he followed as fast as the footing would permit. Half an hour later, with the day as fully lighted as it ever would be, they came out of the canyon's head and reached a high meadow where the pass road forked. One way led on to the reservation. The other turned for Cherokee. When Benbow stopped here McGinnis and Howland and Gray came up. The four of them read that story closely.

"Split."

"Gore's lost some of his boys. They're travelin' out. Cherokee's the way Gore's heading."

"How you know it ain't Gore who's headed for the reservation?"

"He'll never leave as long as he's got men."

Gray said quietly: "I agree with that."

They swung down the Cherokee trailing, following the definite tracks of Gore's diminished outfit. A mile

194

onward they came upon a discarded hat. Benbow dismounted and nudged it over with his boot and saw its sweatband clotted with blood. There was a deep dent in the soft snow shoulders beside the trail, where somebody had fallen, and had been lifted again. He pushed ahead, caution holding him to a walk. Second-growth pine crowded against the trail on either side and the way was winding and tricky, affording the risk of an ambush. Sheltered thus by the trees, they had a little release from the wind but the snow kept driving down, turning the day duller and duller. And then, near nine o'clock in the morning Benbow halted again. One of Gore's men sprawled full length before them in the snow, dead.

McGinnis said: "That was Joe Lane. He came on Running M two years ago. I remember him well."

Joe Lane lay face upward and somebody, touched by pity, had crossed his arms. There had been a sudden confusion in Gore's party here, for horses' hoofs churned the snow in all directions.

"Split again," said McGinnis. "Most of 'em hit south toward the reservation, accordin' to this sign."

"Yes," said Benbow. But he kept watching the trail that led straight on to Cherokee. There wasn't any break in its smooth surface—no indication of passage that way. A pair of Gore's men had apparently broken back in the direction of the Two Dance; the rest had lined out for the reservation.

"Old Apache trick," said Howland. "They'll all join again down there. That's the way we want to go. This bunch ain't far ahead. If we hustle—"

"Gordy," said Benbow, "you take half the outfit and go that way. The rest of us will try Cherokee. If there's no business to be had we'll catch up with you."

"They wouldn't stop in Cherokee."

"Anyhow," said McGinnis, "it's damned poor business splittin' our party. Cash is a smart soldier. Maybe that's what he wants us to do."

Benbow shook his head, not immediately speaking. He let his glance remain a moment on the dead Joe Lane, trying to analyze the story, trying to understand why Gore had left him here. It was a deliberate thing, or else it meant they were breaking up in confusion and had no time for Lane. And that fresh, unmarked trail leading toward Cherokee meant something, too. Cash Gore was a clear image in his mind—the narrow and red-rimmed eyes as cold and as weighing as in actual life. Gore would never bend and he would never surrender. He nursed his hatreds like an Indian; and in him was a nerveless cunning.

"No," said Benbow, "he won't leave the Yellows. Not until all hope is gone for him." And moved into the Cherokee trail. Gordon Howland broke off to the south with half the outfit; the other half followed Benbow, with McGinnis audibly dissatisfied.

"I lay a bet we're walkin' into a trap."

Once again George Gray broke his habitual silence: "No—I think Jim's right. Cash wouldn't leave until he had his crack at Jim."

Half an hour later the trail curved down a gradual slope and fell into the lower end of Cherokee's single street. Stopped at the edge of the timber, Benbow had a long look at that snow-blurred street. Half a dozen horses stood in front of the hotel; and one man stood by the horses with a rifle cradled across his arm, too indistinct in this weather to be identified.

"They're eatin' in the hotel," said Benbow. He turned back, motioning to his party. "We circle and get behind the hotel."

McGinnis shook his head again, made spooky by doubt and that impelled Benbow to say, gently: "I think he's in the hotel with Kell and Riley. I'd scour hell to round 'em up. The rest don't matter to me. Turn around, Nelson. We circle."

196

18. The Flame Rises

After Gore had gone from Rand's house, the latter stood irresolutely against the wall listening into the yonder run of the wind with a growing care. He had whipped out the light and though the fireplace threw some glow across the room, he stood well away from its reflection, half expecting Gore to put a shot through the window. Gore had lost faith in him and he knew the Running M foreman's way of summarily acting upon his suspicions.

He stood in that attitude for a good twenty minutes and then still nervous and unsure he crawled over to his bunk in the corner and stretched out. A swift explosion of wood in the fireplace sent him upright on the bed and for a while he sat that way, a fine sweat covering his forehead. Presently he rose and locked the door and returned to the bunk.

Tired as he was, sleep seemed impossible. By temperament a restless man, he had a vivid mind that tortured him now with all the things it held, with all the thoughts it kept reviving. He laid a palm over his eyes, as though to break up the images flashing brighter and brighter across his inner vision; and he spoke aloud: "Never mind—never mind." But the sound of his voice was high and unnatural and brought no relief.

For him there was no hope at all. He had reached the end of the trail as long ago, in his more bitterly candid moments, he had known he some day would. There was in him that sense of prophecy he could never control, and a strange faculty that stood aside and saw realistically what the ungovernable and undisciplined side of him was doing. Sometimes he had made his resolutions. After a bad night at the poker table he had made them. After some of his escapades with women he had made them and sometimes, in Benbow's company, he had made them feeling the shame of his position. It never mattered, for recklessness soon erased his good intentions and his strong appetite for the sensations of life broke through his little moments of honesty. Some balance wheel had been left out of him.

He stood in a ruin entirely of his own making, his hopes and his fears inexorably tangled. He was gripped and shaken fiercely by a morbid self-hatred. He had killed Price out of pride. He couldn't face the disgust in Price' eyes; he couldn't endure the thought of Price telling Benbow how much he knew. It was this last thought that had driven him to pull the gun on Price, for even in his most bitterly quarrelsome moments he needed Benbow' loyalty and could not face the prospect of losing that loyalty.

Yet he knew he was soon to lose it. Somehow the valley had caught wind of him. Connie knew. And as soon as Benbow, riding out against Gore, began to untangle the treachery that threaded every trail in the Yellows, he too would know.

So, he had no chance of surviving this coming war, and it was the necessity of making up his mind to some definite move that ragged at him and perplexed him and left him confused. He was through on Hat and he was soon to be through with Benbow. He had no remaining friend, then, in the valley; no welcome at any ranch. And his partnership with Gore was over, with Gore's mind frozen against him and the threat of a killing in the wind.

Every road was closed except the one Price Peters had pointed out. He could still saddle up and leave the valley

But as he thought of it the little devils of his mind woke his pride and his recklessness again. He remembered how many doors had once been opened to him and how easy his way had been. He recalled all that he once was—and what he would instantly be admitting if he fled—a man who had betrayed his friends and made his profit out of a ranch that would one day have been his own. To run would be to acknowledge that. Wild anger rushed through him, knocking down the little sanity he owned. And then fear chilled his nerves and made a lump in his stomach and the sweat came again to his forehead. Thus, spun in the vortex of this terrible, desperate unreason, he fell into a fitful sleep. . . .

He found himself suddenly awake, standing on his feet in the middle of the room's cold blackness. The fire was dead and the wind rushed along the walls of the house and rattled up the loose boards and went banging away among the movable objects in the yard. The half-blizzard had swung around and now came blowing up from the direction of the Running M; and out of that quarter he thought he heard the wind-stretched and distance-thinned rumor of gunfire.

He lighted a match and got out his watch, warned by the faint gray shape of the windows. It was near six o'clock then and suddenly there was in his mind one driving impulse, which was to pack the dead Price Peters to some other quarter of the hills so that suspicion of the killing would not fall on him. He had no idea what had borne this impulse to him, but it was there when he woke and it pressed him in a way that would not let him alone.

He ran out of the house to the barn and found his horse standing there with the saddle still on; he had left it in front of the house the night before and had forgotten it. The sound of firing came on distinctly, and then died. Moving around the barn's gray gloom, he haltered another horse and slapped on a pack rig and led both animals down past his house into the Ramparts trail. He pushed his way up through the snow, and had a bad

199

fifteen minutes lashing Price to the pack rig. Afterwards, in the saddle, he sat still considering where he ought to go. The firing had originated somewhere in the canyon above Running M, which meant that Benbow had struck Riley's settlement. The country that way wasn't safe. In the open valley it might be, since the heavy run of snow and the blanketing grayness of morning was still shelter from prying eyes. And it was on the other side of the canyon somewhere that he wanted to leave Price.

He dropped from the Ramparts into the open valley, to discover immediately that Running M was afire, three separate yellow-red blobs of light swelling out above the darkness and the screen of snow. Immediately he retreated farther into the valley and thus circled the burning ranch. Daylight crept dismally through the violent weather when he closed in upon the Ramparts and bucked his way up its stiff slope to the trail. At this point he was not far from the Gannon ranch. Behind him lay Granite Canyon and behind him, at the end of the lead rope, followed the grisly fact of a murder, that fact haunting him and burning its terror deeper and deeper into his brain.

It was his intention to ride straight along the Ramparts to an abandoned cabin well down by the edge of Hat, but the light of the morning, feeble as it was, made him more and more fearful and caused him to change his mind. There was another trail leading upward toward Cherokee and this he decided to take when he reached its junction directly ahead.

He had, in fact, reached that junction and had swung into the trail when a voice reached out from the rear and challenged him.

He jerked himself about in the saddle—afterward knowing it to be a fatal motion—and thrust his glance back against the dim-showing pine trunks. For a moment he saw nobody; and then a man stepped out from one of the pines and called again: "Who's that?"

Wind distorted the voice and the snow blurred Rand's

eyes. He couldn't identify the man, but his reaction was to snatch up his gun and throw a shot back there and to slash his spurs across the flanks of his pony, driving it on at a violent jump. The pack horse, wrenched by the sudden tightening of the lead rope began to buck and then the rope slid from Rand's fist and when he looked behind again he saw the pack horse trotting toward the Ramparts trail. And a gun began to bang methodically and persistently through the wind.

The shots were wide of the mark, slapping against the close-ranked trees. For a moment Rand came to a full halt and searched the wild reaches of his mind for counsel. It did him no good. The violence of his fear grew greater and greater, with the rush of the wind and the pounding reports of the gun drowning out the last of his coolness. It went this way until he could no longer stand it. Throwing his spurs into the horse again he fled up the trail toward Cherokee.

He knew there was no longer any safety for him in this country. His only possible chance of survival now was to reach Cherokee and head out into the reservation country. He doubted if the half-hidden marksman had identified him, but the bolting pack horse bore his brand—and Hat's posse would soon be on his trail. It was the breaking of the lead rope which inexorably damned him.

Later, traveling fast on a half-exhausted pony, he circled Karen Sanderson's meadow and struck straight for Cherokee. He felt the town was safe, since Benbow's posse was engaged with Gore off to the east in the Granite Canyon district; and though he would have preferred to avoid the town he knew he had to stop there for a fresh horse.

Cherokee was a town that had been literally cut out of the pine forest, with the trees marching down within ten feet of the hotel's back entrance. Dismounted there in

201

the pine's shelter, Benbow waited for his outfit to crowd around him.

"This door goes into the kitchen. The dining-room is on the left of the kitchen. They're still eating. One man's out on the street with the horses. Izee—you take a couple boys and duck down the side of the building and nail that fellow. And keep the street clear. We go in through the kitchen, as fast as possible."

Izee nodded, wiggling his finger at two men to stick with him. McGinnis and George Gray were beside Benbow, with the rest of the outfit close behind. Benbow said, softly, "Brace yourselves," and then left the trees. Izee and his two followers jumped at the sound of his voice, like racers leaving the mark, and went down the hotel's side on the dead run. Benbow reached the kitchen door and wrenched it open. A pale old fellow swung away from the kitchen—some strange expression licking its heat across his eyes. Benbow pushed him aside, and made a long dive at the dining-room door. The scuffle of boots whirled up a telltale racket in the kitchen and when he reached the door he hit it hard and low with his shoulder and drove it out of its latch, afraid of time's swift passage.

The door sprang back and he was in the dining-room, with Nelson and George Gray at his rear and with Nelson howling: "Stand fast!" It was a narrow room, a long table running down toward the lobby exit; and at the foot of that table he saw four men's faces swing in a white blur. All this he caught in fractional smears of motion. Ben Kell started to rise. Indian Riley dropped a cup and tried to run, his short and heavy body caught between table and chair. One man yelled and made no move at all; and the fourth, already risen, wheeled like a cat and threw himself out of the dining-room, his boots pounding across the lobby floor.

Kell was on his feet but motionless, his giant's body straining for action and yet locked against it. Benbow called, "Easy, boys," and watched all those three faces freeze. Indian Riley quietly placed both his hands on the

202

table and said in a voice so easy and so indifferent that Benbow never forgot it: "I guess that's it." The third man followed Riley's action, his cheeks as pale as paper. The escaping man went through a side window of the hotel, leaving the crash of splintered glass behind him; outside one gunshot ripped the steady whine of wind. That was all. Some of Benbow's men were careening back through the kitchen in an effort to cut off the fugitive. The others had pushed into the dining-room. Silence fell, dry and inflammable. Benbow saw the giant Kell's eyes throw out a hot light and knew the man was ready to make a try. It was Riley who said in the same toneless way: "Never mind, Ben. What the hell? They'd like to kill us."

Benbow walked behind Riley and reached down to the man's holster. He lifted Riley's gun, emptied the cylinder and threw the gun into a corner, and went around to Kell. "Arms up, Ben," he murmured, and watched Kell's huge muscles stir beneath his shirt in rising. He got Kell's gun and the third man's gun. He said: "Walk into the lobby."

Riley got slowly out of his chair. He was a copper-skinned man, with a long full mouth and eyes as black as obsidian. There was wildness in him—a primitive wildness—and a daring. He was smiling a little as he walked into the lobby and his voice was the voice of a man schooled to hide whatever he might feel. They all went into the lobby, and stopped there.

Riley grinned at Benbow. "Your turn now, Jim. Well, it goes like that. You're sure hell for fightin'."

Izee tramped in from the street, obviously angry with himself. "I missed that fellow by the horses. He's gone."

McGinnis called: "Where's that other boy who ran?"

"Never came out the front door," said Izee.

"Let 'em go," Benbow said. "They took their chances and they had luck. That's all right." He stared at the third man caught in the dining-room; this one's face was altogether colorless and his eyes were sprung marble-round. His nerve was gone and it was hard for Benbow to

203

look at that staring, half-deadened expression. He said irritably: "Who are you?"

Riley said carelessly: "Frankie ain't much, Jim. I only took him on a month ago."

"He's a rustler," pointed out McGinnis definitely.

"Not much of one," grunted Riley. "See for yourself. He's lost his sand and he can't talk. He's small potatoes. Let him go."

McGinnis said immediately: "You know the rules, Benbow. You laid it down. No exceptions."

The rest of the outfit, having scoured the street, came back into the lobby. George Gray said: "Five horses. That accounts for this bunch. Three men here and two that got away. Where's Gore?"

But Benbow had his mind busy with this undersized Frankie who stood there before the crowd and slowly shriveled. Frankie was young but he knew what was ahead of him and fear sent its anesthetic along his nerves and the surface of his eyes showed a greater and greater dullness.

"Frankie," murmured Benbow, "how old are you?"

The answer was a long time coming, so long that the intervening silence grew painful and Izee cleared his throat and looked at the floor. "Twenty-one," whispered Frankie.

"No exceptions," warned McGinnis.

Benbow didn't hear. For him there was a break in the dismal run of the hours, a need for some warmth after all the brutal riding, for some kindness after the cry of men's voices in full pursuit. It didn't show on the broad-boned face, but it was in the soft slide of his talk. "Take your horse and go, Frankie."

McGinnis protested: "No, Jim. No!"

Feeling flooded across Frankie's pinched cheeks. He drew back his head, his lips stretching wide. He was trembling at the knees, he was breathing like a man starved for air. He sighed, "Thanks," and looked around at Indian Riley and said, "Thanks," again, in an exhausted voice. Riley shrugged his shoulders, showing

204

nothing to the kid but scorn; and after that Frankie stumbled out of the lobby and in the dead silence they heard him ride down Cherokee's street.

McGinnis said bitterly: "I don't like it."

Benbow was curt with his answer. "Be quiet, Nelson."

McGinnis whipped a gusty breath out of his nostrils and showed a plain affront. But he didn't say anything more. Ben Kell's eyes were sullen in the way they slid around the crowd, covertly looking for a chance. Indian Riley was soundlessly laughing.

"I never doubted you was tough, Jim. But I didn't know you had a heart." He quit laughing and shook his head, a faint wistfulness breaking his contained manner. "I wish—" and then shrugged his shoulders. "Well, let's get this done."

Benbow said: "Where's Cash?"

Indian Riley stared expressionlessly at him. "Don't ask me dam' fool questions."

There was in Cash Gore an acute perception of trouble, a kind of animal's intuition. After he left Rand's cabin, the warning of something in the wind was very strong. He thought about it all the way back to Running M, and afterwards kept turning it over and over in his head. He had studied Benbow through the last two years with a deep interest and knew how the man's mind worked; and now he weighed Benbow's probable reaction to all the recent happenings, trying to strike an answer. There was no answer, but the smell of the night was bad and so, because he never disobeyed these intangible rumors when they came to him, he suddenly made his decision, called out the crew and left Running M. This was around three in the morning. Going up the canyon, he joined with Riley. Near six, just before daylight, he started back to scout the ranch. It was then that he ran directly into Benbow's men and precipitated the fight.

Much as he had expected trouble, it caught him off

205

guard and the wickedness of Benbow's attack upon Riley's settlement snapped the backbone of his outfit. They went up the pass road pell-mell and when he gathered them up at the Cherokee trail crossing he knew that he couldn't hold all of them. Two of the Running M crew and one of Riley's riders were dead in the settlement; and Joe Lane, sitting like a drunk in the saddle, had a bad crease in the side of his face. It was the sight of Joe Lane that broke his party exactly in half—the dissenting bunch simply pulling out in the direction of the reservation. He didn't try to argue with them.

Later, not more than a mile from Cherokee, Joe Lane rolled out of the saddle, a dead man before he struck the snow; and that sight and the grisly feel of the day broke up his party again. There was a little show of trouble here, for Gore drew his gun and laid it on the crowd that wanted to drift. He said: "I've fed you whelps a long time."

One man said, boldly: "Go to hell, Cash. I don't die for thirty dollars a month. You got eggs to fry. You fry 'em."

Indian Riley laughed at that, and still was laughing when they left. Gore rapped out: "What's so funny?"

Riley said: "I guess we're through in this country, Cash. Benbow's kind of tough. I was thinkin'—fun don't last forever. I didn't know that."

"We'll see," said Cash.

Riley stared at Gore with a shrewd consideration. "He's in your craw, and you want your try at him? Sure. Well, you're fast, Cash. Maybe you're faster than he is. I recall, though, that the man is lucky. Well, luck's a thing a man can't fight. I think ours has plumb run out. We better drift."

There were six of them. Cash and Riley and Kell; the kid Frankie, and Joe Rambo and Dode Perris. They were all seasoned except the kid Frankie. Nobody knew why he stayed. After the second bunch had left, Cash took the others along that trail a little way and had each man break into the timber toward Cherokee, in this manner hiding their tracks. They came together again at the edge of town and rode directly to the hotel for a meal.

It was a town Cash trusted; it was his kind of a town. And he held no particular fear of Benbow at the moment, believing that Benbow would be dragging the country and following the major tracks. Yet the smell of the wind was still bad to him and the spookiness that had kept running along his nerves during all the evening still controlled him. He finished his meal before the others and went out and led his horse down to the stable. The man there, Ambrose McRae, was a friend and Cash wanted a fresh horse; and so he was in this stable when Benbow hit the hotel with a clatter that could be heard all down the street. Crouched in the darkness of the place, Cash saw Dode Perris make one long leap to the saddle and rush away, a single shot exploding at him and missing him. Nobody else came from the hotel's front door and Gore understood that the game was up with Riley and the others.

He ducked back to where his horse stood, hearing Benbow's men shouting forward. For the briefest lag of time he considered his chances, and then in one swift heave he ripped off his saddle, unbuckled the bridle and kicked his horse into a stall. McRae stood at the door, throwing back his low and urgent warning. "Comin' this way." Gore hurled his gear behind a stall and threw himself up to the loose hay piled behind the runway. He was buried in it when Izee's party ran in to have a look.

Benbow repeated his question: "Where's Cash?"

Riley's face was an inexpressive, moon-round surface. He said nothing and Benbow, stirred by an admiration he could not help, knew that Riley had already crossed out any hope of living. It was to be seen in the way the outlaw so quietly and so fatalistically wrapped a calm about him. Silence ran on, with Benbow's crew turned very still and very attentive. Benbow wheeled back into the dining-room and considered the table there. He had caught four men at the table, but there were five plates before him. The fifth plate had been used. He thought about that and afterwards remembered the man who had guarded the horses. It explained this extra plate.

Yet when he returned to the lobby he wasn't quite satisfied. He couldn't shake from his head the deep belief that Gore wouldn't retreat until the last shot had been fired. Lifting his eyes beyond the ring of valley men he saw Sawmill Baker, who ran this hotel, posted in a corner. Sawmill held the key to Cash Gore's whereabouts; and Sawmill, though nobody else knew it, was friendly to Hat. Yet Benbow understood he couldn't ask Sawmill the direct question without putting the hotel man in a hole. Cherokee was a town that would always be a refuge for the toughs and Sawmill, if he valued his life, had to keep his mouth shut. Benbow liked Sawmill too much to embarrass him.

McGinnis seemed to be thinking about Sawmill also, for the Diamond-and-a-Half man pointed a finger at Sawmill and said: "Gore been here?"

Sawmill said quietly: "Gentlemen, I run a hotel and I can't answer your questions."

McGinnis, thoroughly angry, simply bawled: "You'll answer it or you'll get your backbone stretched."

"No," said Sawmill, "he hasn't been here."

Benbow kept his eyes on Indian Riley's face when that answer came, trying to locate some faint stir of emotion. There was none; and Ben Kell's expression was, as before, sullen and sly and hard.

Izee said: "He might of been here but he ain't now. We rummaged all the buildings."

"Been upstairs?" said Benbow.

Izee showed a faint surprise. "Why, no," he answered; and then went immediately toward the stairs. A pair of Diamond-and-a-Half men walked with him.

"He's not here," called Sawmill Baker.

The group stood still, listening to the search party's

208

footsteps drag along the upper hall. Doors slammed open. Izee called down: "Nothin' at all."

Riley broke his long silence. "I'm straight with you boys. Cash ain't in town."

"He didn't run," stated Benbow.

Riley stared at Benbow. "No," he answered, "he ain't the runnin' kind. I always kinda liked him for that."

"Who killed Arizona?"

Riley shifted his feet and said impatiently, "Let's get this over. I know what's comin'."

Benbow said quietly: "I'm sorry, Riley."

McGinnis lifted his head, listening for something. He wheeled away from the group and went to the front doorway—and stood there, his head poked carefully around the casing. Riley shrugged his shoulders at Benbow's talk. "I went into this business with my eyes open, Jim. If I'd gotten away, I'd still be at it. You'll get no regrets from me." Then he thought of something else. "But listen. I didn't kill that Travelin' Kid. I want you to know it. He never amounted to anything, one way or another. It was tough business—and I'm glad I ain't got it written in my book."

Benbow looked at Kell. "You tried to trap me behind Dunmire's stable, Ben. I heard your voice. It was a bad mistake—for you."

Izee came across the lobby. "Nothin' at all," he repeated. "I—"

McGinnis whirled from the door, jumping for Riley. He seized Riley's arm. "You go stand in that door. Everybody else keep away from the windows—and keep still. Come on!"

Riley said, "Why?" suspiciously, but McGinnis pushed him at the doorway. The rest of the crowd had backed toward the lobby's side walls. Benbow called, "What is it, Nelson?" Nelson only shook his head, watching Riley go as far as the door and stop there. Considering all this with a quick interest, Benbow observed the way Riley looked up the street and then suddenly wrenched his head about to shoot a strange, half-grinning glance at McGinnis.

McGinnis breathed: "Use your head, Riley."

Riley drawled, "Yeah, I know," and squared himself at a rider coming down the street.

From where he stood, Benbow had only a vague view of a long pair of legs straddling a horse. The rider had turned in at the hotel porch, and had stopped. Izee's breathing lifted and fell and the silence began to sing, to turn thin. A voice said: "Where's Cash, Riley?"

Benbow jerked his shoulders high and stiff, and started forward. But he only took one step, for Izee suddenly got in front of him and drove his arms against Benbow's chest. Izee muttered savagely, half furiously: "Damn you, keep still!" Benbow knocked Izee's arms down. He didn't move again and he didn't speak, yet all the angles of his features were sharp and deep and a sudden blaze of yellow rage poured out of his eyes, and played on Izee wickedly. Men's breathing seemed to have stopped. Riley was speaking carelessly, almost laughing.

"I thought you was supposed to meet him this mornin' at the ranch."

The man outside said: "He tell you that?"

"Sure. Wasn't that the agreement?"

"Why didn't he keep his mouth shut? What you doing over this way? I expected you'd be in the canyon."

"Just a side trip," said Riley. "You want to see Cash? He's in here, eatin'."

The long legs swung down from the saddle and hit the porch. Riley wheeled back from the door, his grin suddenly shining across the room, strange and narrow and bitter. And then Clay Rand was in the doorway, his high and thin body stopped there, and freezing there.

19. What a Man Must Do

He had seen the shapes of men along the wall and he had been warned by the deep silence of the lobby—the deep and gray and waiting silence. The light was bad in here and his eyes had been pin-pointed by the long ride through the snow. So it was a dragging interval of time before his vision began to clear and his traveling glance struck the near-by McGinnis, the impact of it seeming to sway him back on his heels. There was that fractional delay, that terrific smash of recognition, that wild moment of understanding. Then his glance came on and identified Benbow standing like a statue in the middle of the room. Poor as the light was, Benbow saw Clay Rand's ruddy and arrogant face even then sealed beyond expression. It was like that.

Riley said, in a scornful way, "When I despise a man he's pretty low. Lower than me. Here's your hound dog, McGinnis. Waste no sympathy on him."

McGinnis' voice bit like a bullet into Rand. "What you want to see Gore for?"

Rand suddenly had composed himself. His voice was careful and cool. "That's my business."

"Your mistake," said McGinnis. "It's our business. I want straight answers from you, Clay."

"I've sold beef to Running M," said Rand. "I want my money before he gets away. What's wrong with that?"

"How'd you come to sell him beef?"

"It would be the first beef Cash ever bought," put in Riley, dry-toned.

Rand said: "I'm not familiar with his reasons. He bought it and I sold it."

"In the middle of winter?" said McGinnis.

"Sure."

"A lame story," growled McGinnis.

"Maybe—but I'm telling you."

"Wait," said Benbow.

McGinnis wheeled around and Clay Rand's mouth closed and made a thin streak across his ruddy skin. The room was altogether still. Izee looked carefully at Benbow's eyes and then turned away. The air in this place was heavy and hard to breathe. Benbow never let his glance fall aside from Rand; it compelled Rand to look at him, it was like a force holding Rand's chin up. When he spoke his voice was as barren of expression as a man's voice could be.

"Did you hear shòoting in the canyon this morning?"

Rand said: "Yes."

"See Running M go up in fire?"

Rand hesitated and then made up that delay with a swift "I saw that."

"Then you knew we were on Gore's trail, and the chances were strong he was over in that quarter of the Yellows. What made you figure he'd be here instead?"

"Cherokee's his hangout."

Benbow paused, then said: "Last night on the ranch I told you we'd be riding. I said I wanted you to be along with us. You disappeared directly after that. Why?"

"Connie and I had a quarrel. I was sore. So I went home."

"You went straight home. You didn't see Gore last night, or this morning before daylight?"

"I never saw Gore."

"Did you have an agreement to meet him this morning?"

212

"No."

"A minute ago," pressed Benbow, "Riley said you were supposed to meet Gore on the ranch. You said, 'Why didn't he keep his mouth shut?' What did you mean by that, Clay?"

"I don't want Gore to go around telling lies about me."

Benbow quit talking and the silence came down again like a crushing weight over all of them. Rand lifted one hand and dragged it across his face. McGinnis said harshly: "You believe that story about selling the beef, Jim?"

"I've got to believe it. There's no proof he didn't."

Indian Riley broke in. "I'm telling you it ain't so. Cash never got his beef that way."

"I can't take your word on it, Riley," Benbow said slowly.

McGinnis blurted out irritably: "Every man in the valley knows Rand's been crooked for a long tme. Everybody knows it but you, Jim. Ask Izee."

Benbow stared at Izee, who only nodded.

Rand said, with a repressed bitterness: "If I'm so damned disagreeable to you gentlemen, I'll get out of here."

"No, by Judas!" exclaimed McGinnis.

But Benbow broke in. "I'm not willing to believe he's been crooked unless it's proved. It hasn't been proved. Let him go."

"Wait a minute," said a voice in the doorway, and as everybody whipped around Joe Gannon limped into the lobby and shook the snow from his coat. He made a gaunt, chilled shape in the room and there was the stamp of exhaustion and illness on his work-hollowed face. He had something to say, and said it in a voice that wasn't steady.

"I was up above my house, on the Ramparts. I saw him come by and turn into the Cherokee trail. He was leadin' a horse that had something lashed in a pack rig. I knew he was crooked two weeks ago, because Eileen overheard

213

him talkin' to Gore. So I challenged him to stop. He threw a shot at me and I threw some at him and then he got out of there in a hurry. But he broke his lead rope and the pack horse came back my way. I got it on my place now. I also got what was lashed to the pack rig." He stopped a moment, his voice feeble and without strength. "It was Price Peters. Shot below the heart. My God!"

Into that stunned quiet Rand's sudden and deep gust of breath was like a blast of steam. He made his violent whirl toward the door and was half through it when Indian Riley, all the while watching Rand closely, drove his solid body straight at Rand and nailed him to the casing with the full smash of his shoulders. Nelson McGinnis ran up and half the men in the room jumped over there. Clay Rand's voice was rash and savage and turned mad then, howling below the melee. Somebody hit him across the head and his voice quit; and then the fighting was over and Rand was again on his feet, a little stream of blood running down his white cheeks.

McGinnis wheeled around, speaking to Benbow: "No exceptions, Jim."

Yet even then the crowd waited for Benbow to speak. It was his presence that constrained them and it was the gray and bloodless show of misery on his face that held them still. A long, long interval before he broke that stillness, lifting a hand in a gesture all of them understood. He said, in a weary voice, "No exceptions," and watched them close around Rand and Riley and Kell—and lead them out. Somebody said, "The stable," and afterwards they filed down the street. Izee gathered up three of the racked horses and took them along; and a man ducked into the saloon and came out in a moment with a pint of whisky.

Following behind, Benbow saw all this. And stopped in the stable's arch, he saw the men of his own outfit throw three ropes up over one of the stable's high beams. They were tying Riley's hands, and Kell's—and Rand's. Riley looked indifferently at the three ropes and said: "Do man a favor, Jim. Put that yellow-haired dog on another beam. Kell and me—we're a little particular."

They took down one of the ropes and threw it over a beam farther back. Nobody was talking and the feeling of sickness crawled around while Hat's riders knotted up the loops and squared them underneath each man's right ear. There was some trouble getting these men, so trussed, into the saddles; afterwards they backed the horses directly beneath the straight fall of each rope— and tightened and tied the ropes' free ends to adjoining stall posts.

They stood like that—Kell and Riley paired, and Rand sitting alone behind them. One of McGinnis' men opened the pint whisky flask and offered Riley a drink. He said, evenly: "This'll be the first time I ever refused whisky." Kell bent down and took a long, deep pull; and afterwards Rand emptied the bottle.

The quietness in here got worse, all the men standing back and waiting. Something had happened to Kell, some oddness closing him out from the world. But Riley's poker expression never broke. He said: "Hell will be hot, which is a comfort. I ain't been warm since midnight. When you whip out those horses, whip 'em hard. I want this job well done."

"Riley," said Benbow. "I admire you."

"I wish," said Indian Riley, with a touch of sadness. "I wish—" But his broad shoulders lifted and fell and he closed his mouth, and fatalism covered him completely. He never spoke again. Everybody was waiting here, not knowing why. McGinnis reached up and took a pair of loose halter ropes from a stall post and looked at Benbow. But he moved around Benbow and handed one of the ropes to a Diamond-and-a-Half man, motioning that one back to Rand's horse, himself moving behind Riley and Kell.

Benbow said distinctly: "I'd never ask a man to do something I'm not willing to do," and reached over and took the rope from McGinnis. But he turned then and

215

walked on until he stood near the head of Rand's horse; and stopped there, looking up at the man who had so long been his partner.

Rand had nothing in his eyes that eased it for Benbow; nothing of softness or of regret, nothing to remind Benbow of all their riding days. Yet Benbow remembered them—remembered all the fun and all the laughter, and all the high excitement. It was when they had been young and the world was as they wanted it to be. Long, long ago. And his thoughts turned to Connie and his mind went black and he saw Clay Rand as a stranger sitting high and straight and pale on the horse and he whipped himself around and took two paces forward and drew back his arm and sent a slashing blow across the rumps of Riley's and Kell's horses. And plunged toward Cherokee's street. He heard certain sounds run their grisly tune together—the "tunk" of the ropes whipping tight, the snap of bone and the groaning of the beams beneath all this weight, and afterwards a faint threshing and a faint strangling. Silence settled behind him and he plowed up through the snow of Cherokee's street with his head bent over, seeing nothing.

He went back to the hotel and got his horse and led it into the street, and stood beside it, nothing yet clear in his head. The rest of the outfit came out of the barn and passed by him, on the way to their horses behind the hotel. In a little while they rode back. McGinnis said: "We're going down to see how Gordy Howland is."

Benbow watched them ride away. Izee cut out of the column and came back, and looked at Benbow, and then whirled off. Presently they were gone. Somebody crossed the porch at a slow step and when he looked around he saw Joe Gannon swing into his saddle with a distinct effort of muscle and ride up the street, bound back for the valley.

Benbow walked into the hotel and found Sawmill Baker standing in the exact middle of the floor, seeming to listen and seeming engaged in hard debate with himself.

216

Benbow said: "I want the truth from you, Sawmill. Was Gore here?"

Sawmill slowly nodded. "He came here with those other boys and ate in a hurry and vamoosed toward the stable. I thought he was in there, but if you boys didn't locate him I guess he went out the back way."

Benbow murmured. "It isn't finished," and dragged a heavy hand across his face.

Sawmill cleared his throat. "Jim," he muttered, "I'm sorry as hell—"

Benbow wasn't listening. The sharp edge of something scraped across his mind and roused it. He had stood in the stable, watching Riley; and he had backed into a stall and laid his hand on the rump of a horse stabled there. The rump had been wet and warm.

Sawmill said: "I knew about Clay—"

Benbow made a quick downward gesture with one of his arms and wheeled from Sawmill, his boots gouging up streaks of sound that rolled hollow echoes along the deserted lobby. He passed through the doorway, his glance swinging up and down Cherokee's street with a hard and grasping care. He dropped one foot to the lower steps and he was stretched out like that when a voice said, "Benbow," evenly, and stopped him dead.

The street showed him nothing. His horse and the horse of the pale outlaw who had bolted through the hotel's side window remained at the near-by hitch rack. Directly across the street the saloon's door swung gently on its hinges, indicating the recent passage of a man. Snow slanted thickly down and the light of the day was dull. He held his body still and he held his arms still, with all his senses pitched abnormally sharp and with all his nerves drawing tight. The voice came again, unhurried and quiet—and fatally sure: "Benbow."

Benbow's traveling glance whipped back to the edge of a house adjoining the saloon and at last found Cash Gore.

Gore's shoulder rested against the building edge, as though he had been long waiting in that attitude. The distance was a good eighty feet, with the snowfall and the gray shadows making him a thin and obscure shape; nor could Benbow discover any clear expression on that man's cheeks. Taciturn and secret-minded he had always been, and so he remained now. There was in Benbow's head, crowded as it was with warning and with all the messages of trouble, a moment's wonder. Gore had been there, watching the hotel door, and Gore had had his chance for a quick surprise shot, and had refused it. It was a puzzle to which he never knew an answer for Gore, straightening away from the building's edge, whipped up a gun and fired.

The long sullen voice of that shot was in his ears and the snap of the bullet's passage through the hotel wall was in his ears when Benbow lifted his own weapon and took deliberate aim, and drove his shot home.

He didn't fire again, knowing that this single shot had to be good. Gore, missing one, would never miss another—if another came. The muzzle of Benbow's gun kicked up and he held it poised like that, with its powder smoke rolling back into his nostrils. The silence got longer and longer, and Gore once more had his shoulder tilted against the edge of the far building, as though tired, as though again waiting. A fresher wind ripped up the loose snow and flung it across the air in a series of white, ragged breakers, hiding everything over there. Benbow's mind acutely registered the passing moments, and at the end of those long, long moments the snow cloud dissolved and he saw Gore lying full length at the base of the building.

Sawmill Baker ran from the hotel and crossed the street and bent down; and one man rushed from the saloon and went up to join Sawmill. The two of them crouched head to head, and presently Sawmill looked back to Benbow and struck a straight line through the windy air with his finger. Benbow put away his gun and went directly to his horse and climbed into the snow-covered saddle, and rode out of Cherokee, bound back for the valley.

A mile below Cherokee, Nelson McGinnis' party ran into Gordon Howland who was returning with his men. Howland said: "They passed Buckman's shack on the run. We never caught up. They're headin' out of the Yellows and it's all over. You find anything in Cherokee?"

Izee, who had come this far in greater and greater doubt, suddenly turned his horse about and left the group, racing back to Cherokee ahead of them. Coming into the settlement he discovered Sawmill Baker and the saloon man and Ambrose McRae crowding around the dead Gore; and he listened soberly while Sawmill told him the story. He made no comment on that, for there was something else heavily weighing Izee's thoughts. He said: "Which way did Jim go?" When Sawmill pointed up the street, Izee whirled that way and left Cherokee behind.

He followed Benbow's tracks as they cut down through the trees, passed Karen Sanderson's place, and afterwards struck straight for Joe Gannon's ranch. Once Izee sighted Benbow at the end of a straight alley, but he instantly drew his pony to a slower pace, and in that manner came out upon the Ramparts trail. Here he stopped, watching Gannon's yard and watching Benbow's horse waiting beside the house. A quarter hour later, after Benbow reappeared and rode into the valley, Izee descended the slope and found Eileen standing at the house door. Benbow had even then vanished in the thickening whirl of the half-blizzard. Eileen was crying.

Izee got painfully from the saddle and stamped into the house and when he saw Price laid out on a corner couch he took off his hat and went over, not saying anything. Gannon sat in another corner of the room, speechless and exhausted. Eileen turned in from the door. Izee presented his back to both of them, his sturdy shoulders

219

sagged down. It went like this a long while; until Gannon spoke in as dreary a voice as Izee had ever heard:

"I guess Benbow will remember my part in this business a long while. Izee, did I do right? I got to know."

Izee slapped his hand at his pants pocket and drew out a handkerchief and blew his nose. Eileen was crying again, in a way that was soft and terrible.

"Did I do right?" called Gannon, his tone rising and breaking.

Izee clapped on his hat and whirled for the door, never showing his face to either of them. When he answered Gannon he threw his words over a shoulder. "You got nothing to regret. It was a thing that had to come." He stopped to think about that, and to think about Gannon who had never been liked. And when that pause had dragged out he said, quietly, "You're all right, Joe," and went back to his horse and cut through the weather. When he raised the vague shape of Benbow, he settled down to a patient pursuit that carried him all across the valley. He saw then that Benbow wasn't going to Hat, which was as he suspected. At this point he halted, watched Benbow fade on toward the Two Dance hills, and at last disappear. Izee turned westward in Hat's direction, bucking the drifts.

The long detour around Hat brought Benbow into Two Dance just as full dark howled across the world. Lights were glittering through the snow-smothered air, and a train's whistle beat against the wind hoarsely and grew fainter in the distance. He took his horse into the stable, meeting Bert Dunmire there. Dunmire said: "Tough luck, Jim."

"What?"

"A Block T man just got in with the news." He stared at Benbow's face and added: "You better get yourself a drink."

Benbow wheeled out of the place, crossing the street. He stopped irresolutely in front of the Cattle King and plunged his hands into his overcoat pockets, and

220

remained there with his head tipped down. A man came from the Cattle King and looked carefully at him and said, "Hello, Jim," and went on, without receiving an answer. A man and a woman hurried up the walk from the depot, the woman laughing in a resonant, pleased way. He heard this vaguely, and didn't actually see them until Karen Sanderson called his name. He recognized her then, and was faintly interested in the man who came to a quick and soldierly stand and showed Benbow a pair of bright-blue eyes.

Karen said: "Jim, this is my husband, Fritz Sanderson. He has just finished serving his years in the German army."

Fritz Sanderson bowed exactly from his hips and took Benbow's hand. He said, in precise English: "You are the Benbow my wife has written me about several times." His eyes were interested and gravely thoughtful.

Benbow said: "I didn't know this, Karen."

She looked at him, her smile dying, her lips softening. She murmured: "It was not of interest to anybody, was it? It has been a long wait, but life in Germany is hard these days, and so I came here to find a place. We have a new country now and there will be no more army."

"Fritz," said Benbow, "you are lucky."

Fritz bowed again from the hips, and said: "For the consideration you have shown my wife, I am in your debt, and hope some day to repay."

Karen put out a hand, touching Benbow's arm. Her glance came across to him, straight and gentle, and honest. "You see," she murmured, "I have kept Fritz informed."

Benbow said, "Luck," and went on toward Faro Charley's, leaving these two people definitely behind. They turned to watch him go, and Sanderson quietly observed the way of his wife at that moment. He said: "A good friend, so? But he has trouble."

"There's been a fight in the mountains."

"I did not know there was war in America."

221

"It will take time to tell you, Fritz. But this man is great—and he has lost something."

Sanderson said gently: "It has been a long wait. You have had hungers, Karen. But not for food."

She said, "Yes," and met her husband's eyes without hesitation. "Yes."

"It is so," he murmured. "But now I am here."

"And I am happy. Let us eat. We'll not make it home tonight."

Benbow went into Faro Charley's, the sudden heat of the place at once sinking into his muscles and loosening them. There was a table of Mauvaise men in one corner, and Faro Charley stood behind the bar. That was all. Benbow put his elbows on the bar and let most of his weight drop there, his legs seeming to lose life. His eyes stung and the big muscles running along his shoulders and arms were like sheets of lead. Faro Charley reached behind and laid a bottle and a glass on the bar without comment. But there was something about the man's reserve that sent a spark of interest through Benbow and made him speak clearly:

"Faro, I don't blame you much. But a good man used to sit in here and lose his money. It was one of the things that turned him bad. I'm telling you I don't blame you, or hold you responsible for another man's life. But I can look back now and see what I should have done. I should have run you out of Two Dance. Maybe it would have helped. When's the train come through here?"

"Which way?"

"Any way."

"One o'clock."

"Give me a hundred dollars, Faro. I'll send it back sometime."

He poured a heavy drink and let it go down; and dropped his head again, the weight of his body pressing more urgently against the bar. There was somebody coming into the place. Indifferently looking over the room he saw Izee stand a moment at the door, and then

222

walk on to where the Mauvaise men were playing. It occurred to him, as the vaguest of thoughts, that Izee was a fool for riding around the country in this weather; and afterwards chairs scraped the floor and the Mauvaise men were leaving and Izee was leaving and Faro Charley laid a hundred dollars on the bar. Faro said: "I'm no man to truck for anybody, but you could have my shirt if you wanted it, Jim. Let it ride like that." He faded beyond Benbow's closing vision.

For Benbow was looking inward at some of the bitterest pictures his life had ever furnished him. It was the picture of Clay Rand sitting pale and speechless on the horse in Cherokee's stable, with a rope around his neck and nothing in his heart that would come out. It was the dead face of Price Peters on Joe Gannon's couch. It was the warm smile of Connie as she paused on Hat's porch and looked up to Clay in a way no man could mistake. And that was the end of it. That was the picture that would stick, and torture him, and never let him alone. He remembered then what Jack Dale had said: "You've got something ahead of you that will take your heart out. I'd warn you, only you'll come through it." This was what Jack Dale had meant. It had taken his heart out and he had come through it. But he had nothing left.

A hand touched his arm. A hand pulled him around. And Connie's voice said, "Jim," and he turned to see her there before him, the rose stain of the wild wind on her cheeks and her eyes shining out an emotion he didn't understand. They were alone here, with the Mauvaise men gone and Faro gone.

He said: "Connie—Connie, don't look at a man like that."

"I've heard the news, Jim."

He said: "You'll remember me the rest of your life, for what I've done to you." He was straight on his legs, his black hair unkempt and his cheeks dark with beard. There was a gauntness and a thin-edged exhaustion showing along his face. The shadowing across his eyes

223

held no hope.

Connie's hand gripped his arms hard enough to bring a faint change to his face. She said: "I sent Clay away from Hat last night. I knew what he'd done then. And I can tell you something else. Hat is so empty when you're not there! I found that out. It's always been like that, only I have just found it out. Why don't you tell me you want me! How far does a woman have to go?"

He said, dully: "Connie—"

"It began a long time ago," she murmured. "And it's got to end this way. Jim!"

He had been holding the empty whisky glass in his hand. He put it down carefully, and brought her towards him, like a man reaching for something he is afraid he may lose.

Izee surreptitiously looked in through the saloon door and saw that, and went slowly up the street, enormously relieved. It was the way he wanted it to be—each of those people having something the other needed. It was a thing Jack Dale had hoped for and so now, somewhere along a high green trail, Old Jack must be pleased with what he saw in Faro's saloon. Izee wasn't an imaginative man but he thought then that he could hear Old Jack's long, hearty laughter ringing up against the Pearly Gates. It was his fancy. Afterwards Izee remembered Mary Boring, and the fancy died and he stopped on the walk, borne down with his own personal troubles.

There was an Omaha drummer hurrying up from the depot, a fat little fellow with two huge sample cases in either fist. Izee stepped in front of him, bringing the drummer to a startled halt. Izee said gruffly: "Friend— what do you think about marriage?"

The drummer looked at him, suspecting the worst. He said: "What?" And went by Izee rapidly.

"Well," growled Izee, "I'll be damned if I know either."